MYSTERIOUS INVITATION

THE WHOLE BOOK

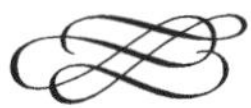

BERNICE BLOOM

Bernice Bloom

PROLOGUE

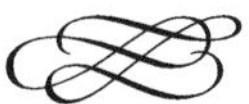

From Beddows and Plunkett Solicitors

Dear Ms Brown,

We are sad to announce the death of **Reginald Charters***. His funeral will be held at Gower Chapel next to Gower Farm Hotel, Llanelli.*

In accordance with the deceased's wishes, we request that you arrive on Wednesday by 3pm, prior to the funeral on Thursday morning. You will be free to leave from 3pm Thursday.

All your expenses will be paid, you will stay in the smart Gower Farm Hotel and you will be more than adequately compensated for your time.

We urge you to attend.

Huw Beddows and Geraint Plunkett

Directors, Beddows and Plunkett Solicitors

PRESENT DAY: THE MYSTERIOUS INVITATION

'Hi, Mum, it's me,' I said, as I plonked myself inelegantly on the edge of the squashy sofa, and listened for my mother's dulcet tones to come down the phone line.

'Oh, hello, love. How are you?'

'I'm OK, mum, but I've just heard the bad news about Reginald.'

'About Reginald? What bad news?'

'Mum, he died.'

'Your father's godfather?'

'Yes. I got an invitation to his funeral.'

'Oh no, that is awful news, Mary. I had no idea. You're sure he died?'

'Well, yes. It would be a bit odd to get an invitation to his funeral if he hadn't.'

'Oh, that is sad. He had come out of hospital and was feeling much better. How did he die?'

'I don't know, Mum, that's kind of why I was ringing you... you tend to know this sort of thing.'

'I didn't even know he'd died. Let me call Rosalyn and check. That has really thrown me. How awful. I will call you right back.'

I put on the kettle the guyand read the card again. Definitely Reginald and unquestionably an invitation to his funeral. The service would take place in a village in South Wales. But why on earth was I invited? I hardly knew the man. And why in Wales? And why did I have to turn up at 3pm the day before? So many questions.

The phone rang as I poured my tea and I wedged my mobile between my neck and ear as I added milk.

'Reggie's not dead,' said Mum. Her tone was a touch accusatory. 'I gave Ros a hell of a shock just now, suggesting that he was. She rushed up to check on him to find him sitting up in bed reading *The Telegraph*, feeling better than he has for years. Why did you say he was dead?'

'I was invited to his funeral, that's why I thought he was dead. It's not an unreasonable assumption. Hang on.'

This was crazy. I picked up the card and read it to Mum.

'Reginald Charters?' she said. 'I thought you were talking about Reginald Oates.'

'Oh.' Now I was more confused than ever. 'I don't know. I saw Reginald and thought it was dad's godfather. I don't know any other Reginalds.'

'Well, sweetheart, it's not our Reginald.'

'This is so odd, mum. It is addressed to me personally, and they have my address and everything. But – I swear – I have no idea who this guy is.'

'You must know him or you wouldn't be invited to his funeral.'

'I don't know him. I've never heard the name before.'

'Well then, why have you been invited to his funeral?'

'Good question, Mum,' I said. 'I haven't got the faintest clue.'

An hour later, I arrived at Mum's front door clutching my laptop, a notebook and the invitation that had caused such consternation. I had been googling the name 'Reginald Charters' for the last hour to no avail. I couldn't find any possible link to anyone of that name. In fact, there were very few Reginald Charters listed on the internet. There was someone mentioned in a big tome all about the modern media, a man listed in a marriage registry in Canada three years ago, and some World War 1 pilot who couldn't possibly be my Reginald because if he'd fought in the First World War, he'd have to be about 122 years old by now.

Mum and Dad were in the sitting room, looking as confused as I was feeling.

'You must know this man,' said Mum. 'Perhaps you met him when you went on that safari trip? Or on the cruise? What about that old man you met on the cruise who was travelling abroad to say farewell to his old comrades. Could it be someone related to him?'

'I don't see how,' I said. 'I met Frank on the cruise and got to know him quite well but he died soon after we got back. I never got to know any of his friends or family or anything. Why would any of them invite me to a funeral?'

Dad shook his head and went back to watching repeats of Morse, while Mum and I set ourselves up in the back room –

laptop open, phones out and books spread across the table. It was as if we were running a murder investigation.

'What about the yoga weekend you went on?'

'Nope. I met a yogi, banged my head, lay there as some bloke's tackle fell out of his shorts when he was coming down from downward dog, then came home again.'

'Was the yogi called Reginald?'

'Nope.'

'What about the bloke with the runaway testicles?'

'Nope.'

Mum and I sat there looking at one another, discombobulated and unsure what to do, when my phone rang. It was Ted, my long-suffering boyfriend. 'I better take this,' I said to Mum. 'I haven't seen much of Ted recently; he gets funny with me when I don't take his calls.'

I was hoping this would be a cue for Mum to leave the room and let me talk to Ted in peace. I thought she might go and, you know, make me a lovely cup of tea or something. But – no. She sat there looking at me, so instead of exchanging words of endearment with my beloved, I told him about the mysterious invitation.

'Read it out to me,' he said.

I read it and waited for his verdict.

'Have you rung the solicitors who sent it?' he asked.

'Oh, no. I haven't. Do you think I should?'

'Err...yes,' he said, a little patronisingly. 'I'd have thought that would be the first thing you'd do.'

I looked at the table in front of me, set up like a major incident room and thought – yes, he was probably right, that should have been the first thing we did, though that wouldn't have been as much fun as going full-scale detective with Mum.

'I'll call them now, and let you know what they say.'

I ended the call and told Mum what Ted had suggested.

'OK, you do that while I put the kettle on.'

I rang the number on the letter and a soft Welsh accent drifted down the line.

'Beddows and Plunkett Solicitors, how can I help you?' she said.

I went through a rather wordy explanation of the invitation and my confusion.

'I understand,' she said. 'Let me put you through.'

Next to answer the phone was Huw Beddows, one of the partners in the firm. My ridiculous enquiry had sent my call straight to the top.

'I'm sorry to trouble you,' I started. 'It's just that I've received an invitation to a funeral and I don't believe I know the guy who died. I wondered whether you could help.'

'I certainly can, Ms Brown,' he said.

How did he know my name? I hadn't given it to the receptionist.

I could hear Mr Beddows shuffling papers around on his desk before coming back on the line.

'OK,' he said. 'Well, I can tell you that Mr Charters specifically asked, on his deathbed, for you to be at his funeral.'

'What?'

'Yes, it was his dying wish.'

'But – I don't know this guy. How can he want me at his funeral?'

'I didn't know Mr Charters personally but he made it clear in correspondence, which he put together from his hospital bed, that he was very keen for you to be there. He only invited six people and you are one of them. We will send you a first-class train ticket and can pay for you to stay the night before the funeral. We will pay for all incidental expenses associated with travel and subsistence. We also request and advise that you come to the will reading the morning after the funeral.'

'The will?'

'Yes.'

'I have been left something in his will?'

As I said that, Mum re-entered the room, teacups shaking on the saucers she was carrying, as she stared at me wide-eyed.

'Yes, I believe you have been left something but I'm not at liberty to discuss any of the contents of the will until it is read formally.'

'OK,' I replied.

'All the information will be sent to you, Ms Brown, along with tickets and a generous expenses allowance. Taxis will be booked to take you to the accommodation and you will be compensated for any loss of earnings.'

'Right,' I said. 'It still seems odd though. And can I just ask you something?'

'Of course.'

'How did you know I was Mary Brown? I didn't give my name to the receptionist.'

'Because you were the only one who hadn't rung.'

'Sorry?'

'The other five people who are coming to the funeral have already phoned up.'

'Oh, OK. What did they phone up for?'

'To ask about Reginald Charters, to say they didn't know who he was and to ask why they had been invited to the funeral.'

'What? Really? No one going to this funeral has a clue who the deceased is?'

'That appears to be the case, Ms Brown.'

'And you can't tell me any more about Reginald Charters?'

'I don't know anything about Reginald Charters,' said Mr Beddows. 'I never met him. I was instructed by a private detective who liaised with Mr Charters as he was dying. They have given me envelopes to hand out and strict instructions to follow but other than that, I know nothing. I am as much in the dark as you are. To be honest, I've never known anything like this in my life before.'

PRESENT DAY: THE MYSTERY DEEPENS

The next morning my tickets arrived along with an envelope with £200 in it for 'incidental expenses'. Everything had been planned in extraordinary detail: 'Come out of the station, a taxi will pick you up there, next to Joe's Ice Cream Parlour which is next to the solicitors' office.'

I honestly don't think the government's Cobra meetings are as well organised as this.

Ted had stayed the night so we flicked through the contents of the stiff, brown envelope together.

'Are you going to war, or going to a funeral?' asked Ted, when he saw the detailed notes and explanations. There was something quite unnerving about the formality of it. If it weren't for the bonus £200 tucked inside, I would have been quite weirded-out by it all.

'What do you think?' I said to Ted.

Ted was silent as he took it in. 'To be honest, I'm not at all comfortable. They have given you every detail in the world about how to get there but told you nothing about why you are going. Does that not strike you as odd?

'Are you sure it's a proper solicitors' firm? I do not see how it makes any sense to go to some remote place to attend a funeral of someone you don't know. And I certainly do not think you should be taking the £200 from them, you don't know what they will want in return.'

'It's for expenses,' I said.

'What expenses? Everything you could possibly need is in the envelope.'

'Snacks and things, I guess.'

'No one could eat £200 worth of snacks on a British Rail journey.'

'Is that a challenge?' I asked, but Ted wasn't in the mood for such light-hearted exchanges. He raised his eyebrows as if to suggest that I wasn't taking this whole thing anywhere near seriously enough.

'When I rang them, it seemed like it was a proper company,' I said. 'I mean, there was a secretary and she put me through to the partner of the law firm.'

'That could have been two nutters sitting in a flat in Birmingham,' said Ted. 'I just think it's weird.' Ted flicked through the notes in front of him. 'I'm going to ring them now and see what's going on.'

'They're not going to be open yet, are they? It's only half past eight. I doubt there will be anyone there till nine.'

'Well, I'll ring at nine then. I want to talk to them. You can't go gallivanting off without us being really sure this is all legitimate.' He looked at the tickets again. 'You're supposed to be leaving the day after tomorrow. I can't let you go off to some remote village in some part of Wales I've never heard of with a bunch of people we don't know because of some weird dead bloke you've never heard of.'

'Well, yes, when you put it like that, I guess it is a bit odd.'

'A bit? It is insane. Can you get a couple of hours off work this morning, so we can try and find out a bit more about this?'

Getting time off work can be really difficult because I work in a DIY and gardening centre, and if I'm not in, someone else has to work for me, but I knew Ted was right.

'I'll message Keith and see what he says.' I sent a text through to my boss to let him know that a relative had died (I couldn't say 'someone I don't know has died'), and explained that I had to go to the funeral and I really needed to sort a few things out first. To my amazement, he came straight back to say he was sorry to hear about my loss and of course it was OK to come in late.

'Now I'm more worried than ever,' I said to Ted. 'Why is Keith being nice to me? This is all so damn odd.'

'Just go and have a shower, get dressed, come back down here and we're going to talk to the solicitors' firm as soon as it opens,' said Ted. He was getting all assertive and controlling. It wasn't a side of him I was used to seeing.

'Whatever you say.' I gave him a salute before running through to my bedroom to shower and change.

I returned half an hour later – fragrant and clothed.

'Have you seen this?' Ted asked, pushing a letter across the table to me. 'It was in the envelope.'

In scratchy, old person handwriting, the letter said:

My Dear Mary,

What a shame I shall not meet you at the funeral, but I am delighted you can attend. This will be a joyous occasion and you will leave feeling full of happiness...uplifted and rejoicing.

This will turn out to be a weekend that you remember for the rest of your life, I GUARANTEE YOU.

Reginald

'Oh. My. God! It's a note from the dead guy.'

Ted read the letter too, his brow furrowed in concentration as he scanned the inked lines.

'I'm still not convinced. I need to check this out properly,' he said. 'Come and sit here.'

He indicated the seat next to him and put the phone on the table in front of us, clicking it onto loudspeaker. We leaned over it like the French Resistance and Ted dialled the number.

'I was thinking, while you were in the shower, I should come with you. I think it would be much safer if I was there, too.'

I was torn by this announcement. On one hand, I thought it was rather lovely that he wanted to come and keep me safe, and it would be nice to have company on the journey. But the other part of me was quite looking forward to the solo adventure of going off on this bonkers trip: to the funeral of someone I didn't know without having a clue why they wanted me there. It appealed to my sense of madness.

'I'm sure I'll be safe,' I said. 'If I don't feel safe, I can just leave.'

'You will be in the middle of nowhere with a bunch of people you don't know,' he said harshly.

A secretary answered the phone in the solicitors' office and

Ted got to work, explaining his concerns. He was put through to Huw Beddows and he repeated his distress at what was being asked of me. I had never seen him so forceful before. It was quite sexy to watch him, to be honest; he wanted to know exactly what was going on, and said that he would be coming with me.

'It's not really the sort of event where partners will be present,' said Huw. 'She'll only be gone for a couple of days and it would be much easier for everyone if she came alone. The others will be coming on their own. Nothing to worry about at all, sir.'

'That makes me more worried than ever. What sort of nutter insists that people must come alone?'

Ted didn't wait for a response from Mr Beddows.

'So, a guy said on his deathbed that he wants a bunch of people who don't know one other to turn up in the middle of nowhere without giving a clue as to why he wants them there and they must come unaccompanied.'

'Yes,' said the solicitor. 'I know it sounds odd and I do not know why he has invited the people he has. All I can do is assure you that Ms Brown will be safe while she is here. She will be staying at Gower Farm Hotel, which is lovely. You have my word that this is a genuine request from a man on his deathbed who wanted to invite these people, I'm sure everything will be revealed over the course of the time that she's here, but I understand Mr Charters had deeply personal reasons for wanting them to come.'

'If this is some dodgy scheme, I will find you and kill you,' said Ted.

There was a silence on the end of the phone.

'Did you hear me?' asked Ted.

'It's not a dodgy scheme. We have been a solicitors' firm in this village for over one hundred years. I have been working here since I was a 21-year-old fresh out of university; my father, Llyr Beddows, owned this firm before me. This is an unusual situation, I accept, but there is nothing dodgy about it.'

Ted finished the call and googled the solicitors' firm, as I had done the day before, and established that – yes – it had been in the village for over a hundred years, and the partners of the firm, and their descendants, had been there for decades.

'It seems legitimate and I'm sure you'll be safe, but do you want to go?' he asked me.

'Obviously I'm intrigued,' I replied with honesty. 'I'd like to know why I've been invited; I think it's worth me going.'

'All right, but you have to call me if there is anything dodgy at all, OK?'

'OK,' I reassured him.

'And you have to tell me what all this is about. As soon as you know – call me.'

'OK,' I said, preparing to leave for work. Ted hadn't done anything this morning that I hadn't already done, and we were none the wiser about why I'd been invited but, somehow, because it had been Ted who'd asked, we both felt that I was safer.

1943: PRISONERS OF WAR

'Closer together.'

Marco winced as he felt the tip of a gun jab him in the side.

'Move. NOW!'

There was nowhere to move. He couldn't get any closer to the guys either side of him. The truck was packed full of soldiers; shoved in like sheep being transported to a slaughter-house. Marco shuffled in his seat, doing his best to move up so he didn't earn the wrath of the British soldiers sent to control and humiliate them. He edged towards Lorenzo, his closest friend – the man he had fought alongside in the most dreadful conditions. The guard stared at him, and Marco dropped his head, looked down at his filthy trousers, and scuffed boots and remained silent. Returning the stare would only result in angering the man. He had no desire to anger anyone. Not ever. And especially not now.

The truck trundled on, along roads full of potholes that sent them swaying from side to side, crashing into one another, unable to sleep though weary from fear and physical exhaustion. Marco was desperate for water and something to eat. He had not washed properly for what felt like months. He had been serving in Africa where they had been rationed to a single cup of water for washing. It was nowhere near enough for them to clean themselves properly, and they had railed against it. Now he would do anything for that one cup of water. Just a drop of water.

He never thought it would be like this. None of them had.

When he left Italy to join the army, he had pulled on his uniform with pride, his head full of images of heroism and glory, painted in his mind by the dozens of war films he had watched as a young boy. He'd read the tales of soldiers returning from the first World War, but their sanitised accounts had given him no clue as to how horrific it would be. He had imagined ration packs and whistling in the showers. He had not considered days without being able to clean himself and becoming so hungry that he would be reduced to eating flesh from camels that had been blown up by landmines. He and Lorenzo had faced daily bombings and attacks. He ought to be glad British forces had captured him rather than being forced to stay there any longer, fighting for his life in scorching, oppressive conditions.

But he wasn't. He did not feel glad at all.

At least he had known what awaited him when he had risen each morning in Africa; here he had no clue what would happen from one moment to the next. He had no idea what hovered at the end of this long journey through a rainy, bumpy foreign land. He guessed they would be worked, and starved, to death. He did not imagine he would see his family again.

As the lorry trundled along, he thought of his mother and the way she had clung onto him when he left, the sound of her cries still clear in his mind. The sight of his father's face – tight and full of pain as he tried valiantly not to let his fears and despair show. Marco was their only son. When he had gone to war, it had broken their hearts. He squeezed his eyes closed at the memory. Would they know he had been taken prisoner? Or would they assume he'd died on a foreign battlefield like so many others? He said his own silent prayer that he would live, if not for himself, for his mum.

Marco kept his eyes shut, trying to think of their lovely house in Naples...how spotless his mother always kept it, all the friends who came round, the great big meals she'd host with enough food for dozens more, and wine flowing freely late into those warm Italian nights.

'Off!' shouted a voice, interrupting his thoughts of home. An unfamiliar man pulled open the doors at the back of the truck. 'Off. NOW!' he repeated in an arrogant tone given more menace by his severe countenance. He embodied everything Marco feared about the British.

Marco joined the others in climbing off the truck and marching into an old hut that did nothing to keep off the cold and rain. They were handed thin blankets and told to sleep on wooden planks lying on the floor. Marco walked over to the place he had been allocated. He was handed water that he drank in one fierce, grateful gulp, but no food. Then he lay down on the wooden slats, wrapped the blanket around him, took one look up at the armed guards who stood at the door, guns cocked, and he closed his eyes. He would probably be shot in his sleep, but for now, he was alive. He needed to focus on that...for now he was alive.

Morning came abruptly with the shrill blast of a whistle and the sound of angry voices blaring through the room.

'Up, up, up,' came the growls, as a gun slammed into his shoulder. Marco jumped to his feet and was told to shower, then handed a uniform to wear – it was wine-coloured with a yellow circle on the back and knees. He did not know what it represented or where he was going next.

After a cold shower, he and the other Italian prisoners were made to march back outside, and forced onto a cattle truck. It was 6am; he had not eaten for days and felt dizzy with fear and starvation. If they wanted to kill them, they were going the right way about it. Marco sat in the truck as it went down the bumpy lanes. He peered out through the back at gorgeous countryside, the beauty of the place outside providing such a vivid contrast to the scene inside the truck where starving and exhausted soldiers sat in fear for their lives.

Then the truck stopped.

An Italian-speaking soldier stood at the front and addressed them. He explained that they were in a country called Wales and they would be working on farms, helping in whatever way was required of them. They would be dropped off, some in small groups, some on their own, and they would have to work hard 'or endure the consequences.'

'You will be collected at the end of the day and taken back to the camp.' Then the truck rumbled on, stopping every so often as names were called out and men climbed off and met their new masters – farmers who looked surly and confused by the men being foisted on them.

'Lorenzo Alberto,' the soldiers shouted, and Marco's closest friend moved to the back of the truck and jumped out, offering a quick backward glance to Marco as he did.

The truck continued, down the narrowest of lanes. 'Marco Stilliano,' came the shout. Marco stood up and walked to the back of the truck, clambering out and making his way forward, where the officer with a clipboard ticked him off and reminded him that if he put a foot out of line he would be shot.

'You understand me?' asked the soldier.

Marco nodded.

'I said, do you understand me?'

'Yes, sir,' said Marco, looking him in the eye. 'I understand you.'

Marco walked toward the farmer standing with what he assumed were two farm hands near a sign saying 'Gower Farm'. Neither of them appeared to be remotely pleased to see him. It was no wonder, really, he knew he must look a terrible state. He shook hands with the farmer and walked with him toward the house, watched as he went by the soldiers on the truck.

'Do you speak English?' asked the farmer.

'I speak some,' said Marco. 'I will learn more.'

'Good, my name's Tom and these are Ken and Keith who work with me on the farm.'

'I'm Marco,' he said, staggering a little as he shook their hands.

'Are you OK?' asked Tom. 'Is something wrong?'

'No, I am fine. I will work hard,' said Marco. 'I promise to work very hard.'

'Have you eaten?' asked Tom. 'You look thin. Have you been fed?'

'No,' said Marco, 'but I will be fine. I can work hard.'

'Irene,' called Tom, as they reached the farmhouse. An

incredibly pretty woman came out and approached them. Tom said something to her in a language that Marco could not understand and she looked at him and smiled. A kind smile that reminded him so much of his mother.

'Hello, Marco,' she said. 'I hope you are well.'

'Hello, ma'am,' he replied. Then she disappeared from view.

'Sit here,' said Tom, going after her. 'Stay with him, boys.'

Keith and Ken sat either side of him on the low stone wall, then Tom came back out with a flask and something wrapped in tinfoil. 'Eat this first,' he said.

'Thank you, thank you,' said Marco as he tore open the foil to see a huge chunk of bread. In the flask there was soup, it was salty and weak but in that moment, it was more delicious than anything he had ever tasted before. He ate the food in minutes and looked up at Tom. 'Thank you,' he said. 'I will work very hard, I promise. You are kind people.'

'I'm sure you will,' said Tom, then he issued an instruction to Keith. Marco could not understand a word of it.

'We're speaking Welsh,' explained Tom. 'I've told Keith to take you to the back field and show you what to do.'

Marco felt like a different person now he had eaten something – stronger and more alive than he had in days, and he threw himself into working as hard as he could. He had been labouring for what felt like a few hours when he heard Tom's voice, as the farmer approached on his tractor.

'Hey, you can stop now,' said Tom. 'We don't want to work you to death. The others are all down at the end of the field having a lunch break. Come on.'

'I can work,' said Marco. 'You already gave me food today.'

'No, you will have a break for lunch every day and a break

for tea in the afternoon,' said Tom. 'We might be at war but we're not savages. Come on. Food time.'

They sat in a circle and Tom handed out the food prepared by Irene.

'What's it like being at war?' asked Keith. 'Is it exciting?'

'No,' said Tom. 'It's not fair to ask that.'

'I don't mind answering,' said Marco in a voice barely more than a whisper. 'It's not exciting. Very frightening. It's quite horrible, but I had to fight for my country.'

Marco dropped his head as he spoke.

'I think that's enough war talk,' said Tom. 'How about you tell Marco something about the history of the farm?'

But Keith was too fascinated to let it go.

'Do you support Mussolini? I mean, it's one thing to fight for your country, quite another to fight for Mussolini. He's an evil bastard.'

'Come on, that's not fair,' said Tom. But Marco raised his hand.

'No – it is fair. I support Italy. Not Mussolini. I fight for my country, my friends.'

Along with many of the prisoners, Marco had a great antipathy to the warmongering policies of Mussolini and to Fascism in general. He tried to explain this to Keith in his broken English. Keith and Tom nodded and Marco realised they understood him. He smiled broadly, delighted to be able to communicate with these lovely people who had taken him in. Ken was sitting a little apart from them and had not said anything to Marco since he had arrived. Marco did not know whether the man just did not like him, or whether he was shy.

By the time Marco had been at the farm for a week, he felt

like he belonged. He was more and more grateful for the decency and kindness of Tom and his family as the days went by. He still did not understand everything that Keith said because he spoke so fast, but he was getting there. He was starting to understand the words that Tom used regularly and starting to make sense of his gentle, lilting accent. Tom delivered everything he said slowly, to help Marco understand, and he spoke with real warmth and with great kindness in his eyes.

Ken was the only one who Marco struggled to get along with. He had asked Keith whether there was anything he was doing to upset the slim, rather miserable man who he shared his days with. Keith explained that Ken was shy. He had been in an accident a few years previously when he drove over a body on the narrow farm track coming back late one night. The police discovered later that the body was already dead by the time Ken ran over it so there was no suggestion that Ken had killed anyone, but the whole incident had hit Ken hard, and led to him withdrawing into himself.

By day, Marco would work as hard as he could for Tom, and learn as much English as he could from his hosts, when they were not speaking Welsh, and at night he would collapse and sleep soundly.

The accommodation, back at the POW camp, was not as bad as he had first feared. On that first night, they had been forced to sleep on a wooden floor, but when they returned from working on the farms, they found they had been moved to the centre of the prison, which was a mass of buildings containing proper beds and with a proper roof.

He would chat to his friend Lorenzo about their experiences, and compare notes on the days they had endured.

Lorenzo was working for a more aggressive, less friendly farmer than Tom, but a man who was reasonable and fair. He ate regularly and was treated fairly. That was all that any of them wanted.

Marco found his life had a pattern to it now; a routine. He was eating properly and exercising relentlessly. Muscles were beginning to form where once he had been skin and bone, and colour returned to his cheeks thanks to being outside all day. Though he and Tom were from different countries and on different sides in the war that was tearing through Europe, they had found common ground in the simplicity of working the land.

'Lunchtime,' said Tom, and Marco laid down his tools, wiped his hands on his uniform and climbed onto the tractor next to his boss, sitting quietly as they drove through the field to where the workers were assembled. A big chunk of home-made bread dipped in lard and a sliver of fruit pie sat in the box, waiting for him.

'Please say thank you to Irene,' he said. 'This is so lovely food. Like my mamma used to make.'

They all laughed at his kind words delivered in a strong Italian accent.

'Where are you from, in Italy?' asked Tom.

'Napoli,' he replied shyly. 'My parents are still there.'

'When did you last talk to them? Do they know you are alive and well?'

Marco just shook his head. His parents did not know where he was. They had no idea whether their only son was dead or alive.

'I have lived here all my life,' Tom said, sensing that he had upset the boy. 'As you know, I live here with my wife Irene and our son, Tom Junior. You haven't met him yet, but you will.'

Marco smiled. 'It is nice to have a wife,' he said. 'To have a family, a son with your name.'

'I'm sure you will one day,' said Tom. 'Once this war is over, you'll have a family too.'

'I will have a son called Joe,' said Marco, emboldened by the confidences shared by Tom. 'He will be called Joe after my grandfather; he lives with my mother and father in Napoli. I have no brothers and sisters, but a lovely life. My father runs an ice cream shop. The best ice cream in the whole of Italy. The whole of the world.'

'I'm sure your father and grandfather must be very proud of you. You are a hard worker. I like that.'

Marco smiled and nodded. He had the warmth of the sun on his skin, food in his belly and gentle conversation. He felt alive again. These people had saved him.

'Thank you,' he said. 'Thank you for everything.'

1943: GOWER FARM

Six months later…

'Hey, Marco. Can I have some?' said a cautious little voice. Marco glanced down at the small boy looking up at him as he ate his sandwiches.

'Of course.' Marco handed the little boy the one remaining sandwich in his small, tin box.

'No, Tom Junior, leave Marco alone.' Irene raced up to them. 'Let him eat his food, you little monster.'

'Hey, it's no problem at all. Of course he can have some,' said Marco. He knew how difficult it was to get hold of food of any sort with the rationing that was going on. The least he could do was share the food they had kindly given him.

'There you go,' said Marco, lifting Tom Junior onto his lap and watching as the boy's eyes lit up when he bit into the soft bread and tasted the saltiness of the scraps of meat they had saved from the previous day's meal.

'Thank you, you're very kind, but those were for you,' said Irene crouching down beside him.

'It's really not a problem,' he said, jumping up with Tom Junior safely in his arms, when he realised there was nowhere for her to sit.

'Please – sit here,' he said, holding Tom Junior on his hip.

'No, goodness, Marco, you've been working since 6am, you're entitled to have a sit down.'

'Please take it; I will not sit down while a lady stands. My father would never forgive me. Please, have my seat.'

Irene sat down reluctantly, and smiled up at Marco. He was such a kind man, a real gentleman, well brought up and a joy to have working on the farm. He had made a huge difference in the six months he had been there – throwing himself into the work and blending in so well with all the family.

Tom Junior still clung to Marco, so the handsome Italian sat down on the grass in front of Irene, putting her son on his lap while they spoke. He'd become close to the family in the time he'd been working on the farm, and had a particularly close relationship with the young boy who loved to be read to by the Italian soldier.

'Tell me all about your book - the Call of the Wild,' said Tom Junior.

'Goodness, stop hassling the poor man,' said Irene. 'First, it's his sandwiches, and then it's that damn book again. He needs a break.'

'It's not a problem at all,' said Marco. 'I have it here.' He pulled out of his bag a small book with a bright yellow cover and saw the look of delight on Tom Junior's face. The book was a novel that his father had given him when he was a little boy in Italy and he had kept it close by ever since. The book had been shot at and lost then found again, it had been through battles and been across countries. Now it was one of his most prized possessions.

'Tell me all about the squadron leader,' said Tom Junior.

The star of the book was Squadron Leader Reginald Charters – a man who seemed to get himself into the most extraordinary number of adventures. In book after book, the squadron leader would be saving lives, leading his men into battle and saving children from certain death. He was swash buckling, brave and handsome...and Tom Junior loved to hear the tales. Marco turned the page and prepared to read.

'Before you start, Marco, I've been talking to my husband,' said Irene, while Tom Junior devoured the remains of the sandwich, licking every finger one by one to make sure he got every crumb.

'Is everything OK?' said Marco. The way Irene mentioned her husband had him worried. The last thing he wanted to do was upset these hosts who had been so kind to him.

'Yes, everything is perfect, Marco. In fact, I would say there is just one thing you could do to make us happy.'

'Of course,' said Marco, ruffling Tom Junior's hair when he realised the young boy was staring up at him. 'You've been so kind to me, of course I'm happy to do anything you want. Would you like me to rebuild the fence down at the bottom field where the sheep got out? I can easily take some of the men down there this afternoon. We can work a longer afternoon than usual and get it finished.'

'No, that's exactly the opposite of what I want you to do, Marco. What I would really like is for you to take some time off this afternoon. Tom and I are going to the Mart – the place where we sell sheep. Please have a few hours to yourself. Use the outhouse near the farmhouse, and have a sleep, or read, whatever you like. But you must stop working these insane hours. OK?'

'I do not need a break,' he said, more bluntly than he meant. He hoped they had not noticed how tired he was. He had tried hard not to show it, and to work diligently to keep them happy.

'Yes, you do, Marco. I insist you take a break. You said you would do whatever would make me happy. I am telling you that would make me happy.

'Also, would you please write to your mum and tell her you're OK? I will put some paper and an envelope on the dining room table for you. Leave the letter there when you have written it and I will post it for you.'

'Thank you,' said Marco. 'You have been so kind to me, I want to work hard for you every day. I would feel bad doing nothing.'

'You mustn't feel bad. I would love it if you spent some time relaxing and enjoying yourself, and Tom would too. Now – you better get back to your story before Tom Junior explodes with frustration.'

'Of course,' said Marco, turning to the first page where the big picture of Squadron Leader Reginald Charters in his fine uniform, sat proudly on the page.

At 3pm, Marco waved off Tom, Irene and Tom Junior, chasing after the truck, loaded with sheep, as it went down the narrow winding road, making faces as Tom Junior squealed with delight.

He walked into the house and sat down at the table. He had no idea what to write to his mum, but he picked up the pen, regardless, and looked down at the lovely writing paper all set out for him. He knew that anything he wrote would have to go through censors, so he couldn't say too much, but he could tell his parents that he was safe, and being well looked after.

By the time he had finished, he had written around three pages – telling them all about his role in the war so far, with the horror removed so as not to upset his mother. Along with the sanitised version of his fighting experiences, he told them about the farm and how kind the Gower family had been – teaching all about farming, from tending to the land, to milking the goats and looking after the sheep. He told them that Lorenzo was well too, and he hoped that everyone at home was smiling and happy.

Once the letter was finished, he put it into the envelope and lay it on the table, before taking a quick look around the room. He had not been in there before…it was lovely, warm and sunny with walls adorned with pictures painted by Tom Junior. The young boy had painted pictures of his family, and of the animals on the farm. Then, in one picture, he had drawn a huge ice cream and labelled it 'my favourite food in all the world.'

Marco stared at it. He knew everything there was to know about ice cream. His father ran an ice cream parlour at home in Italy, and since he had been a boy; he had understood what it took to make the finest desserts in the country. Tom had not mentioned how much he liked ice cream before.

Marco knew what he would do with his afternoon off - he would make them some of the delicious, natural ice cream that his father served in his shop. But would it be OK to use some of Irene's precious milk? With rationing and scarce resources, he did not know whether he should. Then he looked at the gorgeous picture again. He was sure they would be pleased if he left them a treat. So he headed outside and milked the goat, churning up the milk, freezing it then churning it again. He added nuts, berries and honeysuckle, and some icing sugar, mixing all the ingredients in a bag, then churning it, heating it, churning it, heating it, crushing it and leaving it in the freezer overnight with a note in his best handwriting, telling them what he had made for them. By the time he finished, he heard the sound of the truck at the gate, and rushed out of the farmhouse and down the long lane to join his fellow prisoners and head back to camp.

The next day when he arrived at the farm, Irene greeted him at the gate and gave him a huge hug. Marco noticed the admonishing looks from the soldiers on the truck. They hated the prisoners of war to get too close to the farmers they worked for, and particularly the farmers' very attractive wives.

'That was the loveliest ice cream I have ever tasted,' she said, once the truck had trundled away. 'It was amazing. How did you manage to make something so delicious without any ingredients?'

'It's like the ice cream my father makes in his cafe at home,' he said. 'I used to help him and I still remember how it was made. I used the things I found on the farm. I milked the goat. I hope that was OK?'

'Of course that was OK. It was very kind of you, and it was delicious. Can you believe that we ate half of it for breakfast? Tom Junior would not relax until he had tasted it. We have saved you some. Come in and have some ice cream.'

Marco cautiously followed Irene, waiting at the farmhouse door, unsure whether he should go inside.

'Come in,' she said. 'Come on, you know everyone here.'

'Hello, Marco,' said Tom Junior whose face was covered in ice cream. The dogs had gathered around the table, hoping for scraps. Irene shooed them away and showed Marco to a seat, then she spooned more ice cream out for everyone and silence descended over the breakfast table as they enjoyed their indulgent treat.

'Do you know the story of Gelert the dog?' asked Tom Junior, looking up at Marco. 'Daddy is going to tell me the whole story, right from the beginning. Do you want to hear it?'

'Of course,' said Marco, loving the way in which Tom Junior climbed onto his lap and looked up at him. He glanced up at Irene and Tom, as if seeking their approval for this. They both smiled.

'Right, well, Gelert was a lovely, kind dog, who belonged to Tom the Great,' started Tom Senior.

'Yes,' said Tom, giggling to himself. He loved it when his dad changed the names in the stories they read together.

'The dog had been given to Tom the Great as a gift from Queen Irene of Carmarthen who was the most beautiful woman in all of Wales.'

Irene shook her head and smiled at Marco.

'Except when she's cross,' Tom Junior whispered. 'She's not very beautiful when she's cross with me.'

Marco laughed, and Tom Senior continued. 'Well, this dog was a fine and loyal dog, and one day Tom the Great left the dog in the house with his baby, when he went out to do some farming. He thought the baby would be safe with the dog, but when Tom the Great returned, the baby was missing, the cradle had been overturned, and Gelert had blood all over his mouth.

'You are a very naughty dog,' said Tom the Great, thinking that the dog had attacked the baby. 'Very, very naughty dog.'

'Tom the Great was so angry with the dog for killing his baby that he pulled out his sword and killed the dog. Then, as soon as the dog was dead, Tom the Great heard his baby crying. The baby was not dead; he was hidden under the cot, completely safe. Next to the baby was a dead wolf.

'Tom the Great realised that the wolf had attacked the child and Gelert had killed the wolf and moved the baby to safety. Gelert the dog was a hero. Tom the Great was heartbroken by what had happened.'

'Now make the story nice,' said Tom Junior. 'Make it nice like you did before.'

'OK,' said Tom Senior, as Marco ruffled the boy's hair. 'Well, Tom the Great was horrified by what had happened and turned to look at the dog he had killed. He looked closer and realised the dog was not dead, his whiskers moved. Then the dog stood up…it was fine. Everyone was absolutely fine and Tom the Great was made king of the entire world.'

As Irene, Marco and Tom Junior cheered at the happy news, Marco heard the familiar rumbling of the truck pulling up the farm track towards the house.

'I wonder what they want?' said Marco, feeling nervous. Had they come to remove him from the farm because they saw him hug the farmer's wife? Or perhaps they heard that he had spent the previous afternoon making ice cream instead of working the land. He moved to stand up, but Tom beat him to it.

'You stay here,' he said. 'I will deal with them.'

Minutes later, Tom came back in. 'Well, Marco, it seems that Italy have changed their allegiance in the war. We're now all on the same side.'

'Oh my,' said Irene, while Marco sat there, speechless.

'They can't repatriate everyone all at once, so it's been suggested that you stay working on the farm for now, until they know how your regiment will be redeployed for the Allies. I suggested to them that you come and live here, with us, and you will be available for redeployment when the time comes. Does that sound OK?'

Marco dropped his head into his hands. He was overcome with joy.

'Please come and live with us. You can be my big brother,' said Tom Junior.

'I'd love that,' said Marco, turning to face Tom. 'You've been incredibly kind to me right from the start. Thank you.'

'You're welcome. Keith and Ken are moving back to work on their own farm because their father is ill, so we will be busier than ever. Now go and write to your mother, tell her that this is your new address and she can always reach you here. I will ring Llyr Beddows – the man who runs the local solicitors, and ask him what we have to do, legally, to make sure it's OK for you to stay here. He'll know…'

'Thank you,' said Marco, hugging Irene and leaning over to shake hands with Tom. 'You are incredibly kind people. I will never, ever forget what you have done for me.'

PRESENT DAY: OFF TO GOWER

'You're going for one night,' said Ted, as he loaded my enormous case into the back of his car and walked over to sit in the driver's seat. 'One night. Do you really need all this stuff?'

'I don't know,' I said. The truth was that I had no idea what I needed or what was going to happen. I had packed a black outfit to wear to the funeral, but besides that, I didn't know what we would be doing.

'I had to pack lots of things,' I told Ted as he drove off toward the station. 'What if I'm invited to a party or something?'

'It's a funeral. I don't think there'll be much partying going on.'

'Ah, but we don't know, do we? I need to be prepared for every eventuality. I need the right shoes for the occasion without having a remote clue what the occasion is.'

Ted glanced at me despairingly as he cut through the early morning traffic.

'And it's a luxury hotel, remember, it's bound to have a lovely spa, so I've got my gym and spa stuff so I can come back feeling all healthy.'

'Why do they need you to be there today if the funeral isn't till tomorrow?'

'I don't know,' I replied. 'You spoke to the solicitor more than I did; I guess it's just to tell us about the guy who died and why we've all been invited. Hopefully by this evening I'll know what's going on.'

'It's very intriguing,' he said. 'I'm still a bit worried though. You will be careful, won't you?'

'It's very intriguing,' I replied, ignoring the 'be careful' bit. 'Mum's rung everyone in the family and no one has a clue who he is... This is all a complete bloody mystery. Dad has no family at all, really. As you know, he was adopted when he was a baby. He has a half-brother who was adopted by a different family but the two fell out years ago and have not spoken for decades. It's so bloody complicated, but he says there was definitely no Reginald hovering around.'

Ted dropped me at Esher station and from there I got a train to Reading and then on to South Wales. I had never been to Wales before but I had googled the place and it looked amazing. And I have watched lots of Gavin and Stacey and think Catherine Zeta-Jones is beautiful, so I was hopeful that I would enjoy it.

Having negotiated the first part of the journey with relative ease, I sat back on the train to Wales, shut my eyes, and thought about the bizarre scenario ahead of me.

Explaining to work why I couldn't come in had tied me up in the most ridiculous conversation.

'You don't know him, or you do know him?' Keith had asked, with understandable confusion.

'I don't know him, but I have to go to his funeral and while I'm there I assume I'm going to discover that I do know him, and I'll find out why.'

'It seems odd,' Keith said.

I told him he wasn't the first person to say that.

In the end I said I'd take three days off as holiday because I couldn't work out how I could claim them as bereavement days when I didn't even know the guy who had died and certainly couldn't claim he was a close relative. Luckily Keith had been quite enchanted by the mystery of it all and was very keen for me to go to find out what this was all about, so I only had to take two days holiday.

I opened my bag and laid out some snacks on the train table in front of me. They looked so lovely, sitting there urging me to eat them all in one fell swoop. I had bought a big bag of jelly babies because I read somewhere that jelly babies have absolutely no fat in them so footballers and rugby players eat them at half time. I do not know whether this is true, and I am sure I do not want to look like a football or rugby player, but they must be quite good for you if nutritionists are letting leading sports people have them.

More importantly, they tasted delicious – as if sunshine had been melted down and shaped like babies. What's not to like about that?

I could resist it no more, I poured a pile of them into my hand and shoved them all into my mouth, feeling the gorgeous sugary taste as liquid fruitiness ran down the back of my throat.

This is the problem with sweet stuff, isn't it? It tastes so bloody nice and makes you feel wonderful.

I ate a Twix next then regretted it straight away and pushed the rest of my snacks into my handbag to take with me to the Gower Farm Hotel.

At Llanelli station, I was the only person to get off the train, and I stepped onto the deserted platform as if I was in some film from wartime... I was half waiting for the steam to clear to reveal my family, running to greet me after I had been away, fighting for my country.

Sadly, there was no steam and no loving family, so I trundled along the platform, dragging my wheelie case behind me, and making a considerable racket as it bounced along on the uneven surface. They could probably hear me coming from half a mile away.

As I approached the main doors to the station, searching for Joe's Ice Cream Parlour, a kind-looking man dressed like an old-fashioned porter came out to see me and helped me with my bag, placing it in the boot of the taxi sitting outside with my name in the window.

'Have a lovely time, dear,' he said in a beautiful Welsh accent, and I was driven away as if I were a movie queen.

To say that the taxi took me out to the back of beyond would be to underplay the remoteness of the place to which I was taken. Dear Lord, we drove down tiny farm tracks where only one car would fit and had to pull over into the bushes if any other car came towards us. As we went along, the taxi driver told me tales of a tramp who once came and lay down on the ground in one of these lanes and was run over by a farmer's help in his tractor.

'Terrible business. We thought he'd be done for murder, we did,' he said. 'But they worked out the chap was dead before the tractor hit him. How do they work out that sort of thing?'

'Oh, I don't know,' I said, surprised he had taken me for someone with an in-depth knowledge of forensic medicine. 'Perhaps they can tell how long the body's been dead?'

'How do they do that then?' he asked.

'Well, I'm not an expert, but I'm sure they can tell. I've seen Miss Marple lots of times and they can always tell when the person died. Perhaps they examine the contents of the stomach and can see how much food has been digested?'

'Good God, is that what they do, Miss Marple?' he said. 'That is horrible if they do that, horrible.'

'Yes, well, I suppose they have to find out the time of death to help them find out how someone died. My name is not Miss Marple, by the way. I think you got confused there.'

'Right you are,' he said. 'We used to have lots of prisoners of war here during the war. It was probably one of them. Italians they were.'

'Right.' I wasn't sure how to respond to the snippets of local history being scattered in my direction, so we sat in an uncomfortable silence until he pulled into a narrow track leading up to a farm.

'I don't think I'm supposed to be staying at a farm,' I said.

'No, this isn't a farm now. It used to be Gower Farm many years ago, but these days it is a very fine hotel. You'll like it.'

'Oh good.' I peered out of the window as we went past fields of sheep that gave the very distinct impression that this was, in fact, a farm. Then we went past hay barns, tractors, and a chicken coop.

'You're absolutely sure that this isn't a farm?' I mean, I am not a country girl but even I was able to discern farm-like features.

'Here we go then,' he said. 'This is the hotel I was told to bring you to.' He beeped his horn loudly and the large front door creaked open. A woman came out and stood nervously next to the building that resembled, in every way, a farmhouse.

'This is Miss Marple,' said the taxi driver.

'Oh, I thought you'd be Mary,' said the woman, stepping slowly and cautiously toward me. 'We're not expecting a Miss Marple. Have you booked?'

'I am Mary,' I said. 'There's been some sort of confusion about the name.'

'There's your bag then, Miss Marple, enjoy your stay,' said the taxi driver.

'Thank you,' I said, flustered, as I tried to explain to this terribly kind Welsh lady in a brown cardigan and matching brown jumper that I wasn't Miss Marple and hadn't pretended to be Miss Marple, and I was, as she predicted, Mary Brown.

'Very well then,' she said. 'I'll call you Mary, if you don't mind. I am Gladys. Come inside.'

'Sure.' I walked behind her, observing the flammable nest of a hairstyle, made rigid with so much hairspray that the slightest spark would have seen the whole thing go up in flames.

PRESENT DAY: MISS MARPLE ARRIVES

Dragging my large bag behind me, I trailed after Gladys, following the sway of her tweed skirt and the padding of her sensible shoes on the ground, as she walked into the reception area.

'You're staying on after the funeral, are you?' she asked in quite a strong Welsh accent that I was struggling to understand. Then she looked at the size of my case. 'I have only booked you for one night. You plan to stay longer?'

'No, that's fine, one night is all I'm staying for,' I said. I found myself leaning into her in order to hear and understand every word.

'You must be pissed here, after your long journey,' she said.

'Sorry?'

'I said 'you must be pleased to be here after your long journey'.'

'Oh, yes, pleased – yes, very pleased,' I said, and I smiled and nodded warmly. This was going to be a fun couple of days.

'Is everyone else here?' I asked.

'Most of them are. Let me take you up to your room and you can freshen up, then come down for drinks before lunch in twenty minutes.'

'OK,' I said, walking up the stairs carpeted with some swirling monstrosity in faded yellow and brown. I followed Gladys to my room and watched as she opened it by clicking on the latch. No electronic key, not even a normal key.

'How do I lock my door?' I asked.

'There are no locks,' said Gladys. 'You're quite safe here. I'll see you downstairs soon.'

The door emitted a creak like the whine of a dog in considerable distress as I pushed it open. I surveyed the heavily floral linen on the bed in the corner of the room. The flowers on the duvet were pale blue, the flowers on the wall were candyfloss pink, and underfoot were hideous swirls of brown and yellow. Never, in the history of womankind, have so many colours and patterns competed for attention.

There was a small dressing table in the corner that looked as if it had come from the early twentieth century. It was horse brown and thickly lacquered. Like everything else in the room, it was in spectacularly bad taste.

Atop the table sat a gaudy old alarm clock, ticking loudly as if counting down to the end of the world.

It was not the sort of room one associated with a luxury hotel; in fact, there was nothing about this place that brought to mind any thoughts of indulgence. I peered out of the small leaded windows at acres of fields, cranking one of them open to get a better look. It was beautiful outside, to be fair. Nothing but rolling fields as far as the eye could see.

I sat down heavily on the bed. This was obviously a beautiful part of the world, but this 'hotel' was nothing more than an old-fashioned farmhouse with none of the thrills or glamour that one would expect of even the most standard hotel. I did what I always do when feeling slightly disappointed or under pressure, and pulled out all the snacks I had saved and laid them on the bed.

As I put my bag back down onto the floor, I noticed an envelope on the rather tatty bedside table. I picked it up and looked inside:

'Please meet downstairs for a late lunch at 3pm. Drinks will be served at 2.30pm,' it said.

I looked from the note to my crisps and back again. It was almost lunchtime, I shouldn't eat anything really. But then again, circumstances like these allow for a little leeway, surely? I took some crisps out of the bag and crunched into them, feeling the gorgeous cheesy flavour fill my mouth. God, that was lovely. There was nothing as fabulous as food for making you feel instantly better, happier and more relaxed. The problem was that there was also nothing quite as effective as food for making you very, very fat.

I leaned my hands on my stomach that hung over the waistband of my trousers and instantly regretted the reckless snacking. I pushed against it, pulling my stomach in as much as possible, holding it in and saying a silent prayer that it would stay like that. The prayer didn't work though, it never does. I breathed back out and my stomach rolled over the top of my trousers again so I took another handful of crisps to escape the feeling of hopelessness.

Then I put my hand back into the envelope to recheck the timings on the note, and realised there were other pieces of paper there, including a letter in the same old-fashioned penmanship as the letter that had been sent to me at home. Reginald's writing:

Dearest Mary,

If you are reading this note, you are here – in the Gower Farm Hotel. I am so incredibly delighted. This was once a farm that meant so much to my father.

It is appropriate that you should be here because you mean so much to me. Everyone at this funeral means so much to me.

Your relative and the relatives of everyone here saved me from pain and misery and brought me to life again.

Reginald

What the hell?

I read the note again.

So, my relatives had helped him somehow. They had saved him from pain and misery. There were other notes in the envelope. I loosened my trousers further, and sat back on the pillows, tipping the contents of the envelope onto the bed.

There was a list of everyone who was here and would be at the funeral along with photographs of them. I looked down the list at the unfamiliar names. At the bottom, it said, 'Tom Gower (not yet traced).' What did that mean? What did any of this mean?

Also in the envelope was an article about a writing course held in 1973.

It said: 'Learn from one of the best teachers of playwriting in the world: Andrew Marks. Degree not essential but preferable.' Then there were all the details of where the course would be taking place…in Bristol, of all places, at somewhere called the Bristol Playhouse.

Why would someone leave a cutting about a writing course held in 1973? Moreover, how could it be so significant that it had caused him to invite six people he did not know to his funeral?

I sat back on the bed, letting the notes and papers from the envelope fall onto the sheets next to me. My trousers were digging into me and my top was too thick in the warm room. I took my clothes off and lay on the bed in my bra and knickers, then I picked up the phone and rang Ted.

'So, who is he?' Ted sounded all excited. 'Have you been told yet?'

'No, it's all getting weirder by the minute. This place doesn't look like a hotel at all – it's more like an old farmhouse – all creaky and old-fashioned.'

'But you were told it was a luxury hotel – you took all your spa stuff. Is there no spa there?'

'Um, no,' I said. 'Nothing even remotely resembling a spa. We're in the middle of nowhere.'

'And you think it's a farmhouse? Why do you say that?'

'Err…sheep, chickens and tractors everywhere.'

'Yep, well, I guess that does make it sound like a farmhouse. Have you asked them why they said it was a luxury hotel?'

'No, I haven't seen anyone yet, only the lady on reception and I can barely understand a word she says. The accents they have here are so strong.'

'So there's no more news on anything?'

'Sort of. There is an envelope next to my bed, with an article in it about a writing course in 1973. I think it is supposed to be some sort of clue, but I don't know how.'

'Let me just get out of the office and I will talk to you outside – tell me what it says.'

I could hear Ted marching through the office as I told him about the contents of the envelope.

'Well, there's the advert for the creative writing course. I can't see any names on it that seem relevant, or any facts or figures that help me to understand this mad situation any better. I wonder whether the others all have the same article as me. It might mean something to some of them.'

'Gosh, Mary, that's so weird though. What was the name of the guy running the course? I'll google it, and see whether I can find anything out.'

'Andrew Marks,' I said, spelling it out.

'I'll check him out when I get off the call. What else have you got?'

I told him all about the handwritten note, reading it out to him slowly as he wrote it down.

'I don't think that's a clue or anything. I think it's simply a note from him.'

'Yeah,' Ted agreed. 'I don't understand why they are giving you clues though, do you? Why not just bloody tell you who this guy was?'

'Well, that would be nice,' I said. 'They haven't told me anything more than the letter I got through the post told me. And the taxi driver thought I was Miss Marple.'

'Miss who?'

'Marple – you know the TV detective.'

'Oh, right. Why did they think that?'

'A bit of a language barrier, honestly, Ted, and the accent. The accent is impossible.'

'And what about the others?' asked Ted, wisely opting not to grill me further on the circumstances that led to me being called Miss Marple. 'Are they there yet?'

'Yes, they're here, but I haven't seen them. I'm upstairs in my room.'

'Go and find out who's there,' said Ted. 'Then it will all become clear.'

'I've got a list of who's here,' I said. 'But it doesn't really help very much because I've never heard of any of them.'

'Oooooh...go through it. We need to work out what the link is between all the people there. I bet it'll be obvious whose funeral you're attending.'

'Do you think?' I was not at all convinced. But I did like Ted's childlike excitement about the whole thing. I reached over to pick up the piece of paper.

'OK...well it says here that the people invited to the funeral are Matt Prior, who looks about seventeen in the picture. He's doing a carpentry apprenticeship and lives in Wales.'

'OK,' said Ted, I could hear him scribbling down everything I said.

'Then there's Sally Bramley who looks a bit like my mum. I guess she is mid-fifties. She's a PE teacher according to this, and she lives in Ascot.'

'Right,' said Ted.

'Then there's a Julie Bramley – I don't know whether she's related to the other Bramley but she's very glamorous. Works for a magazine in London. Looks like she has had a lot of work done. A bit like Pamela Anderson – you know – the one who used to be in Baywatch. And there are two more – Mike Sween – he's very handsome.'

'Oh yeah,' said Ted.

'No – I mean he's a handsome older man. He's, like, fifty or something – about my dad's age, so don't worry – but he looks like a TV presenter or an actor or something. He has dark hair that is probably dyed and a dimple in his chin. He is from Wales, but now lives in Twickenham.

'Then there's a really old guy called Simon Blake. He's a theatre director and lives in Bath.'

'Right.'

There was an elongated pause while Ted was clearly thinking through the information I had given him.

'So, there's a mixture of ages, genders, geographical locations and jobs? None of them have anything in common.'

'Yep, that's about the size of it,' I said.

'Mmmm… Although – hang on – read me the details of the playwrights' course you mentioned.'

I pulled out the sheet and read it.

'Bristol?' said Ted.

'Yes,' I replied.

'Isn't that near Bath?'

'I don't know. Why?'

'Well, didn't you say there was a theatre director there from Bath? He might have something to do with the playwrights' course?'

'Brilliant!' I said. 'You should be a detective.'

1945: THE END OF THE WAR

'Hey, you guys, come here, come here,' shouted Irene, jumping up in the passenger seat of the tractor and waving her arms over her head. Tom brought the vehicle to a stop and Marco ran across the field toward them, holding Tom Junior's hand.

'It's over. It's over. Germany has surrendered.'

'What?' said Marco, stopping in his tracks.

'It's true. It's all over.'

'Oh my God. Are you sure? Are you really sure?'

Marco threw Tom Junior into the air and shouted with joy.

'Remember it,' he said to Tom Junior. 'May 7th 1945. Never forget that, Tom. Will you? Remember it forever...the day the war ended.'

He spun round, holding the young boy aloft. 'Never forget it, Tom. Never.'

The two of them climbed up and sat next to Irene on the

tractor and they headed back to the farmhouse. 'I won't forget it,' muttered Tom Junior. 'I'll always remember.'

Tom Junior was seven years old. He had grown into a bright and inquisitive boy, helpful on the farm and hard working at school. Marco knew he would make a real success of his life. He wondered whether the boy would remember him, in the years to come. They had been in each other's lives so much for the past couple of years...seeing one another every day. Would he be remembered by any of these people? He knew he would remember them forever.

'What are your plans then?' asked Tom when they arrived back in the farmhouse kitchen.

'I'll go back to Italy,' said Marco. The thought of seeing his parents filled him with joy, though he felt so sad at the prospect of leaving Llanelli. This beautiful part of the world had become his home.

'Have you been writing to your mother regularly?'

'Yes,' said Marco. The truth was that he had only sent a few letters even though he had received loads from his mum.

'Write to her. Invite her to visit us with your father,' said Tom. Irene turned and smiled at her husband. He wasn't normally as sociable, and he didn't extend invitations easily, but she knew how much he had come to love Marco, and didn't want him to leave. Marco was a joy around the house as well as being so incredibly helpful on the farm.

'Yes,' agreed Irene. 'Please invite them, Marco. That would be lovely. And invite your friend Lorenzo – we haven't seen him for a while.'

Four weeks later, Marco's mother and father arrived on the farm. His mother, Anna, with a shawl wrapped tightly around her shoulders, and his father knowing only a handful of English words. Anna gasped when she saw her son – bigger, stronger and more handsome than ever. She threw herself into his arms, sobbing and overcome with joy.

He introduced his parents to the couple who had become his surrogate mum and dad, and to Tom Junior who clung onto Marco as if he thought they'd come to take him away.

'We've organised a little party for you tonight,' Marco told them. 'So you can meet the new friends I've made here.' He spoke in Italian, which felt somehow strange after so many years of speaking English and struggling to understand Welsh.

'There's no need. Tell them not to go to so much trouble,' his mum said. Marco knew that his mum wasn't much of a party animal and was aware that being the centre of attention at a get-together thrown in her honour would be very daunting, but he also knew how keen Tom and Irene were on welcoming them properly.

Despite Anna's resistance to the idea, by 7pm the following evening, Gower Farm had been transformed. Candles flickered and welcome banners danced in the breeze. Marco had made loads of delicious ice cream, there were sandwiches and stacks of Welsh cakes. He had not seen such a spread since before the war. Irene had been baking bread and cakes all day. He was flattered and deeply grateful to her. The party was to celebrate the end of the conflict and the visit of Marco's parents. Tom and Irene were determined to make it the best party ever, and locals drifted in through the evening – all carrying parcels of food to add to the collection, and bottles of beer to share.

Marco walked round checking that everyone was OK, and introducing his mother and father to all the people he had come to know so well while in Wales. His parents smiled as introductions were made, but he knew how shy they felt being paraded around, so once they had met everyone, he took them back over to Tom and Irene, and gave them all chairs to sit on, so they could chat comfortably, away from the madding crowd.

'I'll see you later. You all behave yourselves now. No getting into trouble while my back is turned,' he said, jokingly.

'Not like we used to then,' said a voice behind him. He swung round. His great friend, Lorenzo, was walking through the party with the trademark swagger that took Marco straight back to memories of their youth together.

'Lorenzo. This is magical. Come here.'

Marco pulled Lorenzo into a warm hug.

'So good to see you,' said Lorenzo. 'How's everything been?'

'Great. Tom and Irene have been brilliant. I have stayed working on the farm. I could not be happier. How about you?'

'I've been OK. I moved off the farm I was on, and have been working in Swansea. Do you know it? It's not far from here.'

'I've heard of it,' said Marco. 'Come on, let's get you a beer.'

The two men walked over to the small, disused hen house near the main house. It had been converted into a bar and dance hall for the evening. Marco reached for a glass of beer and turned to hand it to his friend.

Then, he saw her. The most beautiful sight his eyes had ever fallen upon – a gorgeous raven-haired woman – small, slight and delicate, standing near the door, gazing out into the warm summer's evening. Marco stood and stared for a while.

'Am I going to get that beer?' asked Lorenzo.

'Sure. Here you go.'

'Who's the girl you keep staring at?'

'I don't know. I've never seen her before.'

'Go and talk to her,' he said. It was just like the old days, when the two of them would cruise around the coffee bars on their scooters, looking for girls.

But it was so much harder now. He felt like a different person since the war...more serious, less able to engage in flippancy and playfulness.

'I don't know how to,' said Marco.

'I do.' Lorenzo walked straight up to the girl and put his hand out.

'I'm Lorenzo, this is my friend Marco. He is famous in Italy. His dad makes the best ice cream in the country.'

'Nice to meet you,' said Marco, his face burning with embarrassment.

'Can I get you a drink or anything?'

'I'm fine,' she said. 'But thank you.'

'I'll see you later,' said Lorenzo, walking away, whistling to himself as he clutched his beer in his hand, and headed outside.

'I live here with Tom and Irene,' Marco said. 'What's your name?'

The woman went bright red. 'I'm Madelyn.'

She spoke with a strong Welsh accent. Marco knew that if they had met when he first came to the country, he would never have understood her.

'Do you live locally?'

'I am on the farm on the other side of the valley. I live with my mum and dad, and my brothers – Ken and Keith. They used to work on the farm. I think you know them.'

'Ken and Keith? Yes, I know them. They were here when I first arrived. They left not long afterwards.'

'They used to talk about you,' she said. 'They told me how nice you were.'

'That's good of them. Are they here today? I'd love to say hello.'

'No, they're on the farm. They are running it together because Dad got ill and couldn't do any physical work anymore.'

'I'm sorry to hear that. Tell them I said hello.'

'Of course I will, and can I change my mind about that drink?'

'Yes, what do you fancy?'

And that was it.

Marco and Madelyn spent the entire evening together and Marco was smitten. It turned out that Madelyn was just a year younger than he was and had been born on Dirgelwch Farm where she'd lived all her life, and now worked, organising the sales from the farm shop they had set up even though they had so little produce to sell to customers it had become ridiculous.

'I spend most of my time telling people we don't have what they want. Hopefully that will change now the war is over.'

Marco looked into eyes of melted chocolate and knew, without any doubt, that he would marry this woman.

1950: THE ICE-CREAM PARLOUR

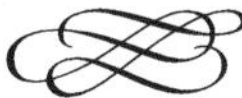

'What's bacio?' asked the little boy with bright blonde hair, standing on tiptoes to peer into the glass-fronted cabinet, while his mother stood beside him.

'He loves your ice cream,' she explained. 'He can't get enough of it.'

'I am glad. Well, bacio means 'kiss',' said Madelyn, offering the boy an air kiss and seeing his nose wrinkle in disgust.

'I don't want a kiss, I want an ice cream.'

'Stop teasing the customers,' said Marco, appearing at his wife's side and draping his arm over her shoulder before addressing the boy. 'So, little man – this is how it works in this ice cream shop: on this side of the cabinet we have the 'fruits of the farm' ice creams which are made from fruits and nuts grown at Gower Farm. On this side are the 'taste of Italy' ice creams – coffee, chocolate, vanilla, and fudge…things like that…flavours that we have a lot of in Italy. Now, if you want a mixture of flavours you have a bacio – a kiss of flavours. So you could have hazelnut and chocolate or toffee…whatever you fancy. If you want three flavours it's a bacio grande – a big kiss – and four flavours is a neapolitan.'

'Dad, Dad,' shouted the boy. 'Please can I have a big kiss?'

Madelyn smiled as she saw the expression of surprise on the face of the boy's father, before the two of them ordered a bacio grande comprised of the sweetest flavours on offer.

The place had been buzzing all day with locals. Because the ice cream shop was on Gower Farm, it was hard to alert new people to the fact that the cafe was there. Madelyn had done her best, and had hung bunting at the end of the farm track, and put notes in the windows of the newsagents in Llanelli telling everyone that a new ice cream shop had opened selling all natural ice cream with fresh farm milk, but it was very difficult to be sure that passers-by knew about them, so they tended to rely on locals.

At 10pm, they shut the shop and cleaned the floors, making sure that all the ingredients were ready for ice cream making the next morning. They had fallen very comfortably into a routine of hard work and determination to make their ice cream shop the best in the world.

'As long as we make ice cream that tastes great, is reasonably priced, and is served with a smile, we will make a success of this,' Marco was fond of saying. 'We have to.'

'Is all the fruit cleaned and ready?' asked Madelyn, as Marco did his final checks.

'Yes, all ready,' he said.

'Come on then you, let's go to bed.'

Their life was busy but enjoyable and Marco thanked his lucky stars every day that he had found himself working on Tom's farm when he had been captured during the war.

He and Tom hadn't been in each other's pockets quite so much since the ice cream shop opened, but they still met up while they could, and Madelyn would often take a tub of ice cream round to the Gower family, and chat to Irene over a cup of tea and a bacio grande.

On Friday night, they had Tom and Irene coming over for dinner, and Madelyn was determined to make a huge success of it. She and Marco had exciting news to share with their landlords and she wanted to cook a perfect dinner over which to tell them. She bought all the ingredients necessary and they asked the staff to cover them in the shop in the evening so they could entertain properly.

Madelyn slipped upstairs to change before dinner, while Marco went over to the ice cream parlour to check everything was OK. At 8pm on the dot, Tom and Irene arrived. Tom was dressed in work clothes, and looked tired and distant, while Irene looked spectacular. She was wearing the most beautiful dress and jacket combination in a lovely powder-blue colour. She looked immaculate. She always did, but on this occasion, more stylish than ever. She seemed to understand clothes so well, and wore them with elegance and élan.

Madelyn made the final touches to the food in the kitchen, and attempted to spruce herself up a little. The sight of Irene in her lovely clothes had made her feel dowdy and unattractive. Marco organised drinks for them all, and invited Tom and Irene to take a seat.

'The ice cream parlour has been packed recently,' he said, handing Irene a gin and sin - her favourite drink. 'The locals have been so supportive.'

As Marco spoke, he saw Tom glance over at Irene and then

look away quickly, but it was enough of an eye movement to let Marco know that something was afoot.

'Is everything OK?' asked Marco. 'I get the feeling there might be something wrong.'

'No, not at all,' said Irene. 'We'll talk about it over dinner. This gin is delicious...just how I like it. Thanks, Marco.'

'Please take your seats when you're ready, and I'll serve dinner,' said Madelyn, rushing into the room and placing the condiments on the table. She dashed back into the kitchen and collected the plates of food: Welsh lamb with mint sauce from the farm, boiled potatoes and vegetables.

'This looks lovely,' said Irene. 'You are very kind to invite us over like this.'

'We're glad you could come,' said Marco raising his glass to salute them. Now, everyone, please get stuck in.

A companionable silence descended over the gathering while they ate their food. Madelyn noticed Irene just picking at hers...barely eating anything. Presumably, that was how she stayed so slim.

'We actually have something to tell you,' said Tom, breaking the tranquility and laying down his knife and fork. 'I don't know how to say this...but we've decided to sell the farm.'

There were gentle gasps from Marco and Madelyn as Tom made his announcement. 'I know it will come as a surprise, but Irene is keen to move and enjoy a new way of life. Her parents live in Llandrindod Wells, and they are getting old. She's keen to be with them.'

'But, I thought the farm had been in your family for generations? Are you sure you want to sell it?'

'Yes,' said Irene, cutting across the chatter. 'We've talked about it for a long time and it's something we're both keen on doing.'

Tom looked down at the table. He seemed sad, dejected, like a man who really didn't want to leave the farm at all.

'Well, I'm sure it will be lovely to be with Irene's parents,' said Madelyn. 'And it'll be nice to have a new way of life. No more terrifyingly early mornings for you.'

Tom smiled weakly. Marco looked from the dejected Tom to the radiant Irene. It was clear who was the keener to move away from farming life. He felt a deep pang of sadness for Tom.

'Obviously, if we sell the farm, we'll be selling your shop with it,' Irene said. 'We've talked to Llyr Beddows and looked at whether we can sell you the shop separately so you'd own that bit of the building, but it's all integral to the farmhouse and the likely buyers are keen to turn the farm into a hotel – *Gower Farm Hotel* they want to call it. I am sorry. There's nothing we can do.'

Marco felt his heart sink, but Tom had done so much for them, he didn't want him to feel guilty about leaving. 'Don't worry, you've given us the best start ever – we've got a thriving business and a loyal customer base, it's about time we moved to the High Street and tried to make a go of it independently. I am sorry you are moving away though. That's very sad. Very sad indeed.'

Tom smiled at Marco, and took a large gulp of his beer. 'You're not drinking tonight, Madelyn?'

'No, not tonight,' she said, glancing at Marco.

It was Tom's turn to be concerned. 'I saw that glance,' he said. 'What aren't you telling us?'

'I'm pregnant,' said Madelyn with an enormous smile. 'I'm going to have a baby.'

'Oh, that's wonderful news,' said Irene, leaping up and hugging the young woman who had become like a daughter to her. 'I'm so pleased for you both; you'll make the most wonderful parents. Oh Tom, now I am heartbroken that we're moving away. You two don't fancy coming to Llandrindod Wells with us, do you? It is a very lovely place with beautiful beaches and spectacular cliffs. We could help you set up an ice cream shop there – it'll be perfect for all the tourists passing through.'

'We can't,' said Marco, shaking his head. 'This place means so much to me. I love it here. I couldn't bear to leave.'

'It is a wonderful part of the world,' agreed Tom.

'We'll help you relocate the shop,' said Irene.

'No don't worry, we'll be fine. As long as we make good ice cream, sell it at reasonable prices and serve it with a smile, we will always be all right. And we are going to have a child... maybe it will be a son, and we will call him Joe. And when we open our ice cream shop we'll call it Joe's Ice Cream Parlour.'

'That's a lovely idea,' said Tom, offering a smile tinged with sadness.

'Tell me about the farm – how are they going to change it into a hotel?' asked Madelyn, eager to stop her husband from becoming too excited about the prospect of a son. She could have a daughter, and she wanted Marco to love a girl just as much.

'I think the plan is for them to keep it so it still has a farmhouse feel, with lovely fields outside, animals and some of the farming outbuildings, and making it as authentic as possible inside, but obviously modernised. We have six bedrooms remember, and there is a big attic and lots of big rooms downstairs. They are convinced it will work.'

Marco looked at the old dresser with the plates sitting on it, plates with pictures of scenes from the local area as well as produce prepared in the farmhouse going back decades – there was a plate depicting a picture of the castle, flowers and plants. One had a couple of lamb chops and potatoes on it which looked exactly like the dinners he'd had on the farm when he'd moved in with them years ago. It seemed such a shame that it would no longer be here as a working farm. He had devoted so much time to it – sweated blood on that land. 'Won't you miss it?' he asked Tom.

'Desperately,' he replied. 'But it's the right thing to do.'

PRESENT DAY: MEETING THE GANG

It was time for me to go down to meet this rather disparate group of people. On the surface it seemed they had nothing in common with me, but presumably I was about to discover the golden thread that bound us together, and to Reginald.

I wasn't sure what I was in for, and though I am a confident person, a feeling of nervousness crept over me as I walked along the creaky old corridor towards the stairs. The walls were slightly wonky and the floor was uneven under the hideously patterned carpet beneath my feet. Crockery plates adorned the walls, all of them featuring scenes from the local area; a castle, beach scenes, flowers and plants. I walked past them, inspecting every one of them, hoping to distract myself from the nervousness growing inside me. One of the plates featured a couple of lamb chops and potatoes. How completely weird. Why on earth would you want a picture of your dinner on the wall?

I turned the corner and saw the wide staircase I had come

up earlier. Thank God. Without any discernible sense of direction to rely on, it was always a moment of wonder when I discovered I was going the right way. The stairs seemed odder walking down than they had seemed when I came up – as if I was descending into some terrible B-movie in which sinister women with their hair in buns would stare at me while stirring pots of boiling water. At the bottom of the stairs, I walked across the oak entrance hall searching for the right room. Then I saw it – a small sign on one of the doors 'Friends of Reginald Charters'. That had to be it. I wasn't sure I qualified as a friend, but I pushed open the large door and peered inside. Faces turned to stare at me. They looked as confused as I felt.

'Hi, I'm Mary,' I said, with a smile. 'Anyone got a clue what's going on here?'

A rather elegant-looking man walked over and smiled warmly.

'Welcome,' he said. 'And no, none of us has the remotest clue what's going on, darling. It's most baffling.' He had an aristocratic, slightly theatrical air and I decided this must be Simon Blake. He was a director and looked every inch his profession, with thinning blonde hair that I suspect was once his crowning glory. Now he clung onto it like a drowning man clinging to a life raft. Every hair seemed to be coiffured and styled to within a millimetre of its life.

He wore a rather shabby, but expensive-looking, linen jacket in a creamy beige colour over green cords, a light blue shirt and navy blue jumper. It was an odd assortment. He was a handsome man, older, and a little frail but still good-looking. He was far too thin though. He could do with eating more. Not that I was planning to advise him about his calorie intake. I think I was about three times his circumference. He had a warm smile and a nice demeanour. And he had made the effort to come over and talk to me while the others just stared fearfully, as if I had entered the room carrying a Kalashnikov.

'Mary, join us for tea and let me introduce you to everyone here. As you can imagine, we are all trying to work out why we have been gathered in this room, and what it is that we have in common. Perhaps you will be the missing piece in the jigsaw that allows us to solve this conundrum.'

'I do hope so,' I said. 'I've never been a jigsaw piece before.'

I saw the tea on the side – a lovely big, old-fashioned teapot with a floral pattern on it, but also saw a bottle of wine. I would have much preferred a glass of wine, but there were biscuits with the tea, and I am very, very fond of biscuits. Would it be acceptable to have a glass of wine and a shortbread biscuit? I decided this was not an appropriate course of action, so I had a cup of tea that I didn't want so I could have the biscuit that went with it. Then I instantly regretted my choice.

'Would it be rude to ask for wine instead of tea?' I said. 'This is such an odd situation; I feel like a little glass would help me to relax.'

'Of course, it's not a problem,' said Simon, turning his back to pick up the bottle, thus allowing me a moment to reach over and grab a biscuit.

'Let's get this bottle of wine open,' he said.

It was at that point I realised no one else was drinking alcohol. They hadn't even opened the bottle. What sort of people were they?

'Oh no, don't open it just for me. I'll have tea,' I said, hoping to God that he didn't take me at my word.

'No, no, if you want a little glass of wine, you shall have a little glass of wine. I'm sure I'm capable of getting this bottle open.' He then proceeded to make an inordinate fuss about going through the drawers of a big oak dresser and trying to summon assistance to find a bottle opener.

'Bottle opener? Bottle opener?' he shouted through the room.

A young man who had been looking at the farm pictures on the far side of the room walked towards us. He was handsome and muscular. He leant over and gently unscrewed the top of the wine bottle and handed it to Simon. 'There you go,' he said. 'It's a screw top.'

'Yes, of course, yes,' said Simon, adjusting an imaginary cravat and running his hands through his manicured hair.

'I'm Matt,' said the young man in a gentle Welsh accent. 'Very nice to meet you.' He went bright red as he spoke and appeared nervous despite his tough-looking shell.

'It's lovely to meet you too,' I said. 'Would you like to join me in a glass of wine?'

'I don't drink,' said Matt. 'It makes me ill. But if I did, I would definitely join you.'

I smiled at him; how polite he was. But fancy not drinking? That was odd. When I was his age, the contents of my veins were eighty percent alcohol.

I thought back to the list of people who would be here today…this had to be Matt Prior. He was in his late teens according to the notes, but he looked older in the flesh, quite different form his picture, perhaps early twenties, but seemed so shy.

As Simon handed me the glass of wine, the door opened and a very attractive woman strutted in. She was tall and slim in a tight-fitting cashmere skirt and jumper combination, and an elaborate collection of gold and pearl necklaces hung around her neck. She was so beautiful and with the tiniest waist I'd ever seen. I put down my biscuit as a sign of respect. You know how people say 'she was really attractive but she just didn't know it'? Well, this woman was beautiful and boy did she know it.

She oozed confidence and sophistication, sashaying through the room, making cold eye contact with everyone as they turned one by one to stare at her. Every inch of carpet she stepped onto became her runway. She was beautiful in a way that made it impossible for me to stop looking at her. She seemed to have been put together better than anyone else in the room.

She was the sort of person who everybody wanted to befriend, to have in his or her social circle, in his or her orbit, so they could feel touched a little by the beauty radiating from her. But, although we all watched her as she walked across the room, she never acknowledged any of us. She let her big blue eyes flick from person to person, but she wasn't looking at us, she was checking whether we were looking at her.

The woman moved to the back of the room, slightly away from us but still within earshot, and peered out of the window as if searching for something far more interesting than any of us could provide.

I smiled at her and she smiled back but it was only her lips that curved into the shape of a smile while her face stayed stationary. It wasn't a smile to embrace you but a smile to distance you and keep you down where you belonged.

'This is all rather tiresome,' she said. 'Does anyone know what the hell is going on?'

'Hopefully we will soon,' I said, eager to make her happy. I always do this with good-looking people. There is a guy called Dave who lives in the flat below me, and I fall apart whenever he talks to me. He is not particularly interesting, but I fall at his feet and would do anything for him (literally – honestly – the things I have done would make you blush!).

'We haven't met,' said the beautiful woman. 'I'm Julie.'

She pronounced her name as if she were French: Zjoolieeee, drawing out the final vowel.

I stared at her.

'And you?' she said.

'Oh. Sorry. I'm Mary Brown.' I put out my hand to shake hers, almost curtseying in the process, but she had turned away and was ferreting in her expensive-looking handbag. The bag might have been from Top Shop for all I knew, but it looked exquisite and costly…everything about this woman looked expensive. 'We've been told that lunch is in half an hour, and that we might like to chat amongst ourselves about the funeral, and the guy who has died.'

'Yes, isn't it utterly daft? Though I understand we're in for some money. Does no one here know him?' she said. 'I mean – surely one of us has a clue who this guy was?'

I felt overwhelmed with excitement that she had chosen me to talk to. Me!

'None of us has a clue,' said Simon, coming over to join us. 'Not the remotest clue.'

PRESENT DAY: BEAUTIFUL BUT BRITTLE

The more I looked around the people gathered in the room, the more I felt like I was in an elaborate Agatha Christie movie. All we needed was the arrival of Hercule Poirot for us to be in a Christmas Special on the BBC. There was the beautiful but brittle woman in Julie, the very handsome and terribly nice younger man, and the theatrical older man. If Christie had plotted this, Julie would definitely be the one who murdered Reginald. Or was that too obvious? Perhaps it would be the daft fat woman in the corner drinking wine and eating biscuits.

'I'm Sally,' said an older woman, interrupting my fantasies. I had missed her arrival in the room because I had been so fascinated by Julie. Sally was quite plain and sturdy and immediately reminded me of a cross between my mum and Clare Balding. 'I'm Julie's sister.'

'Oh, lovely to meet you,' I said. 'Which Julie's your sister?'

'Julie, there,' she pointed to the crazily beautiful woman who was heading towards the doors that led outside. 'The woman you were talking to earlier.'

I was open-mouthed.

'I know – we don't look alike – she got the good looks; I got the good personality. What can you do?'

'Ha!' I laughed and thought immediately that no amount of lovely personality would compensate for not looking like Julie.

Her sister's exit through the back doors, presumably to smoke or get some fresh air, was done with exactly the same dramatic flounce that had accompanied her entrance.

The atmosphere in the room shifted a little when she left, and a kind of calmness descended. Simon walked toward me, refilling my glass (I don't know what happened to that first glass – it seemed to disappear).

'Did you get the cuttings on your bed?' asked Sally.

'Yes,' I said, moving to pull them out of my bag. 'I've got them with me. Did you get some too?'

'Yes, I think we all got them. I spoke to Simon earlier and he suggested that we all go through them and compare notes over lunch. We should be able to work out who this guy was, and then we'll all feel a bit more comfortable about everything.'

'Yes!' I replied. She had hit the nail on the head – we would all feel so much better and more relaxed once we knew who he was. It was hard to feel calm about a situation when you had no idea why you were in it.

'Does anyone have any ideas at all at the moment?' I asked.

Sally and Simon both shook their heads. 'No one I've spoken to has ever heard of this guy,' said Sally. 'I've talked to my relatives and he's definitely nothing to do with my family. I am a schoolteacher and I have been back through the lists of children who went to the school, in case one of their parents is related to this guy. I just can't find any link at all.'

'Me neither,' said Simon. 'I'm completely baffled.'

'He's definitely not related to me,' I said. 'I don't know why I'm here. I am sure they are going to discover they have invited me by mistake, and they were after another Mary Brown. It is such a common name. I cannot believe I was really invited by this guy on his deathbed. How would that ever happen to someone like me?'

'That's exactly what I thought,' said Sally. I felt myself warming to her. 'I was talking to my friend last night and I said to her that I fully expect them to announce halfway through that they got the wrong person.'

'It's interesting that you and your sister have been invited though, isn't it?' I said. 'It makes it sound like there must be a reason in your family for you to have been invited, rather than any of the students at school.'

'Yes, I guess so, but I spent all of yesterday with Mum while she phoned around, and we are absolutely sure he's not related to us.'

Julie came back into the room, smelling strongly of smoke and perfume, her lips glistening with freshly-applied lipstick.

'Shall we see if we can sit down for lunch?' she asked. 'There is no point standing around here any longer than necessary.'

'I think someone is still missing,' said Simon. He appeared to be taking on a leadership role. You know how when a group of people are thrown together, one person emerges as leader? Well that was definitely Simon in this little group. I felt he would be the one to solve the conundrum of who Reginald was and why we were here today.

'I'll just check who's still to come,' he said, consulting a piece of paper. 'A guy called Mike Sween is missing. It says on here that he might be ten minutes or so late.'

'Well he's about half an hour late now,' said Julie. 'Why don't we just go through and get started on this. I've got a few calls I need to make and I don't want to spend all evening faffing around waiting for late-comers.'

'Sure. There's nothing to stop us going through and sitting at the table and having a chat,' said Simon. 'But I'm sure they won't serve lunch till everyone is there.'

'Come on then,' said Julie. 'I might as well lead the way.'

I glanced at Simon and he shrugged at me. Letting Julie do exactly what she wanted was going to be a theme of the day.

PRESENT DAY: EGG & CRESS

'Shall I be chairman?' asked Simon as we all took our seats at a long, sombre-looking, uninspiring, table.

'Sure,' I said, reaching over to take a bread roll from the tureen in the middle. 'That would be good.'

I just wanted us to solve the mystery of why we were there. If Simon wanted to take on the bulk of the responsibility, it was fine by me. I bit into my bread roll. It wasn't half as nice as it looked. The thing was solid all the way through. I struggled to hide my disappointment. There is little in life as annoying to me as bad food.

'Should we not vote? I mean – you can't cast yourself in the role of team leader without us all agreeing,' said Julie.

'OK. We will have a vote. If anyone else wants to do it, that is fine by me. I think we need someone, anyone, coordinating things.'

There was a silence in the room.

'Anyone like to put their name forward?' he asked.

More silence.

'Well, shall I do it then?'

There were murmurs of encouragement while Julie sat back heavily in her seat and crossed her arms.

She was starting to look less attractive as the day wore on.

'Right, OK then. Look – I am no wiser than any of you as to why we have been gathered here today. Clearly the man who died feels he knows us in some way, and wants us to work out how. Now, what I suggest we do is–'

But before Simon could finish his sentence, the big, oak doors at the far end of the room squeaked open and three men came in. The first of the men was exquisitely handsome and beautifully dressed – he looked like an actor or a model or something. That must be Mike Sween. I watched Julie eye him up, and preen herself as he walked past. Behind him strode two older men, one clutching a briefcase, the other holding loose notes in his hand.

'Mike, why don't you take a seat?' said the man with the briefcase, laying his things down on the table and waiting for the guy with the notes to join him.

'Ladies and gentlemen, thank you so much for coming here today,' he said, in a soft, Welsh accent. 'My name's Huw and this is Geraint. We are from Beddows and Plunkett Solicitors and we are handling the estate of Mr Reginald Charters.'

I put the stale bread roll back down onto my plate. This was serious.

'I know this is all very strange, and most of you who I have talked to during the week expressed your surprise and confusion about what is going on here. I am going to be honest and say that Geraint and I have been working as solicitors in this town for almost forty years and we have never known anything like this.

We will run through everything we know, and explain as best we can what will be happening over the next 24 hours. OK?'

'Fine,' said Julie. 'But you must realise that this is all a little tiresome. I am not a child. I have no desire to play silly games. I hope you're able to tell us precisely what is happening.'

'We'll do our best,' said Huw, opening his briefcase and taking out some notes. 'Geraint, is there anything you want to say at this stage?'

'No,' said Geraint, blushing furiously and speaking in a very strong Welsh accent. 'Nothing to add.'

'OK, well there are six of you here. You have been personally invited by Mr Charters. He was very keen for you to come to Wales for the weekend and attend his funeral.

'He was explicit in his instructions, leaving your addresses and lots of detail about you with a private detective who passed them onto us. He wanted to ensure that we invited the right people. Mr Charters wanted you, and only you, to come to the funeral. At this stage in the proceedings, I am instructed to read this note:

Hello dear friends,

A most hearty welcome to Gower – is it not it beautiful? I am sorry I am not there with you but I have gone and stumbled into a premature death. I am a very rich man and have a lot of money to give away...I would like to give the money to you all. How about that?

But before I do that, I want you to guess why you have been brought here...why have I requested your presence out of all the people in the entire world? Try to work it out. I have left you all clues.

You will be handsomely rewarded if you work it out. There is £1 million up for grabs if you can work out why you are here.

Yours,

Reginald

There was a little shuffling and murmuring at that point. Was he suggesting that we would inherit a load of money but only if we could work out why we were there?

'That's all the note says… I will leave it for you to mull over. As I said, we do not know why you have been called here and it seems that Reginald wanted you to try to work that out. We were merely instructed to make sure that you were present and that all expenses were covered and you were treated like royalty.

'The funeral is tomorrow morning and after that I would like to welcome you to our office in the High Street for a will reading and the showing of a video prepared by Mr Charters. I suspect that is when the full reasons for your presence here will be revealed.

'Now my partner, Mr Geraint Plunkett, will talk you through the funeral arrangements.'

'Well, yes,' said Mr Plunkett. He was scarlet, poor man, and in his embarrassment, he had retreated further into a thicker Welsh accent than any of us could understand.

'Could you just say that again?' asked Simon politely.

'We can't understand any of this,' said Julie, slightly more aggressively.

'Anyone want to have some egg and cress?' he said, louder than before, hoping we could all understand him. 'It's very important for someone to have it.'

To be honest, I was famished. There was no immediate

danger of any lunch being served, the rolls were rock hard and I do like egg and cress sandwiches.

'Me,' I said, raising my hand and smiling at him.

'Are you sure?' said Simon, lightly touching my arm. 'That's quite a lot to expect of you. To be honest, I think it's pretty awful of them to ask.'

'No, I don't mind at all,' I said. 'Very, very happy indeed.'

'Diolch,' said Geraint, before quickly saying, 'Sorry – I mean, thank you.'

Then Huw explained that we would have our lunch now. I did wonder how my egg and cress sandwiches fitted into all this talk of lunch, but I decided not to ask.

Talking much more slowly, as if explaining something to a recalcitrant toddler, Geraint continued.

'In the morning you'll head over to the chapel at 9.30am. Mary, I'll come and collect you at 9am, so that you can see the church beforehand and have time for a quick practice there.'

'Practice there?' I said.

'Yes, before you give the head address.'

'Head address?'

'Yes – you just said you'd like to give the address…at the funeral.'

'No I didn't.'

'Yes you did, just now,' interrupted Simon. 'They asked who wanted to do it and your hand shot up.'

'Oh. The address? Oh, I see. Right, yes of course.'

Not egg and cress but a fucking address. How had this happened? Why was everyone so Welsh? No wonder Simon had expressed reservations when I raised my arm.

'I'll leave you to have lunch and I look forward to seeing you all bright and early in the morning. Once again, I'm sorry I have no way of letting you know any more about this rather surreal situation, but I'm sure everything will become clearer as you talk today.'

With that, the two men smiled, turned and left.

'The address?' I said to Simon. 'How can I give an address about a man I don't know?'

'Well, I did wonder,' he said. 'I couldn't quite believe it when you volunteered so readily.'

'That's because I thought he said 'who wants egg and cress?'. For the love of God – I thought he was offering sandwiches.'

PRESENT DAY: LOOKING AT THE EVIDENCE

'Maybe we should start with you then, Mary,' said Simon. 'Do you want to tell us a little about yourself and run through what was in your cuttings envelope? I will write it down in this notebook and at the end, we will try to make sense of how everyone's stories dovetail together and what that tells us about Reginald. Does that sound sensible to everyone?'

'It seems pointless, not sensible,' said Julie. 'What do you think, Mike?'

'Oh, um. I don't know. I have just sat down. I think it would be useful to try to work out why we are here and who this guy is before the funeral tomorrow though, especially if there is money at stake.'

'Let's do that then. Mary, kick us off. Tell us a little bit about yourself.'

'My name is Mary Brown and I live in a place called Cobham

in Surrey,' I said. 'I work at a DIY and gardening centre, and I don't like it very much. And… I am not sure what else to say. I have a friend called Dawn who runs a blog, and I sometimes do vlogs for her, including once going to South Africa on safari and once I went on a cruise. That is the only stuff really that has me into the public eye. No, actually – that is not true. Once I had a bit of an incident with David Beckham's Christmas tree that meant me ending up in the papers and on *This Morning*. But that was a couple of years ago now. Basically, I don't do anything very remarkable, I just go to work and get drunk with my friends and my boyfriend, and I've no idea on earth why I'm here.'

'OK, thank you, Mary. Maybe we will come back to the David Beckham connection if it turns out its significant when everyone else does his or her little talk. Do you want to run through what's in your envelope?'

'Yes – of course,' I said. 'Although it doesn't seem to make a great deal of sense to me. I have a flyer advertising a play-writing course at Bristol Playhouse in 1973.'

'Interesting. Does it say who was running the course, Mary? Was it Reginald, by any chance?'

'A man called Andrew Marks,' I said. 'There is no mention of Reginald anywhere in the cutting, and I even googled the course and couldn't find it.'

'Perhaps it would be worth you reading out what's on the sheet.'

I went through it, relaying all the information.

'OK, I've got that written down. Is there anything else in your envelope?'

'No,' I said. 'Well, nothing else except a note from Reginald and a list of everyone who's here today. That's it.'

I read out the letter Reginald had left and it became clear that everyone had received the same letter – all handwritten.

'Maybe I should go next,' said Simon. 'Because I think the playwriting course might tie in with my family in some way… I have worked as a theatre director in Bath for many years, and Bath is not that far from Bristol.'

His news drew gasps from the assembled group, and a little muttering. None of us had expected to be able to work out who this guy was, but now, suddenly, it felt like we might. There was a shiver of excitement at the prospect. Was the story of Reginald Charters tucked away somewhere in the world of drama and theatre?

'So,' said Mike. 'Let me get this straight – so far we know that Reginald is somehow connected to a playwriting course at Bristol Playhouse in the 1970s and that links Mary to him, and Simon is a theatre director nearby. That's all quite interesting.'

'But it was before I was born,' I said. 'How could I possibly be linked to it?'

'Maybe not you, but a member of your family? Make a note to check with someone in your family about whether they ever lived in Bristol, Mary.'

'Sure,' I said, though I was fairly sure no one I knew had never even been to the theatre let alone attended theatre writing courses on the other side of the country.

'Let me run through my cutting then,' said Simon.

'Mine says 1977 on the top and it's a list of four different plays, all written by different people and performed all over the country. I have googled the playwrights but can't access any decent information on them, which I am surprised about.

'My father was a theatre producer at a number of theatres

and I think these plays might have been put on in theatres he was based in, or overseeing, but that is all.

'I've definitely seen *A Bit of a Puzzler* – that's a great play – written by some guy called Lorenzo Alberto. It was made into a film, I think, but the film was nowhere near as good as the play. The other plays on the list are: *20 Hours to Save the World, Youngest Child* and *24 Hours in Gower*. None of the writers is well known at all.'

He paused and thought for a minute, then hastily re-read the note.

'Hang on, that's how long we're here for,' said Simon. 'Gosh, 24 Hours in Gower. That's us! Has anyone got the original invitation to the funeral?'

I rustled around in my bag, pulling out empty crisp packets and discarded tampons as I hunted through. Then Julie unfolded a copy neatly from her elegant leather wallet and pushed it round the table towards Simon.

I had a pang of guilt about my own messy bag. I should have tidied it out months ago. Why couldn't I be all neat and tidy like Julie?

'YES!' said Simon. 'Here we go – look – it says, 'arrive on Wednesday by 3pm, prior to the funeral on Thursday morning. You will be free to leave from 3pm on Thursday.' He wants us to be here for exactly 24 hours. Isn't that fascinating?

'Let's have a look at the other plays: *Youngest Child*. I wonder how relevant that is.' I asked.

'Let's find out,' said Mike, leaning forward. 'Is everyone here the youngest child, by any chance?'

'I'm an only child,' I said.

'Me too,' said Simon.

'I'm not,' said Julie.

'Ah, that's that theory blown then,' said Mike, sitting back in his chair. 'What about the other plays you mentioned? *A Bit of a Puzzler* – what is that about? I mean – this whole thing is a bit of a puzzler.'

'It's about reality and perception and what's real and what's not,' said Simon. 'It opens with a team of sportsmen running through a tunnel and emerging into a different world from the one they left.'

'Oh God, that sounds familiar. Really familiar. Wow – why do I know that story? I must have seen it or something but I don't really go to the theatre. How come I know it?' said Mike.

'It was made into a film,' said Simon.

'Ah, that must be it,' said Mike. 'What was the other play on your list?'

'It was called *20 Hours to Save the World,*' said Simon... Which is how much time we have been given to solve this puzzle. All those plays do seem to have a relationship to what is happening here today, except the one called *Youngest Child*. We should come back to that later.'

'Do you think he was an actor who starred in them or something?' I suggested.

'Could be, but if he was a famous actor, surely there would be some sort of mention of him on Google?'

'Why don't you ring your dad and ask him whether he was involved in any of these plays, and does he know the writers behind them?' I said.

'He's dead,' said Simon, bluntly. 'And Mum is 96, so she doesn't have the best memory. I will ask her though. She surprises me sometimes and seems to be able to remember things from years ago but can't remember that I went to see her yesterday. Shall we continue to go round the table first and see what everyone's got, then we can all ring our relatives based on all the joint knowledge, and see if we can come up with a picture of who this guy was.'

As we spoke, bowls of miserable soup were delivered – very salty and watery. It wasn't nice at all, and most people left it. When the waitress came to clear away our plates, she looked surprised.

'No one likes it?' she said. 'This soup is called the Pride of Gower Farm Hotel – it was developed in the war by Irene Gower. She and her husband Tom used to run this place as a farm back then. They used to feed it to the farm helpers, and it is unchanged since. All the produce in the soup was grown on Gower Farm.' We nodded and expressed interest in learning the genesis of the soup, but no one drank anymore of it. The bowls were taken away and our pudding was brought to the table. It was bread-and-butter pudding in chipped, mismatched bowls. It didn't bother me that the bowls didn't match each other, there was something quaint and authentic about it, but I did baulk a bit at the chips in the edge of the bowl. It seemed odd. Why would they do that?

The bread-and-butter pudding was as unsophisticated as the crockery in which it was served. The top was lovely and crunchy but devoid of any taste, and there was nowhere near enough sugar in it. When my mum made it for dessert, it glistened with sugar. Underneath the crispy exterior, Mum's pudding was soft and fluffy. It was warm, gooey and gorgeous. This was not. It had a crispiness all the way through which dug into my mouth as I ate it. The currants tasted burnt, which is one of the worst tastes in the world, and its lack of sweetness made it quite unpalatable. Even for someone desperately hungry after being served nothing but a bowl of dishwater soup, I struggled to eat it. I looked around and saw that most of the others were equally astounded by the food they had been presented with.

'We can offer you ice cream instead,' said Gladys, coming in with the waitress and seeing that we had all left it.

'Yes, please,' I said, while the others all murmured agreement. She returned minutes later with big bowls of ice cream for us all. It looked good but I didn't hold out much hope that it would taste nice...nothing else we had been served had; why would the ice cream?

'These are called bacio,' she explained. 'It's Italian for 'kiss' because it's a kiss of two flavours together and was first developed on Gower Farm.'

Oh my God, it was completely lovely. I couldn't believe how delicious it tasted. A silence descended on the table. The soup was horrible, the bread rolls were stale and the bread-and-butter pudding was criminal. But this? This was incredible. I had never tasted such delicious ice cream before.

'Well, that was most pleasant,' said Simon. 'But we should move on with our investigations. Shall we talk to you, Sally? And Julie – you as well. What can you tell us? And what do your cuttings say? Sally, do you want to go first?'

'Well, I'm a teacher and I live in Ascot. I have two children and I work at a local school. I have worked there for twenty years. I've no idea why I'm here today.'

'OK, what's your cutting?'

'Well, it's from 1976 and it's a piece from a newspaper about the number of nurses working in the Bristol area. The only connection I can think is that my mum was a nurse. She lives in Ascot. I know she originally worked in the Coventry area in the

Midlands, but I don't know whether she ever worked in Bristol. I'll phone her and find out.'

'Thank you, Sally,' said Simon. 'The nurse thing is interesting – the only cutting we have had that isn't related to the theatre.'

'Unless he was hinting at a surgeon's theatre earlier?' I offered. 'Perhaps all the theatre stuff is referring to a hospital?'

'Perhaps,' said Simon. 'We shouldn't rule out anything. Julie – would you like to go next?'

'Well, I work for Marie Claire magazine and I live in Putney, right by the river. I spend most of my time socialising in Chelsea. I have done some fairly high-profile things because of being a magazine boss, but I don't know who Reginald was, and – frankly – I am losing all interest in trying to establish his identity. This is a ludicrous waste of time. I bet there's no money to inherit at the end of it.'

'I understand your frustration,' said Simon, gently. 'I think we're all a bit baffled by this, but if we could get all this information together it might really help us to work out what's going on. Let me clarify – did you say you were the editor of Marie Claire magazine?'

'More or less,' replied Julie.

'You are not,' said Sally. 'You work in marketing there. Why do you always have to pretend you're the editor when plainly you aren't?'

'I make lots of editorial as well as marketing decisions. Stop being so petty,' she said to her sister.

'OK. Look, could you just run through what your cutting is.'

'Yes, as Sally said, our mother was a nurse and this cutting is about nurses. It is a piece about how kind nurses are, and how thoroughly decent they are. It doesn't have a date printed on it, but someone has scribbled 1976 on the top of it and it was in the Bristol Post.'

'OK, so, we've established firm links with the Bristol area and the theatre, and now a nurse. Julie and Sally could one of you ring your mum and ask her whether she ever worked in Bristol, and if so, when that was? Might also be useful to ask her whether she ever went to the theatre while she was in Bristol, or knew an actor called Reginald or a writing tutor called Andrew.'

As Sally made notes in her small silver book, and Julie peered at herself in a small hand mirror, the door between the kitchen and the dining room opened and a tall, pale man walked in.

'Sorry to interrupt,' he said. 'My name is Ivor Deg, I'm from the funeral home where Mr Charters is currently resting. Would any of you like to see the body?'

'Good God, no,' said Simon.

The funeral director looked surprised. He clearly had no idea of the peculiar arrangements that had found us gathered in the room.

'Would anyone like to?' he tried. 'It can be nice to see the body to get closure and to see your loved one at peace. I find dead bodies quite reassuring, to be honest.'

There were lots of shaking heads and people looking as if they would rather be anywhere else on earth.

'Is Mary here?' he asked.

I raised my hand tentatively. I had my wits about me this time, I wasn't going to be trapped into any more ridiculous tasks.

'Hello, Mary, are you the deceased's wife?'

'No,' I said. 'I've never met him.'

'Oh, I thought you were giving the address at the service tomorrow.'

'Yes, I am,' I said.

'Right. But if you don't know him, would it not be better if someone else gave the address?'

'Absolutely. I'd be all in favour of that,' I said.

'None of us knows him,' said Simon, and we all clocked the look of bewilderment on Mr Deg's face.

'Sorry,' he said. 'How can none of you know him? I thought the gentleman wanted you all at his funeral.'

'That's right,' said Simon. 'He did, but right now, none of us has any clue as to why.'

1954: THE ARRIVAL OF BABY JOE

'I don't understand what I'm doing wrong,' said Madelyn as she paced around the small cottage, rocking baby Joe in her arms. 'He won't stop crying; whatever I do it's the same. I have fed him, changed his nappy, and winded him. Why won't he stop crying for just one minute?'

'Don't worry, dear, you are not doing anything wrong,' said Marco's mum, Anna. 'Just relax and let him cry if he needs to. Sing to him and cuddle him.'

Anna spoke to her kindly and gently. Madelyn was incredibly grateful for the support that Anna had offered since baby Joe's birth, but she also felt heartbroken that her own mother couldn't be there, supporting her. Her parents had died in a car crash two years ago, and she missed them more than she ever imagined it was possible to miss anyone, especially now she was a mother. She had always assumed she would take to motherhood easily, but it had been hard. She felt exhausted and useless. Her brothers: Keith and Ken came over whenever they could, but they had families of their own, and were so busy on the farm, that she knew it was hard for them to stay for any length of time.

'Madelyn, don't look so worried,' said Anna. 'He's just a grizzly baby – some of them are born that way. He'll soon grow out of it, you'll see.'

Marco's parents had come to live with them after baby Joe was born, and it had been lovely to have them there to cook and care for her while Marco continued to focus on the ice cream parlour. They'd set up in the High Street after Tom and Irene had moved to Llandrindod Wells, and called the place Joe's Ice Cream Parlour, after their son, and Marco's dad and grandfather.

It was a lovely arrangement, most of the time, but sometimes their flat above the shop in the High Street felt packed and noisy with so many people in it. She genuinely loved her parents-in-law but sometimes she wanted to scream. There was never any peace and quiet. The bell rang every time anyone went in or out of the ice cream shop below, and she would hear them talking on the street outside as they gathered in the evenings.

Madelyn hated to moan, and she knew she was lucky that Anna did so much to help but sometimes she longed for the freedom and lightness of the life they had enjoyed when they first got married. They would spend so much time together, just the two of them, curled up around each other on the sofa and going for long walks. No stress; an easy, simple life. She felt weighed down by everything now, and felt it particularly when Joe was being so unbearable.

'Shall I take him for a few minutes?' asked Anna, seeing how low this was making her daughter-in-law feel. 'You go and lie down or have a nice bath.'

'Are you sure?'

'Positive,' said Anna.

Madelyn handed the crying baby to Anna and walked slowly towards her bedroom, yearning for a lie down. She had made it halfway down the corridor before she realised Joe had stopped crying. She was pleased, of course, but also overcome with disappointment and anxiety at her own abilities as a mother. Why had he stopped screaming in Anna's arms when he wouldn't stop screaming for her?

She lay on the bed and cried herself to sleep.

By the time Joe was four years old, Marco and Madelyn realised they were dealing with a child who was quite unlike the other children in the area. The incessant crying had stopped, of course, but Joe had no interest at all in being outside playing. All he wanted to do was to read books and draw.

Joe had a very delicate disposition, hated to get dirty and did not enjoy playing with the boys at school anywhere near as much as he enjoyed playing with the girls. He was an extraordinarily slim boy who was fussy about what he ate and would only consume the tiniest portions.

The only things that really interested him were stories. His parents were forced to read to him repeatedly. Marco would read *Call of the Wild* to him – the novel that his father had given to him when he was little, and that he had read to Tom Junior when he was working on the farm. It was lovely that he was now regaling his son with the adventures of Squadron Leader

Reginald Charters, as he had once regaled that lovely Welsh boy.

Through his childhood and teens, Joe remained uninterested in the life that Madelyn and Marco lived. He said he hated business and hated the world of farming that many of his classmates came from. He became a vegetarian and wrote poems and songs about humanity's cruelty. He thought ice cream was disgusting and wanted nothing to do with the popular ice cream parlours that bore his name.

His great interest was in the arts and he displayed an extraordinary talent for learning poetry off by heart and reading every book he could get his hands on.

While other boys in the area went out and played rugby at the weekends, and trained in the evenings, dreaming of a red jersey and the chance to play at Cardiff Arms Park, Joe was obsessed with Dylan Thomas. He became editor of the school newspaper and his teachers spoke of his writing talent, and how clever he was with words. When he joined his school sixth form he became chairman of the Dylan Thomas Society and instead of watching rugby matches on a Saturday, he saved up to watch plays. The thing he loved more than anything was to write: poetry, short stories and plays. Mainly plays: the theatre meant everything to him.

Marco would encourage his son to join the men for nights out, and to come to local rugby games and support his friends, but Joe had no interest. As he got older, he became more entrenched in his ways and clearer about what he wanted and who he was.

'I love that boy to death, but he's nothing like me at all,'

Marco would say, urging Madelyn to double-check whether she might have come home from hospital with the wrong baby.

'Ah, leave him alone. He is bright and artistic, you should be proud of him. And he's a lovely writer.'

'Oh, I'm proud,' said Marco. 'Just a bit confused.'

Marco tried going to events with his son, but it was all so otherworldly. He didn't understand the people or the excitement of watching a play that had the same outcome every time. He went to watch a series of Oscar Wilde plays with Joe but simply did not get why his son loved them so much.

'How can you watch these plays over and over again?' his dad had said as they sat in their seats once the lights had come up.

'How can you watch sport over and over again?' Joe had countered.

'To find out what will happen. The beauty of sport is that you don't know what will happen.'

'Yes you do – a bunch of rough and artless men will charge around kicking one another. They are just thugs.'

'Thugs? Joe, that is ridiculous, you can't write all sports people off as thugs. And what about Oscar Wilde? He is more disgusting than all sports people put together – sleeping with other men, disgracing his family. It's vile and unnatural.'

'Why does it matter what he does in his own time?' said Joe. 'He's a brilliant writer – can't you just enjoy his talents?'

'Not really,' said Marco. 'Not knowing what he does. I can't believe they legalised it. Homosexuals are disgusting. Did you see what happened to that gay guy who ended up in hospital last week? Doctors operated on him without any anaesthetic. I don't blame them, son. If I were a gay man, I would not go anywhere near a hospital. I would rather die. It's disgusting, that's what it is – disgusting.'

'So no one who's gay can do anything of merit? They will always be judged because they are gay?'

'Yes,' said Marco. 'Now can we go? I've had enough of this theatre to last a lifetime.'

1973: MEETING ANDREW

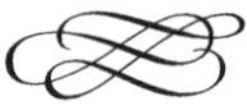

Joe Stilliano stood in the street and looked up at the beautiful Wills Memorial Building in the centre of Bristol.

The quiet, shy boy who'd never been out of Wales stood in front of the grand university buildings and felt like he'd found his place. He would be studying creative writing at Bristol University for the next three years – it was a dream come true. He had studied all of the brochures from universities around the country, and this was the only one with a proper, specialist playwriting department. It was the only course that included a full term of playwriting in it. It was perfect. It was everything he had ever wanted.

He looked at his mother whose anxiety was painted across her face. Her only son was leaving home; fear and sadness consumed her. While Madelyn fretted, Marco looked on impassively. He did not understand why his son wanted to go to university. Not really. No one in the family had been in higher education before, and they had all done OK for themselves. They had a nice life, didn't they? They had a thriving business in Wales with Joe's Ice Cream Parlours in Swansea, Llanelli and Carmarthen now. Each shop needed a manager and staff. He had assumed that's what Joe would do. Enter the family business and help to build it even further.

'Listen, Mum and Dad, I know you don't really understand me,' Joe said. 'I know you think I should stay at home and build a life there, but I'm so happy to be here. I am so delighted to be studying creative writing – you know how much that means to me. I want to make a mark in the world as a writer. I promise I'll make you proud.'

'Oh son, we're already proud, you know that, don't you? Your father and I couldn't possibly be prouder of you. All we want is for you to be happy.'

Joe smiled at his dad and hugged his mum but deep down he suspected that his dad wasn't terribly proud of him at all, because he was doing something that his dad simply didn't understand.

'All I've ever wanted for you is happiness,' his mum repeated. 'Be kind and be good and be happy. That is all. Can you do that?'

'I can do that,' said Joe, as he kissed his mum and dad goodbye and headed off to find his room. He clutched a suitcase containing all his possessions, and on his face was a smile as wide as the ocean. Marco and Madelyn turned and walked away, hand-in-hand, sad but relieved that their only son was happy.

. . .

Joe's first week at university flew past in a blur of new faces and new activities. Life was busy, challenging and fulfilling. He rang his mum and dad to tell them how much he was enjoying himself and regaled them with tales of the stories he'd written and the opportunities on offer.

'Have you made lots of friends?' asked Mum.

'Of course,' he replied, even though that wasn't strictly true. But it was fine. He was happy – he didn't want friends really, they just got in the way of his studies. And it was studying and understanding writing that engaged and entranced him.

'I have to go now, Mum,' he said. 'I'll call you soon, OK?'

He walked down the street and up the stone steps to the large wooden door of the lecture theatre and wandered inside, taking his place at the front of the room as he always did, opening his notebook and preparing to take notes. He was the first person to arrive.

He had no idea as he sat there, that his life was about to be transformed forever.

The lecturer walked out, carrying a pile of books with his briefcase balanced on the top, struggling to reach his desk before dropping everything onto it.

'Morning, I am Andrew,' he said to Joe. 'I'm today's lecturer.'

'Morning,' said Joe, looking up and falling instantly in love. He felt moved to the very centre of his soul. The lecturer was not beautiful but there was something captivating about him. He was a pale man with greying sandy hair and a cropped beard. At a guess, he was around 50 and had sparkling blue eyes that held Joe's gaze, and a childlike smile that belied his age. There was something vulnerable but steely about him.

Other students drifted into the lecture theatre until the place was completely full, but to Joe it felt as if he and Andrew were the only people in the world. Andrew ran through his lesson about the art of storytelling, and as he spoke, Joe's love grew deeper. The knowledge, enthusiasm and sheer joy that Andrew conveyed startled and overjoyed him. He had never known feelings like this. At school, boys had chased girls around and he had kept his distance. He had laughed with them when they described their conquests, but he had not ever really understood what moved them to behave so oddly around girls, and he had never had a girlfriend himself.

Now he understood why. He felt uplifted, excited but terrified beyond belief.

'Right, we'll leave it there for this week,' said Andrew. The lesson had flown past with extraordinary speed. 'But if anyone is interested in coming on a course that I'm holding next Saturday, the information is being handed out. Any questions?'

Joe sat, staring at Andrew from the front of the room, watching him tidy away his things before standing up to leave. Long after Andrew had walked out of the door, Joe rose slowly to his feet, packed up his things and left the building. He had only been in there for an hour… Nothing had changed really, and yet everything had changed.

The leaflet about the playwriting course was neatly folded and tucked inside his diary. Over the next ten days he would battle with himself about whether he should go, sick with anger that he was attracted to Andrew and remembering his father's words about disgusting gays and how vile and horrendous they were; how they'd be beaten by police and abused in hospitals. He knew how much gay men were despised by society. He remembered his father's friend – the local PC Arthur Peters – talking at length about what he would do if he arrested a gay man. 'I could use him for target practice,' he told Dad, as they drank their beers and laughed together. Marco had instilled in Joe the belief that gays were bad and they deserved bad things to happen to them. Did that make Joe bad? He didn't feel it. All he knew was that every time he thought of Andrew, the world seemed in every way brighter, warmer and happier.

Ten days later Joe walked into the Bristol Playhouse where Andrew was running the playwriting course. To the extent that he knew anything about matters of a sartorial nature, he had dressed up and was looking the best he could. He wanted to make an impression on the man who had dominated his thoughts. He had tried to convince himself that this playwriting course would help with his degree and that is why he needed to go. But that wasn't true, and he knew deep down that his presence on the course was entirely because he found Andrew so attractive.

Joe took his place at the front of the small room ten minutes before the lecture started and pulled out his notebook. When Andrew came in, Joe's face lit up.

'We've met before, haven't we?' asked Andrew, shaking Joe's hand and sitting on the edge of his desk.

'I'm in your writing class at uni,' said Joe. 'It's lovely to meet you properly.'

'You too,' said Andrew.

There were probably around 30 years between the two men, but they looked at one another and became locked in a spell of desire.

Other people came in and took their seats, but Andrew didn't move from his position, perched on the edge of Joe's desk. Only when it was time to start did he make his way to the front, offering Joe a secret glance before commencing the class.

The morning passed quickly. Not only was Andrew adorable, but he was interesting; bright, informative and helpful. And when they broke for lunch, Joe decided to do something he had never done before...to make a move. He walked up to Andrew, offered him a most dazzling smile and asked him whether he fancied lunch.

Joe had always been shy, and found it difficult to make friends and get to know people properly, but this felt different, natural. He was compelled and dazzled by Andrew – drawn to him as he had never been drawn to anyone before. Over lunch, they chatted about everything...their backgrounds, their ambitions, the things they loved and the things they hated.

'How many relationships have you had?' asked Andrew.

'None,' said Joe, shyly. He didn't feel the need to lie. 'I never chased girls when I was younger, and I never hung around with the guys who went out looking for girls. It never appealed to me. I didn't see the point. I had lots of girl 'friends' but not girlfriends. I have never been in love. How about you?'

'I had girlfriends when I was younger. I went out with them largely because it was the thing to do. I do not think I ever thought about the fact that I might not actually be attracted to them, or indeed to any girls. I didn't admit the truth to myself for years.'

'The truth?'

'That I am gay. I am attracted to men. It is who I am; there is nothing I can do about it. When I was your age, it was illegal to be gay so it has not been easy. Nothing is easy when you are attracted to men. How long have you known you were gay?'

'Um, I didn't really know I was gay. I don't know that I am. I mean – I just don't know.'

Andrew looked up and checked that no one was watching them, before he reached over and kissed Joe on the lips.

'How was that?' he asked.

'Lovely,' Joe replied, honestly.

'You're gay,' he said. 'Would you like to come out on a date with me?'

'Yes. I'd love to,' said Joe, without hesitation. He felt a light flutter run through him, the sort of flutter of a million songs and poems, the sort of flutter he had never known. He was tapping into experiences today that were totally new. He went home that evening to his small room in the halls of residence and wrote the date in his notebook: 29 September 1973. The date when everything changed. The date he'd got to know Andrew. The date he had fallen in love. The date that would set in motion a catalogue of events that would ruin his life, but through the years, when Joe looked back, he knew he wouldn't change anything, nothing at all, about that date, that moment, and his feelings for that man.

1976: THE ATTACK

Joe stood in front of the mirror and sighed. He didn't know what the meeting today with Andrew would bring. They had not seen each other all summer. Joe had been with his mother in Wales, nursing Madelyn through her final weeks. The cancer had taken every part of her: it had stopped her physically, slowed her movement and eventually closed down her breathing. But she had remained bright and warm until the end. She had smiled when she could, looking at her son so lovingly as he stroked her hand.

'I've had a good life,' she had said. 'A good life because I met your father – what a great man he was – and because of you. He loved you so much, Joe. He thought the world of you.'

'And I of him,' Joe had said, gently stroking his mother's hand. There were so many times when he wanted to tell her that he had met someone and was in love. He thought she might be reassured to hear that he had someone to look after him when she was gone. But what if it just worried her more? What if she had no idea he was gay and went to her death fearful of what the future would hold? So he stroked her hand, and talked about the past, and didn't mention Andrew or what sort of future he would have without her. On what would turn out to be her last day, he had arrived to find her lying on the bed looking so hauntingly fragile that he wanted to sweep her into his arms and protect her forever. Her eyes were barely open, and wisps of hair stuck up from her head.

'Joe, brush my hair for me, would you? Make me look nice for when I meet your father again.'

Joe choked back the tears as he brushed his mother's soft, thinning hair. Her luxurious mane had been destroyed by age and cancer treatments. As he brushed, his mother closed her eyes, a gentle smile had come to rest on her lips and quietly she drifted away.

He had organised the funeral, knowing it would be well attended. His mother and father were such popular people. Joe had asked Andrew to come with him on this visit home because he knew it would be the last time he would see his mother. Joe wouldn't tell her that they were lovers; just that they were friends.

But Andrew felt uncomfortable about it. He thought it would cause too much gossip locally, and that wasn't right. He had said that having never met Madelyn it was better all-round if he didn't come.

Joe had agreed, reluctantly, that this was a sensible solution, but somewhere deep down inside him he felt hurt by Andrew's actions. He was worried that Andrew was pulling away from him and the thought of losing the love of his life at the same time as he lost his mother was unbearable. While he was in Wales, burying his mum, he yearned to have reassurance from Andrew that everything was OK. Joe wrote to him daily, begging him to come, urging him to call and let him know that all was well. In the manner of a million jilted lovers, his desperation for reassurance drove the object of his affections further away.

Joe struggled to understand what had gone wrong after three years of dating. It had been so wonderful to start with... after meeting on the course, they had gone on long walks in the countryside and sneakily held hands when they were out of sight, enjoying picnics by the river and late-night talks. Joe had felt whole, he felt alive and vibrant and as if he were walking on a ground made of the softest clouds. Everything he experienced felt like it had come straight from the cheesiest pop songs. Now he understood why great works of art, great poems and the most popular songs were invariably about love.

Joe felt free and lighter than he had since he was a young boy. He knew what his role in life was – it was to be with Andrew, supporting and helping him. He knew that clearly. Everything made sense now. He was growing intellectually under Andrew's guidance. It didn't matter that Andrew was much older, in fact, it made it better. Joe had been unsure of the world and nervous about the relationship he was embarking upon, so having someone there who was worldly, sophisticated and experienced had made it much easier. Life had been joyful and Joe had thought it would last forever.

He couldn't quite put his finger on the moment when things changed. It wasn't anything in particular...no one thing happened that changed their relationship or created a tension between them that wasn't there before. Joe simply started to feel as if Andrew was not as bothered about coming to see him. Andrew had stopped trying, and no matter that Joe tried twice as hard, hard enough for both of them he thought, it still did not work. Andrew barely acknowledged him at the graduation ceremony when Joe was awarded his first-class honours degree with a distinction for play writing. When they did see one another, Andrew no longer made any effort. The romance had gone and the passion was gone.

Now Joe was back in Bristol, preparing for the next stage of his education – an MA in playwriting. He looked at himself in the mirror; tonight he would see Andrew after their summer apart. He had bought a new shirt, but as he stood there with the stiff material tucked into his new jeans, it looked all wrong. It was too formal. He looked miserable...the whole thing wasn't him at all.

He desperately wanted to look good when he saw Andrew. He ached with desire to see the man he loved, and he wanted to make the best possible impression. But at the same time, he feared an evening of stilted conversation and awkward moments. He feared most of all that he would be dumped. Still, he would go. He would meet Andrew while looking the best he could, and he would hope against hope that everything would somehow, miraculously, be OK.

Joe walked out of the small apartment he was renting next to the university and headed into the chilly autumn evening.

The harsh steps toward winter had begun: flowers no longer sat in the gardens and the warm expectant air of summer had been replaced with a biting chill. He wished he'd brought his jacket.

And some gloves. He rubbed his hands together and blew into them, speeding up his walk toward the park and to the small pub on the other side where he and Andrew had arranged to meet.

As he strode along the pavement, kicking leaves underfoot, his mind was so focused on the meeting ahead of him that he hardly saw the man walking toward him until the guy was in front of him and had blocked his way.

'Going somewhere?' the stranger asked.

'Yes,' said Joe, moving to step round the young man in a black leather jacket. He wasn't a big man but had a menacing air.

'Going to meet your boyfriend?' he asked.

Joe became vaguely aware of other men gathering to the side. He felt fear rise up inside him. They had obviously been watching him and Andrew. Joe was used to rude comments being shouted out at him, of course, but nothing like this. No one had made him feel quite this scared.

'Cat got your tongue?' It wasn't the guy in the leather jacket this time, it was one of the others. Joe turned to look and as he did, he felt a crushing blow to the side of his head.

'Faggot,' came the shout. 'Bloody faggot. Joe Stilliano, you are a fucking faggot. Yeah, don't look so shocked – we know your name, gay boy.'

A kick to his groin left him doubled over in pain.

'Fucking bummer.'

Smack.

'Pervert.'

Whack.

He crumbled to the ground while kicks and insults rained down on him. He prayed he would live through it, and prayed, more than anything, that they would not go after Andrew. Let them beat me enough for both of us, he thought.

'Fucking homo.'

Kick.

'Christ. Is he dead?'

BLACKNESS.

PRESENT DAY: WHO IS REGINALD?

Ivor Deg, the funeral director, could not get out of the room fast enough once he realised that none of the people going to the funeral knew who Reginald Charters was. It was quite the most ridiculous thing he had ever heard. Why were they going if they didn't know him? And where were this Reginald chap's real friends? He smiled a half smile and backed towards the door. Then he remembered.

'Oooh, I have this,' he said, dropping a large envelope on the table. 'I was told to give it to you. Have a good evening. See you tomorrow.'

Simon picked up the envelope and read the writing on the front.

This is an envelope containing the notes for Tom Gower's family. He should be here with you today, but Reginald was unable to track anyone down.

'We'll look in this later, shall we? When we've been through everyone who's here,' said Simon. 'Now, where were we? Um – Mike, do you want to run through a little bit about yourself, and what cutting you've been given?'

'Sure, OK. Well I am a TV executive at SKY, I live in Twickenham and I'm obsessed with rugby, as you can probably see from the size of me.'

He delivered this line with a slight raise of his eyebrows and a gentle look over to where Julie was sitting, staring at him with undisguised lust. In all honesty, Mike was not that big, and I would not have had him down as a rugby player, but it didn't surprise me at all that he worked at SKY. He looked exactly like one of their perfect, white-toothed presenters.

'My sheet of paper makes some sense to me. It is a mock-up of an advert for a bed and breakfast in Bristol. It has a picture of a green B&B over a map of Bristol. My dad ran a bed and breakfast in Bristol for years. It is funny because it was the same gaudy green colour as in the picture. I remember my mum would nag Dad about the horrible colour all the time. 'She'd say: 'Do you know – people navigate their way around this area of Bristol using our business to guide them. They say 'go to the disgusting green B&B and turn left at the roundabout'. Do we really want people talking about our place like that? Using its ugliness as a local landmark? Why don't we paint it a lovely, elegant cream colour and have colourful window boxes. It would look so much better.'

But my dad insisted that the fact that it stood out, and people used it in their directions around the area meant that everyone knew where it was. 'It's good for business, Sarah,' he would insist. 'The first thing you need to do as a business owner is make sure that people know where you are. Well, everyone knows where we are. It is perfect."

So, Mike explained how the B&B had retained its reptilian colour as a result and now here it was again, in front of him.

'I can't ask Dad whether he's ever heard of Reginald Charters because he died a few years ago, but I will call my mum and see what she says. I asked her whether she'd heard of him when I got the invitation and she said she hadn't, but – you never know – I'll try again.'

Simon scribbled down notes as Mike spoke.

'Yes – do ask your mum if she can add anything to the story. Any information would be useful. Now, last but not least, Mr Matt Prior, do you want to tell us a little bit about yourself?'

Matt turned a rather alarming shade of scarlet. 'Yes, my name is Matthew but everyone calls me Matt, I'm 19 and I'm on a carpentry apprenticeship,' he said in a soft Welsh accent. 'I live just outside Cardiff with my mum and dad, and I don't know who Reginald Charters was. My clue is very strange. It is a taxi receipt from 1976 with a smiling emoji along with a cross, like a medical cross, I guess. That's all I have.'

'Ah, a medical cross? I wonder whether that relates to Julie and Sally's mum. Is your dad a taxi driver?' asked Simon.

'No,' said Matt. 'He's a carpenter.'

'OK,' said Simon. 'Could you ring your dad and ask him whether anyone in the family would have been a taxi driver in 1976, and if so which area?'

'Yes, sure,' said Matt. 'I'll ask him.'

'Right,' said Simon. 'This is all giving me a huge headache, but I think we have found some similarities and possible links to the family members. Certainly, we know that the key dates are between 1973 and 1976. Shall we have a break, and ring around relatives to see what they can tell us?'

'Shouldn't we look at the envelope that spooky-looking guy gave us?' said Sally. 'You never know – it might help.'

'Oh yes, of course, I had forgotten about that.'

Simon carefully opened the manila envelope and pulled out some notes.

'Oh,' he said. 'That's not very helpful - nothing to do with B&Bs, nurses or Bristol. It's a cutting from 1943 when a load of Italian prisoners of war came over to Wales to be based on farms.'

'So, do you think he was a prisoner of war?' asked Matt. 'I remember learning about them at school.'

'He couldn't have been,' said Simon. 'He wasn't born until – hang on – um, around 1950ish.'

'Perhaps his dad came over as a prisoner of war?'

'That's a real possibility.' Simon squinted as he did the basic maths in his head and calculated that – yes – the dates worked out. 'But why would an Italian call his son Reginald?'

'So that he assimilated? So he seemed like a local?' suggested Mike.

'Could be,' said Simon, nodding his head. 'Let's all go and make our phone calls and have a little break and come back to this feeling a bit fresher.'

There were murmurs of approval, largely at the suggestion of a break, but also because we knew we had to talk to our relatives. There was a million pounds at stake, everyone wanted to work this out.

'I will see whether we can get some drinks, shall I?' said Simon, looking around the table.

'Yes please,' I said. 'If there are any snacks or anything, that would be great. Lunch wasn't all that wonderful, was it?'

'No, indeed,' said Simon. 'You never got your egg and cress after all, did you?' He smiled warmly at me and ruffled my hair and I decided I really liked him.

'Let's meet back here in an hour, shall we? Six o'clock?'

PRESENT DAY: TERROR IN THE HOUSE

I walked back up to my room, sat on the small chair that creaked alarmingly beneath my weight, so I eased myself off it gently, and went to lie down on the bed instead. I scanned through all the notes I had. Although I knew Mum didn't have a clue who Reginald Charters was, and I didn't feel I had any new information to impart, I thought I ought to make an effort and ring her

'Mum, I'm here, in Wales, preparing for this funeral tomorrow.'

'Oh, how exciting. Tell me – who was this guy?'

'Well, that's the thing, we still don't know, Mum. He gave us some clues, but didn't tell us who he was, he wanted us to guess. We should find out for sure after the funeral tomorrow, but we are trying to work it out beforehand because he said we would inherit his money if we worked it out. It is really strange. I have a bit more information. Can you have a think about this, and work out whether you know anyone who fits this bill?'

I went through everything with Mum, the dates, the relevant places, and exactly what we were trying to find out. She shouted out to my dad in the background, but I could hear him saying he hadn't got a clue, and that I was to make sure I was OK.

'Sorry, love, neither of us knows who this guy could be. The name doesn't ring a bell at all with me, or your dad, I've rung everywhere I can think of and we just don't know him.'

'OK, Mum, but make sure you let me know if you think of anything at all, won't you?'

'Of course I will. You look after yourself.'

'Thanks,' I said. I didn't really want to stay in the room by myself, and was hoping that if I went for a wander around and about, I might see some snacks somewhere, so I headed back down. I peeked into the rooms downstairs, but they were all just drawing rooms and libraries with big white sheets thrown over the armchairs like something out of the Victorian era, so I went back to the room we had been sitting to find Matt, Mike and Sally still there. There was no sign of Julie.

'Hello, do you mind if I join you?' I asked.

'Of course not,' said Sally. 'Have you had any luck unearthing any more information?'

'Not a thing,' I confessed. 'Mum doesn't even recognise the name, and we're not an arty sort of family so we're certainly not the sort of people who go on theatre writing courses or anything like that. I just do not know why I am here. I wish I could help. It would be great to solve this puzzle.'

'It's the oddest thing I've ever known,' said Matt. 'And this house feels haunted to me – don't you think? Everything creaks and the whole place makes me feel uncomfortable. I'm sure my jacket moved off my chair onto my bed, I definitely didn't leave it on my bed.'

'You probably did but just forgot about it,' said Sally. 'Clothes don't move themselves. And any way if there were a ghost…'

Sally was halfway through her sentence when all the lights in the room went out, plunging us into complete darkness.

'Christ,' said Matt. 'I told you this place was haunted.'

'Just relax,' said Sally. 'They'll come back on in a minute. Try not to panic.'

'OK,' said Matt's shaky voice. 'We're here because a dead man we've never met invited us and now all the lights have gone out, but I'll try not to panic.'

'It's probably just the electricity short circuiting,' said Sally. 'I'm sure someone will be down soon to fix it.'

We sat in silence again. I rather hoped Mike might offer to go and investigate but he sat there, not saying a word. My Ted would have jumped up to find out what was going on. And so would Simon. Simon? Where was Simon?

We sat in silence a little longer, then things got scary as a howl came from outside. 'Oh, Christ alive,' said Matt. 'We're all going to die. I knew I shouldn't have come. I just knew it.'

Next there was a creak and the sound of movement outside, followed by the slamming of a car door.

'It's Reginald's ghost come to haunt us,' said Matt.

'What? In a car?' said Sally, dismissively. 'Do ghosts really drive cars?'

Then footsteps…slowly crunching through the gravel. I felt terrified, thinking this could actually be where we were all shot.

The door eased open with a haunting squeak. I didn't want

to die. I dived under the table and I felt Matt drop down next to me. Then the lights came on.

'Hi, everyone,' said Simon. 'What are you doing sitting in the dark?'

I slowly edged myself back into my chair.

'And what are you doing on the floor? Are you playing some sort of game? I haven't spoilt your fun, have I?'

'My God, man, you terrified us,' said Matt. 'I thought you were Reginald's ghost come to haunt us.'

'I went to the shop.' He smiled and held up two carrier bags. 'Mary said she was hungry and I thought we could all do with a snack, so I nipped out while you were in your rooms and thought I'd surprise you with this little lot. Did not expect to come back to find you all sitting in the pitch black.'

There was a loud thud as he plonked down the two bags, and we all looked at each other, embarrassed. Then the door opened and Julie walked in. 'Sorry, darlings, I didn't plunge you into darkness, did I? I was trying to find the outside lights and I think I turned all the house lights off, I put them back on again as soon as I realised what I'd done but they're all bloody complaining out there in reception.'

'No problem at all,' said Matt. 'We all thought it was something like that.'

1976: THE ARRIVAL OF THE ANGELS

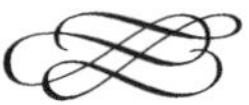

The crowd of men who beat up Joe Stilliano hadn't mean to leave him lying on the ground, begging for his life. As they raced away from him, to a man they felt that they had overdone things. One guy glanced back, terrified of what they might have done. They had beaten this guy so badly that he lay in a pool of blood, his breathing shallow, clearly in pain. The deal had been that they would teach him a lesson after he had been seen poncing around with that other gay guy – the older one. But then they hadn't seen him out and about all summer and when they'd knocked on the door of the flat they had believed to be his, there'd been no answer. For weeks they had waited for him but he hadn't appeared. Then, when they saw him, they reacted – quickly and brutally.

A young man in an old denim jacket wondered whether he should go back. Or should he find a phone box and ring an ambulance?

'Run, James,' shouted Ed, the leader of the pack. He had

been the one to throw the first punch. He was well aware that if James hung around and was caught, they would all be implicated. If the bender died, they would be on a murder charge. He grabbed his mate by the collar of his denim jacket and pulled him so he stumbled into a run. 'Fucking run.'

And so, James ran. He ran as fast as he could away from the man lying in the ever-growing pool of blood.

Joe lay still. Sprawled across the pavement on the quiet street until a taxi passed, stopped and reversed until it was alongside him.

'Are you OK, mate?' asked the driver, getting out before he saw the full extent of the injuries.

'Jesus Christ, mate. Can you hear me? Are you OK?'

Joe could hear the voice through a veil of pain. He tried to nod but couldn't manage to move anything.

'Wait here for two minutes, I'm going to get help,' said the man.

Joe tried to open his eyes…everything was blurred. He closed them and listened as a car drove past, birds tweeted. It was such a quiet street. What if the man didn't come back? When would he be found? He closed his eyes and drifted off to sleep.

Minutes later he woke to the sound of voices: a man and a woman – the same man as before, talking to him, telling Joe that his name was Fred Radex, and he would try to help him.

'What's your name?' asked a soft female voice. 'My name's Daphne and I'm a nurse.' She sounded young. He guessed she was pretty. She sounded like she might be pretty.

'Joe,' he said.

'Good, OK, Joe, there is nothing to worry about. We are going to help you. Can you squeeze my hand?'

Joe squeezed with all his might and heard the nurse give a little yelp.

'Well, there's nothing wrong with that squeeze,' she said kindly. 'I think we can safely say you're going to survive; we just need to get you to hospital. Have you called the police, Fred?'

'No!' cried Joe, as loudly as his bruised ribs would allow. 'Please no. No police. No hospital. I beg of you – do not call the police. Just take me back to my flat and I'll be fine.'

There was no way he was going anywhere near a hospital to be experimented upon by doctors who disapproved of his lifestyle. And he would not allow them to call the police so he would become 'target training'. He remembered the words of Arthur Peters, the local policeman who had described gay men as such. That was not going to happen to him.

'You need medical attention,' said Daphne. 'I can't just leave you, you're really unwell. We need to get you to a hospital.'

'I'd rather die than go to hospital…you have to understand,' said Joe. 'Please don't take me to hospital.'

He moved to sit up but his stomach hurt so much that he rolled back onto his side.

'Let's get him off the street,' said Fred. 'Then we can work out what to do.'

'Can you walk?' they asked Joe.

He struggled to sit up again.

'Hang on,' said Fred. 'I'll just go and get some help.'

Daphne knelt down beside Joe while the man was gone and spoke to him gently.

Did he know what year it was? What was the name of the Prime Minister? How many fingers was she holding up?

He could answer the questions but the fingers meant nothing to him. There was just a blur.

'Andrew!' he said, remembering, quite suddenly. 'I'm supposed to be meeting Andrew in the bar. How long have I been here? He will still be waiting. I need to tell him I can't come.'

'You don't need to do anything,' said the nurse. 'You need to lie very still, then we'll get you out of here and check what damage has been done. I think you'll need to go to hospital, but let's worry about that later.'

Joe could feel his heart beating faster. He didn't want to be taken anywhere except to Andrew. 'He will be cross if I leave him waiting,' said Joe. 'I need to talk to him.'

'He won't be cross when he sees what's happened,' said the nurse, wiping gently at his eyes. 'Can you see my fingers now?' Joe looked out and realised he could.

'Three,' he said, confidently.

'Well done. You have lots of blood in your eyes. Once we've cleaned you up, you'll feel a hundred times better.'

He saw the taxi driver return with another man.

'I'm not going to hospital and I don't want you to call the police,' said Joe. 'Please, promise me you won't.'

'This is Nicholas Sween,' said the man. 'He and his wife Sarah own the bed and breakfast just there – the funny-looking green one. We're going to take you in there and get you a drink of water, then we must get you to hospital.'

'No hospital,' growled Joe. 'I can't go to hospital. Please don't make me.'

The two men glanced at one another, wondering what the kid had against the police and doctors, then they lifted Joe onto his feet. The woman with the soft voice wiped his face again and replaced his broken glasses on his nose.

'We're not taking you to hospital. Just relax. We're going to look after you.'

'No police.'

'OK, no police. Let us just get you off the street and work out what to do.'

Joe moved quietly next to them, leaning onto the men who supported his weight on their shoulders. He was taken to the B&B and into a reception area where he heard a woman gasp and hushed voices talking. Then he was being laid down. He heard them mention hospital and he repeated his heartfelt desire not to be taken to hospital. He would rather die than face the judgement of the authorities. He would rather never recover from his injuries than be forced to discuss with medical staff why he had been attacked, what he had been called and what his private life entailed.

They lay Joe down on the sofa.

'Here, I'm just going to bathe your face,' said Daphne, crouching down next to him. He heard the swishing of water and then felt a warm damp flannel on his face.

'Tell me if I'm hurting you,' said the nurse. 'I'm just wiping away the blood so we can see what the damage is.'

'Thank you,' said Joe. The feeling of her cloth on his skin was painful but he lay there and let her finish. He felt he'd moaned enough.

'I think your nose is broken,' she said. 'And there's a nasty cut above your eye. There is every chance your cheekbone is broken too. They'll fix you up in no time in hospital.'

'No!' said Joe.

'Can you tell me why?' asked the nurse. She wiped the top of his head again with a flannel while she spoke.

'Just take me back to my flat, I'll be fine there.'

'We will do no such thing. Will you tell me what's worrying you so much about the police and hospital?'

Joe struggled to open his eyes. He could see there were two of them standing there.

Daphne sensed his reluctance to speak.

'Nicholas, any chance you could put the kettle on for me and bring me some boiling water?'

When Nicholas left the room, Joe knew he had to tell the nurse the truth.

'They beat me up because I'm gay. They called me names and said they hoped I'd die.'

There was a silence in the room.

'You're disgusted, aren't you?' said Joe. 'You're completely disgusted with me. I do understand. I am disgusted with myself but I can't help it…I was born this way; it wasn't my choice.'

'I'm not at all disgusted,' said the nurse. 'And neither will the doctors at the hospital be disgusted. They will look after you whether you are gay or not.'

'That's not true, and you know it. Most of them think it should still be illegal, and we all know what the police do if they get their hands on gay men.'

'No one will treat you badly, you have to believe me,' said the nurse, but Joe shook his head.

'A few years ago they'd have been able to throw me in jail for being gay. I've heard of lots of people like me who've ended up in police stations and hospitals and been abused and beaten half to death.' Joe was gasping for breath as he spoke, he was close to tears.

'OK,' said the nurse. 'Calm down. Please don't worry. I'll care for you, but you must do as I say, or you'll be very ill.'

'Yes, I will,' said Joe. 'I'll do exactly what you ask me to do.'

'OK. Well, first - where are your parents? Your mum and dad?'

And that's when Joe broke down. He had stayed calm through his mother's last days, coping with the loss of the woman he loved more than life itself. He had organised the funeral and avoided crying throughout it. He had been erudite when he gave his speech. Then he had returned to Bristol to face the certainty of being dumped by the man who'd come to mean more to him than any other man. He had even coped with being beaten up by an angry mob. But now, as he lay there, being tended to by a kindly stranger, the whole thing got the better of him.

'My Mum died, I buried her last week,' he said through gasping tears. 'I've lost Mum and Dad.'

'I'm sorry,' said the nurse, while Joe wailed.

'The man I've been seeing, he's much older than me. I don't think he loves me any longer. He wouldn't come to the funeral,' Joe added, then he sobbed and sobbed while the lovely nurse gently held his head and allowed him to release his pain.

'Where were you due to meet this man?' asked Daphne.

'The Three Ducks, the pub through the park,' said Joe.

'OK, I'll go and see him and explain what's happened. Give me your key, and I'll go and collect your things from your flat as well,' said the nurse.

'Thank you so much,' said Joe, laying his head back on the cushions. She placed a warm blanket over him and padded out of the room.

1976: LOOKING FOR ANDREW

When Daphne walked into the pub, it dawned on her that she had no idea what Andrew looked like. She had relied on being able to walk around, look at the men sitting on their own, and work out which of them was gay. It wasn't so easy. There were quite a few men sitting by themselves, poring over the newspapers or reading books.

She smiled at one or two of them before approaching a small blonde man with two dogs at his feet.

'Are you Andrew?' she asked. 'Waiting for Joe?'

The man shook his head, but she noticed the older man at the next table look up. 'Are you looking for Andrew?' he said, jumping to his feet.

'Yes, hi – I'm Daphne,' she said. 'I'm afraid Joe's been hurt.'

Andrew looked worried. 'Hurt? How? What's happened?'

She explained that he had been set upon by a group of thugs and was at the B&B recuperating. 'I'm a nurse,' she said. 'I'm taking care of him. He is very worried about the fact that you are here waiting for him, so I thought I had better come and explain. Do you want to come with me to see him?'

Andrew dropped his eyes and looked down at his hands, fidgeting in his lap. 'I don't know,' he said.

'He's not expecting you… I just thought I should ask. Why don't you want to come?'

'Our relationship has been over for months,' Andrew said. 'I think it would be a huge mistake to come.'

Daphne nodded. His answer was sensible if not particularly caring. Joe could do better. She stood up to go. 'Whatever you want,' she said dismissively.

'Do not call the police, will you?' said Andrew. 'He'd really hate that. He's got a phobia.'

'Yes, so I understand,' said Daphne.

'I'm sorry,' said Andrew. 'He's a lovely man, but I don't love him and it would be wrong for me to rush to his bedside and pretend that I do.'

Next she went to Joe's flat – a small, sparsely decorated place. It contrasted so much with her own chaotic flat which she shared with two other nurses – it was always full of noise and music and was messy all the time.

Joe's place was so cold and dismal, and he had so few things in it that she decided to pack them all up and take them to the B&B. A young man in a denim jacket, waiting outside, offered to help. He said he knew Joe and asked how he was. Daphne explained that he had been badly beaten up and was recuperating locally.

'Will he be OK?' asked the young man.

'Eventually,' said Daphne. 'But he's not feeling great at the moment.'

Once she had all of Joe's belongings in the car, she drove

back to the B&B and unpacked everything into the room that Nicholas had earmarked.

'Blimey, how long is he staying for?' asked Sarah, helping to carry the piles of books upstairs.

'I think he'll need to stay for a couple of weeks, if that's OK,' said Daphne. 'There's no way he can go back to that flat on his own.'

'Sure,' said Sarah, glancing at Nicholas. It was tough running a Bed and Breakfast. Turning paying customers away for two weeks would be difficult. They would do it, of course, but it would make life hard for them.

1976: A BIT OF A PUZZLER

Joe had spent a week in bed relaxing and was starting to feel much better, thanks to the kind nurse who had come every day to look after him. Now he needed to get up, walk around and stretch his legs. He climbed out of bed, gingerly at first, then walked across the room to the old wooden door, undoing the latch and stepping onto the landing.

He walked cautiously down the stairs. Sitting halfway was a boy, staring disconsolately at the carpet. The boy had his head in his hands.

'Are you OK?' asked Joe, making the boy jump out of his skin.

'No, I'm not, I'm… Wow, what happened to your face? Have you been in a fight? Did you win?'

The boy looked fascinated, more intrigued than scared by the sight of Joe on the stairs.

'It was kind of a fight,' said Joe. 'But I didn't have much of a chance; there were a lot of them and only me. They attacked me in the street and I'm afraid they won. As you can see!'

'Wow,' he said. 'Fighting is awesome.'

'This wasn't really that awesome, I can assure you,' said Joe. 'It was pretty terrible really. Is your dad the owner of this place?'

'Yes,' said the boy.

'Well your dad was very kind and he came and helped me and he let me stay here while I get better. I've been fast asleep for days!'

'I wish my dad was kind to me,' said the boy. 'He hates me.'

'I'm sure that's not true. My name is Joe by the way, Joe Stilliano.'

'I'm Michael Sween.'

'How old are you, Michael?' asked Joe.

'I'm twelve.'

'And why do you think your father hates you?'

'Because he forces me to do homework and I hate it. I have to write a story for English called 'A Bit of a Puzzler' – how am I supposed to do that? I hate making up stories.'

'You may be in luck – I can't do many things very well, but you know what I am very good at?' said Joe.

'What?' asked Michael.

'Writing. Do you want me to help you?'

'Yes please, mister. Come up to my bedroom and I'll show you my assignment,' he said.

Joe sensed that going into a young boy's bedroom was definitely not advisable.

'Why don't you get your books from your room and meet me downstairs and we'll work on the project together? Does that sound OK?'

Michael's face lit up when he smiled. He was going to be very handsome when he grew up, with his mop of dark hair and dimpled chin. Michael raced upstairs to collect everything he needed for his project while Joe sat down at the large dining room table to wait for him.

Five minutes later, Michael came barrelling down the stairs, taking them two at a time. He threw a pile of books in front of Joe. 'This is it,' he said. 'I've got to write a story and I've got to try and make it two whole pages long.'

'Well, luckily, I can help. Now – tell me what's the biggest puzzle you can think of?'

'Well, the biggest puzzle I can think of is that Barry Angel is not in the England rugby team,' said Michael. 'He plays for Bristol and he's brilliant. Even my dad agrees with me. He's the best player and he should be in the team.'

Joe laughed. 'You like sport, do you?'

'Yes,' replied Michael. 'I'm going to play rugby for England one day.'

'Good,' said Joe. 'I will definitely come and watch you play. Well if you like rugby and are going to play for England, why don't we have a story about an England rugby team for your homework?'

'Yes,' said Michael, his face alight at the thought.

'It needs to be a big puzzle for the rugby team, so...why don't we write a story about a rugby team who turn up to play in a big match, but when they run through the tunnel to go onto the pitch they come out in a totally different world. That would be a puzzle, wouldn't it? How did they get there? What's going on?'

'Yes,' shrieked Michael. 'A world with aliens and dinosaurs in it. I want it to scare my sister.'

'I didn't know you had a sister.'

'Yes, she's much older than me and she's staying with Grandma and Grandpa this week.'

'OK, well let's write a story that will scare her then. It could be a world in which all the animals and the trees can talk?'

'Yes,' said Michael. 'And the trees start fighting. But how do we write the story? I'm not very good at writing.'

'Well, we just start at the beginning. Let us start writing about the team all arriving for the match. What shall we call the team?'

'The Sween Rovers,' said Michael. 'That's my name.'

'What are you two up to?' said Nicholas, walking into the room. Joe jumped to his feet, suddenly worried that his kind host might be suspicious of his motives, sitting down and chatting to a young boy.

'I'm doing my homework, Dad,' said Michael, his face full of excitement. 'We're writing the best story ever. Joe's helping me and he's brilliant at stories.'

'Thanks,' said Nicholas, smiling at Joe. 'Very decent of you. I am hopeless at anything like that – not a creative bone in my body. How are you feeling?'

'I'm feeling much better. Thank you. Thanks for all you've done.'

1976: BACK TO WALES

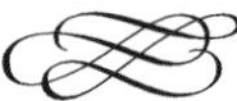

It was almost three weeks before Joe could leave the B&B, and by the time he did, he was feeling stronger than he had for ages. His face bore the scars of his beating and as he moved toward the front door, accompanied by Daphne, Fred, Sarah and Nicholas, he felt sore, but he no longer suffered from extreme pain as he had in his first weeks.

When he reached the door, he stopped suddenly and flinched a little at the thought of going outside. He'd been safely cocooned for so many weeks that fear ran through him at the idea of going into the big, wide, frightening and judgmental world outside.

'OK?' Daphne asked.

'Just a little overwhelmed,' he replied.

'You're going to be fine,' said Nicholas. 'Head up. Don't let anyone judge you.'

'Thank you,' said Joe. 'Thank you so much for everything

you've done. You have been so kind, and so generous. One day I will pay you back for your kindness. I promise.'

'No need,' said Sarah. 'Seeing you up and about and looking so well is payment enough.'

'No – I will. I promise you. I will pay you back one day, all of you. Just you wait.'

Joe hugged Daphne tightly. He still felt soreness in his ribs, but he would not let the shiver of pain stop him from the need to show affection to this lovely woman.

'You take care, lad,' said Fred, shaking his hand. 'You're a good kid. Don't let anyone tell you otherwise.'

'Come on then,' said Nicholas. 'Let me help you with these bags.'

The plan was for Fred to drive Joe to the station in his taxi, then for Joe to head on to Wales. He had given in his notice at the flat in Bristol, and needed to get away from the place for a while. He would live in his parents' flat above the ice cream parlour for a few weeks while he worked out what to do.

His plans to do a Master's degree at Bristol University would have to wait. He did not want to be anywhere where the thugs might find him, and he had no desire to subject himself to a course lectured by a man whom he loved deeply but who no longer loved him.

His relationship with Andrew had been wonderful for two and a half years, but for the last six months of it, it had been difficult. Andrew had stayed with him because he was going through so much…he realised that. And, in many ways, he was grateful to Andrew for not calling it off when Joe was half way through his finals, or tending to his sick mother. Andrew was a good man, and he had transformed Joe's life and made him truly happy for the first time. But he couldn't be around him, because deep-down, despite everything, he still loved the man.

'You stay in touch, OK?' said Fred.

'You saved my life,' replied Joe, in tears. 'I swear. You saved my life. You found me and saved me.'

'Your life shouldn't have been in danger in the first place, with those thugs attacking you like that. I wish you'd have let me call the police. I swear they should be behind bars.'

'I'm sure that's exactly where they'll end up,' said Joe. 'Thanks so much.'

The two men hugged and Joe climbed out of the taxi, waving goodbye before heading to the platform.

Fred turned the taxi round, and waved at Joe in the rear-view mirror.

Joe waved back without turning around. He was terrified and hated being away from the security of the B&B and the nurturing attentions of Daphne.

1976: THE ARRIVAL OF REGINALD CHARTERS

The small flat on the High Street in Llanelli was exactly as Joe remembered it from when he was a little boy. The family had lived there until he was around thirteen, then they had moved out and bought when his grandparents died, and left them the money to buy a bigger place. But they had always kept the small flat. As Joe walked in, he was transported straight back to his childhood. The place was an arrow through time, linking the Joe of today with the small, shy boy of yesteryear. He settled down in the armchair and thought about himself as a little boy in the flat, refusing to come down to the ice cream parlour for his birthday party and hiding under the table so his dad couldn't find him. Nothing much had changed in the intervening years. OK, maybe he didn't hide under the table anymore, but age and a good education had done nothing to erase the fear of socialising that ran through his veins. He had been so unlike his sociable parents…always wanting to hide away and not see anyone. He kicked off his shoes, dropped his head to one side and nodded off to sleep.

When Joe woke hours later to sounds on the street below, he sat up with a start. He had forgotten how noisy it could be when people went into the ice cream shop downstairs. Customers milled around outside in a way that they never hung around outside his Bristol flat. He found it all quite disturbing. Every noise made him leap out of his skin. He yearned for peace and quiet and knew the flat wasn't right for him as a permanent base. He needed to sell it, along with the shops and his parents' house and find his own home... somewhere quiet where he could be alone with his books and his thoughts. Somewhere to sit, grieve, and lament the love he had lost and to work out what shape the future was without that love in it.

A few days later, Joe went to talk to the managers of the ice-cream shops. He told them that he was putting Joe's Ice Cream Parlours up for sale, but wanted them to have the chance to buy them. He offered them huge discounts to help them out, earning himself more hugs, declarations of gratitude and tearful moments than he'd ever imagined knowing. It felt good. Helping people had made him feel alive and valuable. Even with the big discounts he had given, he made a lot more money from all the sales than he ever imagined having in his life. He would invest it wisely. He knew what it would be useful for one day, but not yet. Then he looked for somewhere to live, deciding on mid-Wales where he knew no one and could concentrate on writing to his heart's content.

He decided on a little village called Hay-on-Wye, away from Bristol and away from his childhood home in Llanelli.

Once he had settled in, he set about writing as much as he

could. He wanted to throw all his feelings, anger and emotion onto the page. He wanted to create plays that were wonderful works of art.

He worked night and day on his first play – a complicated work about reality and perception. It was an existentialist piece about understanding change and accepting that we know nothing about the future and what it holds. On the surface, it was a play about a team of footballers who ran onto the pitch and arrived in a new dimension, but it had a much deeper meaning. The place they arrived in was the real world, and the life before the tunnel was all their perceptions, all the baggage they brought to the world.

'The play is about how humans are so far inside the values they cling to that they never look outside them, meaning they operate in a world so coloured by their own views that it's not real,' he wrote in a letter, pitching the idea to a theatre director. 'The 11 men represent all eleven of mankind's failings and insecurities. The players are sure what the world is about until the day they run through the tunnel and onto the pitch. There they live a new enlightened life, a real life, and let go of all their nasty destructive prejudices.'

Joe lay down his pen and smiled to himself as he thought about how this play had its roots in the school project he had worked on with Michael, the young son of the B&B landlord. Michael's homework had been called 'A Bit of a Puzzler' and that is what he would call his play. He picked up his pen again. He would add a dramatic twist to the play and make the footballers turn on one another...they would have to choose one of their number – representing one of mankind's failings – to walk back through the tunnel into the flawed world they had escaped from. Yes. That was it.

He would love to see his play being performed, but he desperately did not want anyone to know he had written it. He had no desire for fame at all. He wanted no attention and had no real need for money. He simply wanted his work to fly. He needed a nom de plume and he knew straight away what name he wanted.

In his bag was the book he always carried with him: *Call of the Wild* – the novel his father had given him when he was little. His dad had been fond of telling Joe how it had been through battles and been across countries and how he had read and reread the book to a young boy called Tom Gower. It had a faded yellow cover – the only possession his father had kept from when he was young. Joe flicked through it and saw the name that had coloured his childhood. Squadron Leader Reginald Charters – that was the name he would adopt. He would become Reginald Charters.

PRESENT DAY: GATHERING THE CLUES

'That was quite funny,' said Simon, as he pulled out all of the notes he'd made, reminding himself of exactly where he was before his kind decision to buy snacks had resulted in everyone in the group almost having synchronised heart attacks. No one else in the group laughed. 'Well, it was funny from my point of view – coming in here to find you all crouched on the floor in pitch darkness. Jolly funny.'

While he shuffled papers, I helped myself to a slice of the angel cake that Simon had bought: it was pink, pretty and very sweet, so it suited my inner seven-year-old down to the ground. I teamed it with a glass of wine and felt all set up for the afternoon.

No one else at the table seemed remotely interested in any of the snacks Simon had made such an effort to provide which, again, suited me down to the ground.

It was a mystery to me that anyone could sit there, all relaxed, while there were uneaten snacks lying on the table. I found it hard to concentrate on anything when there were cakes, crisps and biscuits within arm's length, regardless of how full I was.

The good news was that there seemed to be more of a buzz in the room now, after we had had a break, or perhaps it was the bonding experience of fearing that the house was haunted by the ghost of Reginald Charters. People were more animated; there was murmuring and chatting, and less concern and frustration with the whole thing.

I turned to Matt, sitting next to me, and smiled.

'This is amazing, isn't it?' he said. 'I mean – I wonder who on earth he was, and what this is about.'

'Did you have any luck finding things out?' I asked him.

'No one in the family has heard of Reginald Charters,' he said. 'But I think I can understand why I've been given this clue. I have a sort of inkling about my great Grandfather, but it might be nothing. I will go through it all when we get started. How about you?'

I told him that I called Mum earlier and she was no use at all. She said we had no theatre types in the family and no connections to a taxi ride, a nurse or a B&B in Bristol.

I looked around the room, wondering whether anyone apart from Matt had found out anything that could take us further in our struggle to unlock the mystery. As I scanned the room, I noticed that Julie had moved and was now sitting next to Mike. He had his arm round the back of her seat like a teenage boy on a cinema date in the 1950s, his fingers lightly touching her shoulders, subtly edging down the line of her bra strap.

Julie had reapplied all her makeup, and looked like she was heading out to a top London nightclub not sitting in a rather dismal, ancient room in a farm masquerading as a B&B in the middle of nowhere. Still, who could blame her? Mike was gorgeous and Julie was incredibly beautiful when she was all done up. I was transfixed. Until she turned and saw me staring and I was forced to pull my head away so quickly that I almost gave myself whiplash.

I wondered what it must be like for Sally. Fancy growing up with a sister as beautiful as that. Her teenage years must have been torture. There were four years between them and such a distance in terms of how they looked...their body shapes, hair, the glossy skin, that star quality; Julie had it all. How horrible it must have been for Sally seeing her younger sister turn into such a beauty. I was glad I didn't have siblings; I would not have been able to control my jealousy if I'd had to grow up with someone like Julie.

'Right, let's go through everything, then,' said Simon. 'Mary – would you like to make notes?'

'Sure,' I said, though I was far from sure. I am not very good at practical things like this, and it was very likely I would forget to write down something crucial and ruin everything.

'Here's some paper,' said Matt, pushing a pad towards me. 'Just shout if you want any help.'

'Thank you,' I said, noticing what lovely hands he had – very big and hairy. I like a man with proper man's hands.

'Shall we come to you first, Matt?' asked Simon.

'Oh, OK. Well, mine was a bit of a strange one because I just got a taxi receipt with a smile emoji on and something like a medical cross. I talked to Mum and Dad, and they said that my granddad was born in Bristol but then they moved to Wales when Grandad was a baby.'

'Ah right. Was your dad someone who took taxis a lot? Or your grandad?'

'No,' said Matt. 'But my great grandad was a taxi driver.'

'Oh,' said everyone in the room.

'Ooooh,' said Simon. 'That is interesting. Did your Grandfather work as a taxi driver in Bristol?'

'No, my Great Grandfather, not my Grandfather.'

'Oh,' we all chorused in disappointment.

'Then he's probably too old for our calculations, isn't he?' I said.

'Yes, I guess so,' said Matt. He looked quite dejected. Clearly, he thought he would help the investigations with his revelation that his great grandfather was a taxi driver.

'Well, let's work it out,' said Mike, taking his arm from around Julie's shoulders and leaning his elbows onto the desk. How old are you, Matt, if you don't mind me asking?'

'I'm 19.'

'Write that down, Mary,' instructed Mike in an aggressive tone.

'Certainly, Your Lordship,' I replied. Mike glanced at me before turning his attention back to Matt.

'Do you know how old your Dad is?'

'Yes, he is, like, 42 or 43. It was his 40th birthday a few years ago. Do you want me to find out exactly how old he is?'

'No, don't worry about that for now. So, how old would your Grandfather be then? Do you have any idea?'

'Yes, I know it's his 70th birthday in a few weeks, because we're going to have a party.'

'Great. OK then so that would make your Great Grandfather around 95-ish, would it?'

'I don't know, he died about 15 years ago, when I was little.'

'Right,' said Mike. 'Sorry to hear that.' He was leaning

forward on his elbows. 'I think this works though. Let's say your Great Grandad would be about 90, shall we?'

'Yes, I guess that would be about right.'

'Then we need to work out what year he was born. Mary, can you work out what this year minus 90 comes to?'

'Well, um,' I said, rather taken aback by a request for maths to be done. I did not sign up for this. 'I think it's 1928,' I said, thanking the good lord for calculators on iPhones.

'Right, so what's the year on your taxi receipt?'

'It says 1976.'

'So your great Grandad would have been 48 in 1976?'

There were murmurs around the table.

'If that's what it works out at,' said Matt. 'I don't really know. I'm not very good at maths.'

'I think that's right,' said Mike. 'Could you do us a big favour and ring your parents now and ask whether your Great Grandfather was likely to have been a taxi driver in Bristol in 1976?'

Matt picked up his phone and rang his parents. He spoke in Welsh to them but I could hear him say '1976' and various other words that translated into English. Eventually he put his hand over the receiver and addressed the group: 'Yes, my Great Grandfather would have been working as a taxi driver in Bristol at that time.'

'Bloody hell, I am a genius,' said Mike. 'I should be in the sodding FBI.'

'Write all that down,' said Simon, glancing over at the pad as I did so.

'No, no…not about Mike being a genius…don't write that. Just everything to do with Matt.'

I scribbled out the genius remark and wrote down the details about ages and years. Then I looked up at Simon.

'This is good,' he said. 'Matt, before you hang up, can you just check with your parents whether your Great Grandfather mentioned anything happening in 1976? There's the medical cross on the receipt, so possibly involving a hospital or doctors?'

Matt spoke in Welsh again and shook his head.

'They don't know,' said Matt.

'OK,' said Simon. 'Could you ask them to call you if they think of anything that happened in 1976, anything at all? Also, can you tell me what your Great Grandfather's name was?'

Matt spoke briefly then put down his phone and said his Great Grandfather's name was Fred Radex. We all broke into a round of applause. I don't know why really. We'd discovered that Matt's Great Grandfather drove a taxi in Bristol in the 1970s, but we had no idea who Reginald Charters was, and didn't seem all that much closer to finding out, to be honest. I took a large sip of wine and helped myself to another slice of angel cake. It seemed rude not to.

'Julie and Sally – let's come to you next. Did you have any luck with your investigations?'

Sally spoke, as we all knew she would. The chances of Julie having bothered to make any calls were so remote as to be unworthy of consideration.

'Well, yes, I also had some luck,' said Sally, and I saw Julie look up in amazement. 'You'll remember that my sister and I had cuttings which related to nurses in 1976. Well, it turns out that my Mum was a nurse then and…I never knew this…but she worked in Bristol.'

'OK,' said Simon. 'Well, that's interesting. Very interesting. Did anything happen that she can remember from then?'

'She was only in Bristol at the beginning of her career, then she met my Dad and they moved to Coventry then to Ascot before I was born, but she does remember a few things.'

We all leaned forward a little in our seats.

'One thing she said she remembers is a big fight in the Students' Union when Bristol Uni played Gloucester Uni at rugby. It was a real grudge match and they were fighting in the bar afterwards. A load of rugby players came into A&E with glass in their faces – she said that was horrible. That was one of the worst things she had to deal with because so many of them were badly hurt.

'Another thing she remembers is a black guy being attacked in a racist attack – it was awful. He died and Mum was devastated. She went to the funeral. His name was Ricky. The other thing was a guy who she found in the street who had been attacked for being gay, and he was terrified of going to hospital. They are the things she remembers but definitely none of those people was called Reginald. She says she thinks the gay guy was called Joe but she's not sure.'

'What's your Mum's name?' asked Simon.

'It's Daphne,' said Sally. 'Daphne Bramley.'

There was a silence in the room and I scribbled down everything that had been said. What to make of all this? It did not seem like it was forming any coherent picture.

'Perhaps the taxi driver was rushed to hospital? Or perhaps the taxi driver was one of the guys at the rugby bash at the university?' offered Simon.

'No, because the taxi driver was in his mid-40s,' I said. 'It would be unlikely.'

'No one in my family's ever been to university,' said Matt.

'How old is your Mum, Julie?' asked Simon.

'She's 63.'

'Right, so in 1976 she would have been?' He was looking at me but before I could reach for my phone, he had worked it out. 'Ah, 21,' he said. 'Write it down, Mary. And can you read back what we know so far?'

'Well, um, yes. We have a taxi driver from Bristol and a nurse from Bristol who are related to people in the room and correspond with the clues that have been left, but Reginald's name has not come up at all in connection with either of them.

'Fred is no longer with us, so it's hard to get further information on his time as a taxi driver in the 1970s, but Daphne says she remembers three significant occurrences from her time in Bristol – a huge fight involving university rugby players in a bar, a racist attack and a homophobic attack.

'Daphne thinks the black guy was called Ricky, but she's not sure. She thinks the gay man was called Joe.'

'Right,' said Simon. 'Have you got anything to add at all, Mary?'

I explained that I didn't. The advert for the playwriting course meant nothing to anyone in the family.

'I'm sorry,' I kept saying. 'It's really frustrating but Mum and Dad can't think of anything at all.'

'Don't worry, Mary. Well, I will run through mine, shall I? So, my father was a theatre director. He died about 20 years ago, but according to my mum, whose memory is not the best, he worked with lots of up-and-coming writers and encouraged university students to write for the theatre. What I do not understand, though, is how this all comes together. My cutting is dated '1977' so if we are going to take a literal interpretation of all this – Reginald went on some sort of playwriting course in 1973. Something happened in 1976 involving a nurse and a taxi driver, then a year later he was somehow involved in this long list of theatre productions, most of which appear to be in some way linked to my father.'

'Oh God, this is interminable,' said Julie, from her position in the nook of Mike's arm. 'How the hell are we supposed to come to any sort of conclusion?'

'Don't worry, angel,' said Mike, gently stroking the top of her head. 'Shall I go through mine?'

'Yes, yes, of course,' said Simon, who had clearly forgotten all about Mike. 'I had a cutting of a B&B stuck over a map of Bristol. It is clear to me why I have this, my mum and dad ran a B&B in Bristol for most of their lives. The date on it is 1976, and they were definitely running a B&B then. Unfortunately, my dad's died and mum, Sarah, is in a home with Alzheimer's, so I can't add any more than that.'

Simon shook his head and looked out of the window across the fields. What was this all about? Why were they in Wales? Who were all these people gathered here today, and – most importantly of all – who in God's name was Reginald Charters?

TWO WEEKS AGO: REGINALD'S HOUSE IN WALES

Reginald felt he'd had a pretty decent life. He couldn't complain. Perhaps not the sort of life that many people would choose for themselves; a life largely devoid of human contact and social activity. His had been a life devoted to writing.

'Have you brought anyone with you?' asked the doctor, sitting next to Reginald and trying not to catch his eye. The doctor had done this a hundred times...had this conversation with all manner of different patients, but it never got any easier. It was particularly difficult with this gentleman who seemed to hate hospitals and refused to be admitted for treatment.

'No, I'm on my own,' said Reginald. 'But don't worry – I'm fine. Just tell me what is going on, and let me get out of here. Tell me the truth.'

'It's end stage. I am sorry, Reginald, but it has spread and there's nothing more we can do to stop the cancer. We can give you all sorts of drugs to keep you out of pain and we can make sure you sleep properly at night, but there's nothing we can do to prolong your life.'

Reginald nodded impassively. 'How long have I got?'

'Weeks,' replied the doctor. 'A month at most. I am sorry. I wish I had different news. Cancer is a bastard…it's in your lymph nodes – it's spreading throughout your body.'

Reginald smiled at the doctor and thanked him for his honesty.

'I'm sorry,' repeated the doctor.

'It's not your fault,' said Reginald.

They were at a politeness impasse, so Reginald stood up, shook the oncologist's hand and left.

'We can get you drugs for the pain,' the doctor called after him. 'You don't have to suffer, and we have counsellors to talk to, people who will help you.'

'I'm not in pain,' said Reginald, smiling. 'But I'm very grateful for your concern, and I'm indebted to you for everything you've done to help me.'

'A cancer specialist will call you, just to check you're OK and see whether there's anything we can do,' said the doctor.

'You're very kind,' repeated Reginald as he strode towards the door. He wished to waste no more time. Small talk was all very well and good, but if he had just three or four weeks left, he needed to get cracking – he had so much to do and the last place he wanted to be was in a bloody hospital.

First, he needed to go to the private detective agency on Llandrindod Wells' High Street. He strode in and announced that he needed to talk to someone urgently.

'Shall I make an appointment for you?' asked the receptionist. 'We have lots of time next week.'

'I'll wait,' he said. 'I can't come back next week; I don't know whether I'll be alive then.'

'Oh,' said the receptionist, looking alarmed. 'I'll call Mr Dillon.'

She shuffled off into some back room, then came out smiling.

'Mr Dillon is with a client but he will see you when he's finished. Can I get you a tea or coffee or anything?'

'I'm fine. Thank you for offering, though, that is most kind of you.'

He sat in the waiting room and thought about everything… all the incredible plays he had written but never taken credit for, all the friends he could have met and the lovers he could have enjoyed. But then – if he had lived a normal life, he wouldn't have the body of work he had created. And he could easily make everything right again in death – take ownership of the plays that he was so proud of, and take responsibility for saying 'thank you' to those people who'd made his life more bearable all those years ago. And he would share his plays with the people who meant so much to him….as a final act.

Mr Dillon emerged and announced that his name was Paul, though Reginald had no plans to address him in such a casual way. He was a rather smart-looking man, not what Reginald was expecting at all. He had expected a chain-smoking, ill-fitting suit kind-of-guy…maybe with egg stains down his tie, certainly pot-bellied, and not wearing a neat, light blue lamb's wool jumper, smart trousers and shiny shoes. His hair was cut into a respectable short back and sides and he wore owlish glasses on his face. He looked clean cut, respectable. You would never have guessed he was a private detective...which was useful really.

'You told my receptionist that you might be dead next week. Is someone threatening you?' he asked. 'Do you fear for your life? I am happy to help, if you are, but my suggestion is always that the first point of call should be the police. If you want me to contact the police and work with them, I can but I would strongly advise police involvement. Unless the fears you have for your life are because of something you have done that is not legal. Is that the situation?'

'No, no, no,' said Reginald, smiling at the thought of doing something illegal. 'Thank you for your advice but even if I were about to be stabbed through the neck I would not want the police involved. I am not a fan of the boys in blue. No – the reason I told your receptionist that I had to see you urgently was because I'm dying.'

'Oh, Mr Charters, I'm so sorry.'

'No – don't feel sorry for me, I'm perfectly fine. I have been ill with cancer for a while and now have a few weeks to live. What I need is for you to find some people from my past. I've led a very quiet life, Mr Dillon, I've not made friends, I've locked myself away, but before I became a hermit, I was treated to great human kindness by some people, and I would like to leave their descendants all the money I have. I suspect some will be untraceable but I would like you to do your best.'

'And you need this done quickly?' asked Mr Dillon.

'I want it done within the week and I will pay handsomely for the speed at which I am expecting you to work.'

'OK,' said Mr Dillon. 'We'll certainly try. I can put a few operatives on the case and we will see how we get on. I can report to you in a couple of days. Are all the people in this country, or are we looking abroad?'

'At the time I knew them they lived in Wales and Bristol. They could live anywhere by now.'

'We'll start the research and keep an open mind,' said Mr Dillon. 'We'll come back very soon with everything we have. Now, can I take some details from you?'

'There's something else,' said Reginald. 'It's the youngest descendants of these people that I am planning to leave my money to: the youngest descendants who are over 16. I'd like it to mirror one of the scenes from my play: Youngest Child – have you heard of it?'

'No, I haven't,' said Mr Dillon. 'I didn't realise you were a writer. I'm not much of a theatre-goer.'

'That's a shame. Yes – I am a writer. Not that anyone knows, of course – I have hidden my whole life. I have simply never spoken about my plays before. You are the first, Mr Dillon. I wanted to write without judgement and fear. Now, though, as I am dying, I feel differently and want the world to know. That is why I am telling you. My dying wish is to celebrate the kindness shown by individuals and to celebrate the plays I wrote but never claimed. All the money from the plays will go to charity. We will come on to that though – I am being very distracted, Mr Dillon, I do apologise – we have so much to get through. I didn't mean to bore you with talk of my plays.'

'No problem at all. I'm happy to help you do whatever you want.'

'Thank you. Now, where was I? Oh yes, I would like to have videos of the youngest children as well, and any information about how they live their lives today.'

Mr Dillon wrote everything down. 'We can try and video them in a public place,' said Mr Dillon. 'I'll talk to the operatives and explain your request and they will call you with any updates.'

'One other thing,' said Reginald. 'I don't have a phone.'

'No mobile? No problem, if you let us have your landline, we'll call you on that.'

'No mobile, no landline,' said Reginald. 'I will need you to come to my flat every morning at 10am to update me. I will pay all costs, all fees, and I will tip you wildly if you can make my dying wish come true.'

'We are very good at what we do, Mr Charters. If anyone can do it, we can. Do you want to let me have all the information you have?'

'Of course,' said Reginald, feeling his mood lighten. He had been rather dreading this encounter. Decades of self-enforced solitary confinement had left him ill-prepared to talk to people, motivate them to help him or even look them in the eye. He felt it had gone rather well though, and as Mr Dillon went to call the receptionist to take down the details of all the potential recipients, Reginald sat back in his seat and thought about how much he wished he could be there when they received the news that they had each been left a small fortune.

TWO WEEKS AGO: THE SEARCH BEGINS

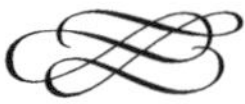

At 10am the next morning there was a loud knock on the door.

Excellent. Reginald liked people who were good timekeepers. He walked slowly to the door and swung it open. He hadn't been feeling very well that morning which was unusual for him. He had coped well with the cancer symptoms but today he felt dreadful, achy, slow and – well – ill. Still, the sight of Mr Dillon and two other men on the doorstep lifted his spirits.

'Come in,' he said. 'Can I get you gentlemen a cup of tea?' As he posed the question, he realised he probably had no tea, certainly he had no milk…milk made him feel quite sick. He had not bought it for months.

'No thank you,' said Mr Dillon. 'We're fine. Let me introduce Bob Kiffin and Mark Bow.'

'Nice to meet you, gentlemen. Now, the important issue – do you have any news for me?'

'We do,' said Mark or Bob, Reginald couldn't remember who

was who now. His memory was ridiculous. He had to write everything down or he forgot it immediately.

'So, you asked us to track down the youngest living descendants of six people: Andrew Marks, a former university lecturer at Bristol University who became a good friend, a taxi driver called Fred Radex, a nurse called Daphne Bramley, an owner of a bed and breakfast in Bristol called Nicholas Sween, a theatre producer called Alastair Blake, and any descendants of the Gower family who owned Gower Farm and then moved to Llandrindod Wells. So far we have managed to find the descendants of two of those people.'

'Oh, that's wonderful,' said Reginald, clapping his hands together. The men could see how delighted the sick, frail old man looked and felt a buzz of excitement that they had been able to bring him such joy.

'First, I have found the two daughters of Daphne Bramley... they are called Julie and Sally. Would you like to hear more about them? One is four years older than the other but I have videos of both because we didn't know we were going to find the younger one when we videoed the older one.'

'Yes, please,' said Reginald, sitting back in his seat.

They played a video on a laptop. It showed a very smart, beautiful woman striding down the street toward a glitzy office. She swung the door open then became distracted by someone she knew, and let it swing into the face of the person behind her. Next there was footage of the detectives talking to people outside the building. Those who knew Julie did not appear to have very much to say about her that was good.

'Goodness, she doesn't look like much fun,' said Reginald, crossing his arms across his chest as it dawned on him, for the first time, that he might be leaving a load of money to very unworthy recipients.

'No one had a good word to say about her. Everyone we talked to described her as 'arrogant', 'jumped up' and 'entitled'. The sister is different, though. Would you like to see the next video?'

'Yes, please.'

A rather bigger, very plain woman was getting out of a car and heading toward a school, carrying bags as she spoke to children and chatted to teachers.

'We couldn't video the children without the school or their parents' permission, but they all love Sally. Other teachers didn't say much and it was hard to video them without them worrying about us videoing any children, but they were all very complimentary about Sally. She sounds like a down-to-earth, warm woman.'

The clip had stopped with Sally's face frozen on it.

'My goodness, she resembles her mother,' said Reginald. 'Exactly like Daphne. That is how I remember her. She had such a soft voice and she looked like that. My goodness, it is like going back in time. She's the older one, is she?'

'Yes,' said Mr Dillon. 'I'm aware you want us to invite the youngest children, so we'll dismiss her.'

'No, no – don't. Invite them both and I will have some fun… create a bit of mischief as I did in A Bit of a Puzzler. I don't suppose you've heard of that, have you?'

'I'm afraid not. I really should go to the theatre more – you mentioned one of your plays before.'

'Indeed,' said Reginald. 'My most successful plays will be coming to life after my funeral. And there will be big drama, BIG drama. How about that?'

'Yes, very good,' said Mr Dillon. 'Now, do you want us to talk to Daphne herself? It won't be hard. She and Sally live near one another in Ascot. We know Daphne gave up nursing years ago and moved out of Bristol when she met her husband-to-be. He's dead now and Daphne is retired.'

'Oh, that's lovely of you, but – no. The greatest way to repay a debt is to look after the youngest children.'

'A line from your play?'

'Yes, Mr Dillon,' said Reginald. 'Very good.'

Paul Dillon smiled, and thought he really should take his wife Daisy to the theatre soon, to see one of Reginald's plays.

'The other person we've found is Mike Sween, Nicholas Sween's son.'

'Mike?' said Reginald; his face was alive with happiness and memories of the past. 'Michael. My goodness, I did his homework with him and the story we wrote became the basis of my greatest play. Michael – such a sweet boy.'

'We have a video,' said Mr Dillon, fiddling with his laptop until an image of a handsome young man filled the screen. 'We asked him what he thought of late-night pop music concerts being held at Twickenham – he lives there,' said Mr Dillon. 'Just to – you know – get him talking. This was his reply…'

'Thanks for asking,' said the handsome face, bursting with confidence and a hint of narcissism. 'I think music concerts are great, exactly what we need to liven up the area. I'm all in favour.'

The clip ended.

'We don't have anything on what he's like. There were no neighbours around and he works for SKY so we couldn't get near his work because of security gates, but we'll keep trying.

He was very nice and helpful to our pretend cameraman, if that helps?'

'No – that's fine. I just wanted to see them. Any idea what happened to Nicholas? He was a nice guy.'

'I'm afraid he died. His wife Sarah is still alive, though.'

The three men left, leaving Reginald to contemplate what to do... It had simply not occurred to him that the descendants of the fine people who had helped him years ago would not be decent or worthy of his charity. Julie seemed most unpleasant. He had a clever idea about how to deal with her...an idea that would give a grand twist to the whole thing. But what if the others turned out to be equally unpleasant creatures? Should some get more money than others based on how they lived their lives? But that didn't suit him at all. He did not want to sit in judgement of them. Who was he to do that? It was very complicated.

The next day Mark and Bob returned, this time without Mr Dillon, and the day after that, with him.

They were managing to locate the descendants of everyone who had helped him. Fred Radex, the taxi driver, had a great-grandson who still lived with his mum and dad – he was sweet and kind and over 16. His life was about to be transformed.

Simon Blake, son of Alastair, the man who allowed him to write and earn without ever revealing his identity, had been found. Reginald knew that Alastair had died because he had worked with him until his death six years ago, and he could easily have found his descendants without too much trouble, but he liked the fact that Mr Dillon's men were doing the whole thing for him and providing him with videos of his son Simon. He doubted whether anyone would ever understand just how much Alastair had helped him by allowing him to write plays and see them produced and staged without ever having to be named as the writer. Alastair went to all the meetings on his behalf and allowed Reginald to write all day and never be forced to see anyone or talk to anyone except Alastair. When Alastair died, Reginald stopped writing...that was how symbiotic their relationship had become.

On the fourth day, only one of the investigators came to see him – Bob Kiffin, a young buck who had the bearing of an over-eager estate agent itching for a sale in order to impress his girlfriend. He had a video with him of a woman called Mary Brown – a jolly, fat woman who turned out to be the youngest living descendant of Andrew...beautiful, lovely Andrew. He watched the video of the woman in her DIY store, messing around with the plants – peering through them to entertain children, laughing all the time, and eating when she wasn't, and he thought how different she was from Andrew – the man he'd loved so much. Andrew taught him what love was, but he could never be described as jolly or happy.

'How are they related?' asked Reginald.

'Quite distantly, I'm afraid. He doesn't have his own children but his brother adopted a boy and the boy's daughter is Mary.'

'Oh,' said Reginald, unable to hide his disappointed that she wasn't a blood relative.

He looked back at the screen where Mary was hiding behind a small potted privet hedge to eat a chocolate bar. 'Yes, that's fine,' he said. It was not so much who he gave the money to as a gesture of thanks for the past that he and Andrew had shared.

'Any news at all on Andrew?' he asked.

'He died ten years ago,' said the man. 'I think he was gay,

actually, not that that is relevant, just didn't know whether you knew.'

Not relevant? His whole life had been strangled by the relevance of being gay in rural 1970s England.

'I'm gay too,' said Reginald, determined to say it proudly and openly for the first time in his life. 'Andrew stood by my side when I first came out. He allowed me to be gay; he told me it was OK to be myself. He supported and nurtured me. He changed me from a shy and confused boy to a happy man.'

'Cool,' said the detective. 'Andrew sounds amazing.'

No judgement, no disgust. Perhaps the world had moved on since 1976.

'There's only one problem now,' he said. 'We can't find the Gower family anywhere. Well – we can – but not the right family. We have found Gowers all over the place, but none of them used to own Gower Farm. Paul's there now, and Mark Bow is talking to people living near Gower Farm. I suspect the man and woman died and had no children.'

'No - they had children - a boy called Tom. Tom Junior he was called. Please keep looking.'

Once the investigator left, Reginald lay on the sofa and drifted off to sleep. He dreamt of happy times: Andrew's warmth, sunshine flickering through the leaves on long walks to the park, and his mother's gorgeous smile...

THE BEGINNING OF THE END

'Mr Charters, are you OK?'

Bang. Bang. Bang.

'Mr Charters?'

Reginald stirred in his position on the sofa. He took a minute to work out where he was and what the terrible noise was before he struggled to his feet and tried to move slowly toward the door, but he couldn't do it, his legs collapsed beneath him.

BANG! Much louder now, then suddenly people were in the room.

'Mr Charters, can you hear me? It is Paul Dillon here. We've called an ambulance; it will be here soon.'

'Not an ambulance,' he said. 'I can't go to hospital.'

But his voice was a whisper that no one heard. And he fell straight back to sleep.

'Good morning, Mr Charters.' A stout nurse with appalling

skin was breathing down on him and making him feel quite nauseous. She lifted his arm to take his pulse, counting under her breath. 'OK. Doctor will be here soon,' she said.

'Where's Mr Dillon?' he asked.

'I don't know a Mr Dillon,' she said.

'He brought me in. I need to talk to him. Please, it's very important; he's helping me to fulfil my dying wish.'

She looked back at the sad old man who had already soiled the bed twice.

'I'll find out,' she said.

'He works as a private detective.'

After what seemed like an interminable wait, Mr Dillon appeared at his bedside with his reliable associates. He smiled when he saw them – Paul, Bob and Mark – his Three Musketeers; they were the closest he had come to having friends for decades. He noticed that Mr Dillon was carrying a bunch of grapes. Perhaps he should have made more of an effort over the years. Friends had always seemed like such hard work. When you paid for people's time, as he was doing with these three, it made it all much less complicated.

'Have you found Tom?' he asked. 'Or Tom's children? Anyone connected to the Gowers?'

'No,' said Paul Dillon. 'I've been out there for days, as has Mark. We've found nothing, it's like the whole family has disappeared into the ether.'

'Really? But how could that happen? I don't understand.'

'It can take a while to find people, I can carry on searching but it might take longer than...well, you know – it might take a while.'

'Keep searching, never stop searching,' said Reginald. 'Now I need you to do something else for me – I need you to get a solicitor here ASAP so I can sign over power of attorney to you.'

'But you don't know me. You can't do that.'

'I know you better than any other person alive today. I trust you.'

While Mr Dillon reluctantly went in search of a lawyer, Reginald subjected himself to test after test from box-ticking doctors with clipboards and charts. He was injected and fussed over. They would take him out of pain, they would keep him clean and they would all know that any day now he would die. Probably sooner rather than later, Reginald suspected. He could no longer walk, nor could he feed himself, and the pain of swallowing and shortness of breath combined to make him feel vulnerable and scared. Not scared of death, but scared of not having everything in place for death.

When Mr Dillon arrived back with a lawyer, the form signing began, and Reginald signed over money and instructions to the amiable private detective in the presence of the serious-looking solicitor.

'Now, I need you to find me someone who can produce a video for me. The video will incorporate all the short films you've made of the people who will be in my will.'

Dillon sent his assistant, Mark, to investigate. While he was gone, Reginald sat back against the pillows.

'I would like to invite the people you've found to the funeral,' he said. 'I want them to be the only people there – they represent the only people in my life who really cared.'

'Sure,' said Dillon. He wanted to add that he had grown to care a little, and that he would not have broken down the door to his flat and got him to hospital if he did not care. He wanted to add that the doctors and nurses all cared. There were many people who cared about him, if only he would abandon his deeply held views that he was alone in the world, and look around him he'd see that. But the man was sick and frail. He would just help him all he could and do his best to fulfil the man's dying wish.

Reginald steeled himself. All he had to do now was make this simple video then he could slip away. He hoped that the money he was leaving to people would enable them to see the world…and live much fuller lives than he had.

'I'm going to create a bit of mischief in my will. You hear that, Mr Dillon? Not everyone who comes to the funeral will get money, you see.'

'Right,' said Dillon.

'All the information is in that envelope I gave you. You know what to do? You pass all this on to the people who come to the funeral, OK? Remember the envelopes we talked about? Use Beddows and Plunkett, those solicitors on the High Street in Llanelli, next to Joe's Ice Cream Parlour and use Degs Funeral Service in Llanelli. It's all in the letters I gave you.'

'Yes – I've got all your notes here about which people to use, Reginald. Don't worry.'

'OK, then we just need to make this video to show after the funeral, and everything is sorted. Agreed?'

'Yes, just the video. Are you up to recording it now?'

'Yes, I'm ready. I have been practising for this moment all my life. Let's go then.'

Mr Dillon straightened the sheets on the bed so that Reginald looked as respectable as possible.

'When you're ready,' said the young nurse who had been given the duty of holding the iPhone to capture his words.

'Can they see me and hear me?' he asked.

'Yes, all ready to go,' she said.

'Hold it up, Nurse, and make sure they can hear what I'm saying.'

'Don't you worry,' she said. 'We can hear you loud and clear.'

PRESENT DAY: GOWER FARM HOTEL

I woke up and knew immediately that I wasn't tucked up in my lovely, comfortable, modern bed at home. I glanced at the terrible decor and the tiny window next to the bed through which a cold breeze was seeping. I pulled back the thick, floral curtains to check that I hadn't left it open but – no. It was just old, allowing a horrible freezing draught to come in. I fiddled with the handle to try to pull it tighter.

Then I remembered.

Oh God.

It was as if I had been shot in the stomach.

Shit.

I had to make a speech…about someone I had never met, but who held me in such high esteem that he was insistent I come to his funeral. How do you write a speech for such an occasion? Bugger. I wished I had written it last night, but after the lengthy late-night discussions I had been too tired by the time I got to bed. At least we had a theory now about why we were at the funeral…however vague it was. We had decided that Reginald was an ageing actor who had lived in Bristol and dated a nurse who he met in a taxi. It did not feel substantial enough to be worthy of a £1 million reward but it was the best we could do.

Now I had to write a bloody eulogy. I pulled out my laptop and googled 'funeral speeches'.

There was a brilliant site that listed touching eulogies that were perfect for funerals. They gave loads of examples of great speeches for mums, dads, husbands, babies and friends, but – perhaps unsurprisingly – there were no examples of eulogies you could make about someone you'd never met before and knew absolutely nothing about.

I clicked on the example of a eulogy to a friend, then cut and pasted it into a Word document. I would go through the eulogy and change it so it related to Reginald. Quite how I would do this, I had no idea; I would have to keep it vague. I scurried through the document, cutting and changing and throwing out detailed sentences and throwing in attributes that felt appropriate until I had a short speech that I thought I could deliver without causing offence. Since it did not appear that anyone who had ever met him would be at the funeral, it did not matter too much – there would be no one around to contradict me if I just made it all up. Nevertheless, I felt a strange loyalty to this man who had brought me to the strange hotel in the middle of nowhere, and introduced me to this odd collection of people. I wanted to do well by him even though I might never know why he had invited me.

I dressed in black and walked down to breakfast to meet the others. When I got to the dining room they were already there, sitting in silence, also dressed in black, eating cooked breakfasts. I took a seat next to Mike and Julie and ordered a full English.

'So, have you got your speech all written?' said Mike. 'I don't envy you that at all.'

'Kind of,' I said. 'I've got something written, but I've no idea whether it's any good.'

'I'm sure it will be perfect,' said Mike, as my huge breakfast arrived in front of me. There was fried bread, fried eggs, fried bacon, fried sausage, fried tomato, fried mushroom and black pudding. There were also beans and toast piled onto the plate and when I moved the toast, I found fried potatoes nestling underneath it. This might be the greatest breakfast I had ever had.

'Will you excuse us?' asked Mike, standing up and pulling out Julie's chair. I noticed that Julie had no plate in front of her, and had been drinking a cup of boiled water. Where was the fun in that?

I finished my breakfast and waited in the lobby to be taken over to the church for the funeral service. I had been told that I would be able to practice first, but no one came at 9am, so I waited with the others until 9.30am and walked over with them. There was a lot of smiling, encouraging and hugging me and telling me not to worry and how brave I was. With every kind word and compliment, I felt more and more nervous about what I had to do. I clutched my notebook tighter as we followed the funeral director out of the hotel and toward the small church and graveyard opposite.

We walked in and all sat on the front pew. There were a few people scattered on the other pews.

'Who are they?' asked Mike. 'I thought we were the only ones coming.'

'No, no one here knows Reginald. They are locals who just come along to most funerals we hold here…for something to do. Except for those three men at the end of the pew over there. I do not think they are locals. They said their names are Paul Dillon, Mark Bow and Bob Kiffin.'

I watched as the vicar walked to the front of the church, coughed gently, looked up and smiled.

I was kind of hoping that the vicar would say something personal about Reginald that I could echo in my speech, but - no such luck. Instead of a warm, personal speech, the vicar thanked us all for coming and said he was pleased that everyone who Reginald had asked to be at his funeral was here, and he was delighted to hand over to me for the eulogy.

Shit.

I walked to the front and could feel five pairs of eyes boring into the back of my head. I looked down at my notebook and out to the congregation, seeing five people at the front, staring at me expectantly and around half a dozen other people dotted around the church. One was knitting; others sat stiffly in their best coats, waiting for me to start. The three men on the far pew had a look of genuine grief on their faces, but as far as I was aware, none of the people in this church knew, or had even met, Reginald.

I cleared my throat and began to read from my notebook.

'Thank you very much, everyone, for coming here today to remember Reginald Charters. I know he would be delighted that you are all gathered in this lovely church to honour him and say 'goodbye'.' I paused. This was ridiculous. Reading out inanities was pointless. I needed to tell the truth.

'This is a very difficult talk to give,' I continued. 'Because I don't know Reginald. As far as I am aware I have never met him, but I know that I am connected to him in some way. He asked for me and for the other five gathered in the front row to come to his funeral. I will be honest – we do not know why he asked us. Last night we spent lots of time trying to work it out, but we still do not understand, not really.

'So this is a crazy situation and this is a very difficult speech to give. What I would like to say to you, though, is that this whole experience has taught me a lot: it has taught me that the little things we do for one another really matter. Somewhere along the line, a relative of mine did something for Reginald that was so special that he sought to offer his gratitude by tracking me down and inviting me to the funeral.

'My relative might not even have understood how great a favour he did for Reginald. We might never find out what happened and why we are here. But we know that relatives of ours meant a huge amount to Reginald.

'It's the little things you do – the favours and kindnesses you perform that are the most important things, and can mean everything to someone.

'What our relatives did for Reginald clearly meant everything to him and I'm glad to be here today to remember him and to be reminded that being good to people, being kind and thoughtful, is the most important thing. Thank you very much.'

I walked back down to my seat, almost light-hearted with relief that it was all over. I had winged it, but I had been honest, and I had reflected the truth of Reginald in the spirit of everything we knew about him.

'Let us pray,' said the vicar. I dropped my head and thought about Reginald Charters...whoever he was.

PRESENT DAY: SEEING REGINALD

'Come in and take a seat,' said the solicitor, ushering us all into his meeting room where a large screen television stood in the corner. 'I hope the funeral was OK. Please sit down and we'll get started.'

We all shuffled along, undoing our black garments in the heat of the office and plonking ourselves onto wooden chairs set out in a line like at junior school.

There was tension, rather than excitement, in the air; we were finally going to find out exactly what this was all about. I think we were all a little about what we might hear. Why hadn't he just told us at the beginning what this was all about? Why did he try to make us guess? Perhaps there was a nasty sting in the tail and we were all about to be shot.

'OK. Well, it's my duty to inform you that we act for the late Mr Reginald Charters,' said Huw. 'We were contacted by his representative last week after his death from cancer. We were given specific instructions to contact you, as we did, and to gather you today for the funeral and for this reading of the will afterwards.'

He was reading from a note, clearly left behind by Reginald.

'Mr Charters requested that I hand out envelopes to you, as I have. In the envelopes were clues as to why he invited you. I am now asked to play this short film to you which will explain everything.'

'How exciting,' I muttered to Sally. She squeezed my leg affectionately and went to say something back to me, but before she could get the words out, an image burst onto the screen.

'Can they see me and hear me?' he was asking.

He was a very old, frail-looking man in a hospital bed.

'Hold it up, nurse, and make sure they can hear what I'm saying.'

A grainy image of the late Reginald appeared in front of us.

'Hello, I am sorry to be so intriguing, and to drop hints and make you work hard to find out the truth,' he said. 'But I wanted you to be intrigued enough to listen carefully when I told you my story, my truth, and explain what these clues mean. And why I have chosen you to come to my funeral. If you had just received a note in the post advising you of my passing and leaving you money, you would not have taken in the magnitude of my story. So, I am sorry for the subterfuge, but I think it was necessary in order to get your attention right from the very start.

'So, what should I say then? Well, first – you haven't worked it out, have you? No way will you have. No way at all. I could not resist giving you 20 hours to work it out, just like in my play *20 Hours to Save the World*. Have any of you seen it? Of course, you have not. If you have, you'll know that the world doesn't really blow up after 20 hours.'

We all leaned forward in our seats, as if being physically closer to the television would make what we were being told somehow clearer. We were all fascinated.

'And just like in the play, your right to inheritance won't blow up after 20 hours. You will inherit money regardless of whether you have been able to work out my link to you all. So that's good, isn't it? As I say, I only made you guess in order to capture your imagination. And for the sheer fun of it, of course.

'Right, I should stop waffling. My name is Reginald Charters, but I was born Joe Stilliano. My father, Marco Stilliano, came over to Wales during the war as an Italian prisoner and worked on Gower Farm.'

There was a gasp from Huw. I turned to face him to see him staring at the screen, mesmerised. 'Joe Stilliano? Marco's boy? Goodness!'

'I changed my name to Reginald Charters after I was badly beaten up for being gay. The year was 1976 and homosexuality had been legalised only nine years previously and was frowned upon. I was regularly spat at and glared at, and one day I was beaten so badly I thought I would die. I couldn't possibly go to hospital or tell the police – I'd heard lots of stories about how homophobic those organisations were and how many young gay men reported crimes only to find themselves beaten up again by angry policemen. Oh, I know you're probably thinking that things like that never happen, but this was the 1970s – a very different time.'

Reginald's voice was shaky but clear. He stopped and a nurse gave him a sip of water out of what looked like a feeding bottle for a guinea pig.

'Sorry,' he said. 'I'm a sick, old man, as I'm sure you can see. Well, after I was beaten up, three people came to my aid: a taxi driver called Fred Radex found me and looked after me before he called Daphne Bramley. The two of them took me back to the B&B run by Nicholas and Sarah Sween and there they looked after me. I never repaid their kindnesses, but they saved my life, I have no doubt of that. I always promised to pay them back. And, as you'll know if you've read my play, *Youngest Child,* you go to hell if you don't help out the youngest child of anyone who does you a favour.'

'Oh yes,' said Simon, nodding frantically. 'That's right – I remember the play now.'

'Sally, Julie, Matt and Mike – I am going to pay you back now for what your relatives did for me,' Reginald continued.

'There are two other people – Mary and Simon. Let me tell you why you are here.'

I could feel my heart beating inside my chest.

'Now, I've only loved one man, a gentleman called Andrew Marks. He made me feel wonderful…alive and worth something. He taught me who I was and what life was about and I loved him intensely for three years before he fell out of love with me. After I was beaten up, I ran away. I never said goodbye.

'Mary Brown – you are the closest family member to him. Andrew never had his own children but his brother, Carl, adopted a boy and that boy is your dad, Mary Brown.'

'Oh blimey,' I said. 'Well I'd never have worked that connection out in a million years.'

'I wish I'd said goodbye to Andrew and thanked him properly for loving me, but I didn't. The reason I didn't was because I was beaten up so badly that I withdrew from the world. I had nightmares every day after I was attacked and was left so terrified that weeks went past when I refused to leave the house. I should have asked for help but I didn't. What kept me going after I'd been loved by Andrew and physically saved by my three angels, was writing. I wrote and wrote, but I had no desire to attach my name to any of the pieces I wrote, so I changed my name to Reginald Charters after a character in a book that my father left for me, a book I loved very much when I was growing up. But then I realised I didn't want my new name to be famous either, so I met Alastair Blake, a theatre producer, and explained everything to him. He allowed me to write plays for him under a variety of names without telling anyone who the real creator was.

'I worked with Alastair for 30 years and managed to avoid all limelight and all contact with the theatre world. I wrote, I earned money – lots of money – but was never famous. Simon, I met you so many times when you were a boy, but you were never introduced to me. Your father kept my identity secret from everyone, even his family.

'He was a wonderful, wonderful man. He gave me the opportunity to do exactly what I wanted to do, and he put on plays I had written that were scandalous at the time, he took the dissension and gave me the money. Even when my plays were made into films – like when *A Bit of a Puzzler* was made into a film called *The Devil's Work* – my identity was kept secret. The writer of that play was Lorenzo Alberto – named after Dad's best friend in the war. They were taken as prisoners of war together but lost touch when Lorenzo went back to Italy.'

Reginald snorted with laughter at this stage, and started coughing wildly. A nurse offered him another drink out of the funny feeding bottle and he carried on.

'So, here you all are...my chosen ones. I have seen videos of you all – I know a little about you all. I believe that you are the youngest generation of the families I wish to support.

'My only disappointment today is that I couldn't track down anyone related to Tom and Irene Gower – the family who took my father in and supported and helped him. I will leave money for their family for when any of them is found. Someone has to be found. I want everyone to keep on looking...they saved my father's life. They were good people. Are you all good people? I hope so.

'So, the good news...my share in the branches of Joe's Ice Cream Parlour, which I sold decades ago, along with my income from being a playwright, has netted me well over £3 million. £1 million of that will be left in trust in the hope that relatives of Tom and Irene Gower can be found. They deserve that. It is what my father would want me to do. A million will be used to provide gifts for all those who have helped me to fulfil my dying wish. By the time all costs, debts and the funeral are taken care of, I estimate that I will have £1 million left that I would like to leave to you. I propose that I give each of you £200,000. How does that sound?'

There was a pause in the video while Reginald cocked his head to one side. We all did calculations on our fingers. Matt was the first to vocalise what we had all realised. 'There are six of us, so that's not £200k each.'

'Have you worked it out yet?' said Reginald as we were all mumbling and trying to do the basic mathematics.

'I couldn't part without one final bit of puzzling mischief, could I?'

A silence fell over the room as we all looked from one to the other.

'One of you won't be getting anything,' he said slowly, leaning in to the camera. 'Just like in *A Bit of a Puzzler* you will all receive a huge amount of money except one of you, and you as a group will decide which person will go home empty-handed. That is why I asked you to stay for the day today. You have a choice to make.

'It's now around 11.10am, if my instructions have been followed properly. You have until 2pm to report back here without one person in the group. The person missing will be the one you all vote off. The person selected need not return. Then I might have another surprise for you. You can't vote for yourself, and you can't opt to share the money six ways – one of you has to be voted out.'

PRESENT DAY: THE FINAL TWIST

'Do we have to do this?' I asked the solicitor. 'It's a really horrible thing to do.'

'You heard what he said. It's one of the absolute conditions of the money being passed over.'

'This is monstrous,' said Julie, and for the first time in two days, I agreed with her. It also felt like it was needless and cruel.

'Please follow me,' said the receptionist, opening the door to another room, and trying to lead us in.

'Where are we going?' asked Simon. 'Can't we stay in here and make our decision?'

'Of course, you're more than welcome to stay here, but we have a boardroom with a large table in it. It is much better for discussing, deciding what you want to do.'

'OK.'

We were shown into a boardroom that had definitely seen better days – I don't know what high-level negotiations took place there, but it was far from impressive. The only good news was that there was a large table full of snacks – I mean, proper snacks – the best snacks – potato skins dripping in melted cheese and bacon, chicken nuggets, sandwiches, crisps, dips, mini burgers and cones of fries. The BEST snacks. I wandered straight over and piled potato skins, crisps and chips onto my plate before realising that someone was talking to me. I glanced up to see them all seated, looking over.

'Are you joining us?' said Julie. 'You had an enormous breakfast, surely you don't need any more food.' She gave me a withering look as she spoke and raised her eyebrows at Mike as if to say, 'look at the state of her'. I put down the plate on the side and went to join the group.

'Where's your food?' asked Simon.

'It doesn't matter,' I said, even though it really, really did.

'No, seriously, Mary – where's the plate you had? What have you done with it?'

'Oh, don't worry – it's over there,' I said, indicating the corner of the buffet where I had dropped it suddenly under questioning from Julie.

Simon stood up and strode to the buffet, picked up my plate and brought it to me. He put it in front of me.

'There you go,' he said. 'Enjoy it, Mary. That looks delicious. Ignore Julie.'

'How about we go back and say we all share the money that's there,' said Julie. 'Just force them to let us all have some.'

'We can't – he'd probably make us all leave without anything,' said Simon.

'Well, what on earth are we going to do then?' asked Julie. 'This is so childish, there is no way we can eliminate one person. That's ridiculous.'

'We will all have to vote. It is the only way to do it. Write the name of the person you think should not receive any money, and I will add them up and the person with the most votes is the one who has to leave,' said Simon.

'We can't do that,' said Julie.

'What else will we do?' I chipped in.

Julie glared at me. 'Haven't you got potatoes to eat?'

She really was the most unpleasant person. I was now damned sure I knew whom I was voting for. Beautiful or not, she had to go.

'Hands up everyone who thinks the best thing to do is to write on a piece of paper the name of the person we wish to eliminate.'

Every hand went up except Julie's. She nudged Mike aggressively until he took his hand down. Even with his forced change of mind, the result was clear.

'Then we write down a name each. Does anyone want to say anything before we vote?'

'Hi, I hope you don't mind, but I would just like to say something,' said Matt. 'This has been the weirdest weekend of my whole life, and I was really worried about coming, and then when I saw how grown-up and posh everyone was, in this really elegant hotel, I got even more worried. But you've all been very kind.'

He was bright red as he spoke. 'And it's really good, isn't it, that our relatives helped this man when he was in great need. I have been thinking – would I do that? I really hope so. It makes me feel so proud, and even if I am voted off – I am glad I came here. I'm really glad I met you.'

'Here, here,' said Simon, raising his glass. 'To our relatives. May we be as kindly remembered as they have been.'

'To our relatives,' we all said, raising our glasses.

'And to Reginald,' I added quickly.

'To Reginald,' we all toasted again, then Simon took control, handing round pieces of paper. 'I know we all think this is very unfair, but it was Reginald's wish, and this is Reginald's money.'

Once everyone had received their piece of paper, Simon spoke:

'There is no need to identify yourself,' he said. 'All you need to do is write the name of the person that you think we should eliminate, and shouldn't receive any money.'

I took my piece of paper and wrote 'Julie Bramley' on it, and folded it up and put it into the envelope that was passed around the table. Not only was Julie the person I liked the least, but there were two sisters… If Sally wanted to, she could give Julie some money. If anyone else around this table was eliminated, they would receive no money at all.

Well, that is what I tried to convince myself of anyway, but – basically – I didn't like her. She was snappy, self-opinionated, and just because she was born beautiful she thought she was better than everyone else. The envelope arrived back with Simon.

'Now, I'm not sure how to do this – whether I should go through the envelope and work out who is the person who has to leave, or whether I should read out the names one by one.'

'Read out the names,' said Julie. 'Then we know it's genuine.'

I thought to myself that it was odd she suspected Simon would not be genuine. I could not think of a more reliable, honest man to conduct this bizarre procedure.

'Fair enough,' said Simon. 'If that's the way people feel, then I will make sure that it's all very transparent.'

He put his hand into the envelope and pulled out a piece of

paper, unfolding it carefully. I knew that it would be a vote for Julie, as they all would be.

'The first vote is for you, Mary Brown,' he said.

'Oh. Me?' I said. 'Right, sure.'

'Yes, sorry, Mary. The first vote is for you.'

I could feel my heart beating in my chest and a dull ache developing in my stomach. It was nothing to do with fears about not getting the money. I have never been very money orientated. It was more about the fact that someone had thought I was the worst person in the group. How could they think that? What had I done wrong? Christ, I gave the speech at the funeral. I tried to be nice to everyone. I could feel tears pricking in the back of my eyes.

'Don't take it personally, Mary,' said Simon. 'It's just the ridiculous position we're in.' The next name to be pulled out was 'Julie', then another one: 'Julie.'

I was glad that the majority of people appeared to be voting for Julie, but all I could think about was the fact that someone had voted for me.

The Julies kept on coming.

Then 'Simon'.

Simon took the news that he had been picked out as someone who shouldn't receive the money with a simple shrug.

All the rest of the names to be pulled out of the envelope said 'Julie'.

'We appear to have reached a decision,' said Simon, looking at Julie.

'Are you really suggesting that I leave?' she asked, aggressive and confrontational.

'Yes,' said Simon. 'This is nothing to do with us; it's everything to do with Reginald. This is what he wanted; we are just obeying his wishes.'

'It does seem very unfair,' said Sally, leaping to her sister's defence. 'Are you sure we shouldn't challenge it? Make a point of refusing to throw anyone out. Perhaps he is waiting to see whether we will throw someone off and if we do, none of us will get any money. He might be playing games to see whether we stick up for the group as a whole? Julie's done nothing wrong; it seems so cruel.'

'Yes,' said Julie. 'And anyway – you got a vote against you, Mary. Maybe you should leave? Or you, Simon.'

'No,' said Simon. 'This is all getting very silly. You have the most votes and I'm afraid you are the person who has to leave.'

'Fine, I'm going. I'd have gone anyway because this is an absolute farce. A waste of the weekend for nothing. The only good news is that I got to vote for Mary.

'I mean, look at the plate of food you had right now – should you really be eating all that food considering the weight you are? You're not even a blood relation of anyone who helped Reginald.'

At this point Mike stepped in. 'Come on, Julie, you are bang out of order here.' Julie stood up, grabbed her beautifully tailored jacket from the back of her seat and stormed out of the room. We all sat there, shell-shocked.

'I think this is cruel,' said Sally, as her sister left. 'Very cruel.'

It occurred to me, once she had gone, that if Julie voted for me and therefore there was only one other vote that was not for her, it meant that either Mike or her sister had voted for her to go. It could not possibly be her sister so it must have been Mike. As we all prepared to walk back into the room without Julie, I turned to him and gave him the biggest smile I could muster.

PRESENT DAY: THE WILL

'Please, take your seats,' said Huw Beddows, as we trooped back into the room. We all sat down exactly where we had been sitting before, with Julie's seat empty.

'Thank you for making a decision. I know it must have been hard,' he said. 'Can I just confirm – Julie Bramley has not come back into the room with you, is that correct?'

'Yes,' we mumbled, then Simon took the lead:

'Yes, I can confirm that Julie Bramley has not come back with us.'

'OK, thank you very much. I'm going to show you the rest of the video now, then I need to take bank details from you and you're free to go.'

He picked up the remote control, scowled at it then pressed the buttons on it as if he had never operated any technological equipment in his life before. Eventually, the screen burst into life and Reginald was back in the room.

'Hello,' he said. 'You're back! Without Julie, I hope. Please tell me you are without Julie. Terrible error if you have thrown someone else to the dogs. So, that is all I've got for you. The clues were simply to make you think about my story and your relatives' places in it. To think about kindnesses you might perform. I wish you nothing but joy and happiness. Look after yourselves. Stay in touch with one another and have wonderful, fulfilling lives.'

Then the picture went and Reginald was gone.

Huw walked to the front of the room. 'Reginald died two hours after the video was made. He slipped away peacefully.'

We sat in reverential silence for a moment, none of us sure how to react. We had known that he died, of course, we had spent the morning at his funeral, but it was still moving to hear his final words and to know the details of his passing.

As we sat there, the solicitors' receptionist appeared at the back of the room and motioned to Mr Beddows to join her. He excused himself and walked over to her, and the sound of whispered Welsh filtered through the room. Then he walked back to the front.

'Ladies and gentlemen, you might have been aware of three men at the funeral, at the far side of the church. They are the private detectives who Mr Charters employed to track you down and fulfil his final wishes. They say they are happy to come in and talk to you about Reginald and tell you anything you might not know. Would that be of interest?'

'Oh yes,' I said, as a chorus of 'yeses' followed mine. We had not met anyone who knew Reginald; it would be great to find out what he was really like.

Huw excused himself and left the room, returning minutes later with three men in thick overcoats.

'These are the private detectives I mentioned. They dealt directly with Reginald and may be able to answer any questions.'

One of the men stepped forward. 'My name's Paul. It is lovely to meet you all. I run a small private detective firm and was visited by Reginald a couple of weeks ago and asked to find you. He didn't have much information about where you'd be or what chance we had, and – as you have heard – we couldn't track down any of the people related to Tom Gower, so we're still working on that. We spent a bit of time with Reginald and got to know him fairly well. We're happy to answer any questions you may have.'

'Thank you,' said Simon. 'Would you mind explaining what happened? And – when he called you, what sort of guy was he?'

'Yes, of course. Well, the first thing to say is that he didn't call, because he didn't have a phone: no landline and no mobile. He came into the office and we had to go to his flat to update him.

'He was very old-fashioned, courteous and a little shy really. He was very nice – I warmed to him, but I felt he had locked himself away for a long time and, as he was dying, he wished he had not. He used fake writers' names on his plays because he didn't want to deal with the attention that his plays would bring him and he regretted that and wanted it put right after his death. He is leaving all the royalties from them to charity.

'He also regretted that he lost touch with people who'd been very kind to him. That's why he wanted you to be here today and to inherit some of his money.'

'Can I just ask you how we were chosen? Julie and Sally were here, but my older sister wasn't invited,' said Mike.

'He asked me to track down the youngest descendants who were over sixteen.'

'Ah, so it was 'youngest descendants' like the play?' said Simon.

'Yes,' said Mr Dillon. 'All of it was based on his plays.'

'So how did Sally end up here? No disrespect, Sally,' I said. I was still confused.

'Well, yes – that was a bit odd, but we were looking for the youngest daughter of Daphne when we found Sally and we made the video about her and collected all her details because we didn't know whether we'd find Julie. When we did track down Julie, we thought we might as well show Reginald both videos. He thought Sally resembled Daphne and was generally more appropriate for the inheritance than Julie, so he came up with the plan for voting off.

'That voting off idea comes from one of his plays – a play that was written way before X-Factor or Big Brother or any of those other voting-off shows. This whole final act that he wrote was the summary of all of his plays.'

'The plays he suddenly decided to take ownership of in death...' said Simon. 'What a beautiful literary flourish.'

'There was no way anyone was ever going to work out how we knew him, though,' said Sally. 'Why did he ask us to spend so long thinking about it, and deliver the clues like he did?'

'Just like he said - he wanted you to know the whole story and really think about how much impact your relatives had. He also wanted you to meet one another and spend time together.'

'Do you think you'll find Tom Gower?' I asked. It was bothering me quite a lot that the detectives had not managed to do this yet.

'I'm afraid I've not been well, so will be taking a few weeks off, but once I'm better and back in the office, it will be a priority.'

'Good,' I said. 'Just one final question – was it his idea to get one of us to do a speech? That was plain cruel.'

'Yes,' he said. 'That little twist made him laugh a lot.'

'I wish I could have met him,' I said. 'It's a shame we never got to.'

'Read the plays,' said Mr Dillon. 'I think he poured every part of himself into the plays. You'll get to know who he was and what he stood for if you read them.'

I nodded. I planned to read them all and learn as much about him as I could. I figured that the more I learned about him, the more I would understand the odd couple of days I'd just endured.

Once we had finished questioning Paul, he bid us farewell and Huw thanked him.

'You're all free to stay here and mingle for as long as you like, but I know that some of you have travelled a long way and are probably keen to get back before it gets dark, so I understand if you need to leave.

'It just behoves me to thank you for coming and to wish you the best in the future. Do stay in touch with one another, and - as Mr Dillon said - read Reginald's plays if you get a chance.'

Huw left the room, and we all sat there looking at one another.

'I think I should go,' said Sally. 'You know - call my sister and check she's OK. I'm giving her a lift back, so I should go and find her.'

'Of course,' Simon said. 'It's been lovely to meet you.'

We all hugged her and she left, followed by Matt, then Mike. Simon and I remained.

'I feel drained after all that,' I said

'Me too. Goodness, it's hard to let it all sink in, isn't it?'

'Yes. I keep thinking about the clues we had. Do you remember when Sally rang her mum and she talked about three significant events that had happened when she was a nurse in Bristol: a rugby club brawl, a homophobic attack and a racist attack?'

'Yes, I remember.'

'Well she thought the guy who was beaten up in the homophobic attack was called Joe. And he was. But we were looking for a Reginald.'

'Oh yes - that's true. Him changing his name and hiding away from the world didn't really help us, did it?'

'No, indeed.'

We sat there for a few minutes longer, then I thought I ought to make a move. Mum would be striding round the house by now, wondering what was going on.

'It would be nice to stay in touch,' I said. 'Shall I set up a WhatsApp group for everyone?'

'Oh, please do, Mary. Then we can all stay in touch and share information as we read the plays.'

'Now I suppose I should go and get my train. It was lovely to meet you.'

'You too, Mary. You have been a delightful companion. Make sure you get up that WhatsApp group for us.'

'Yes, I'll go back to the room and pack up all my stuff and do it right away.'

PRESENT DAY: HOMEWARD BOUND

I leaped onto the train with about three seconds to spare after a very embarrassing run down the platform, shrieking at the driver to wait as I dragged my huge case behind me. By the time I fell onto the train I could hardly breathe. I removed my coat and threw it over my arm before I went hunting for my seat.

The train was packed and there was no first-class carriage, so the solicitors' firm had booked me a seat in carriage F. I seemed to have joined the train in carriage D, so as the train moved off, making every step perilously difficult, I stumbled and staggered through the train like a drunk, heading for carriage F, seat 12A. The task of dragging a huge case full of clothes that I did not wear behind me was proving hellishly difficult as I weaved through, trying to avoid feet, elbows and handbags. In my spare hand, I carried my coat and a healthy supply of snacks.

There it was – seat 12A. The only problem was that someone else was sitting in it.

'Excuse me,' I said. 'I'm really sorry, but you're in my seat.'

'Am I?' said the guy. I felt a bit bad kicking him out – he had a nice spread in front of him – crisps and sandwiches and a big cup of coffee, but there was nowhere else to sit.

He gathered his things together, putting his work notes under one arm, the sandwich and crisps in his hand and the rubbish from the food in the other, then attempted to pick up his coffee. The train jolted and he slipped, spilling coffee all over his clothes and his papers.

He dropped the work and the coffee and attempted to try and clean his shirt with his hands, but his hands were full, so we all looked on in mounting sympathy as he went to throw the rubbish he was carrying into the bin and accidentally threw his sandwich and crisps away by mistake.

'Shit,' he growled. His shirt was soaked, his notes were ruined and his food was in the bin.

'I'm so sorry,' I kept saying as he walked away, covered in coffee.

It was not my fault – he was in the wrong seat – but I am British so I felt hellishly guilty even though it was entirely his own fault for not reading his ticket properly.

I settled into the still-warm seat as my phone bleeped. It was a message in the WhatsApp group that I'd just set up.

Mysterious Invitation WhatsApp Group

Mike Sween

Been doing a lot of thinking since we left the solicitors. I think we should all try to help find the Gowers. They obviously meant so much to Reginald and his dad, and we meant so much to him…it would be nice, don't you think?'

Mary Brown

I am in. I would love to help.

Matt Prior

I'm in if Simon's in. We need him to organise us.

Simon Blake

Dear all, Of course I'm in. I think that's a great idea.
Kind regards,
Simon B

Sally Bramley

I'm in too.

Simon Blake

Dear Sally, How is Julie?
Kind regards,
Simon B

Sally Bramley

In a massive sulk, but she'll get over it. Her boyfriend is worth millions so she doesn't need the money. It might teach her to be kinder. Mary, I'm really sorry for the way she spoke to you.

Mary Brown

Don't worry. It's fine.

Mike Sween

So how are we going to organise this, then?

Simon Blake

Dear all, Let me have a think and I'll come back with a plan.
Kind regards,
Simon B

Mary Brown

Great, looking forward to seeing you all soon for our next adventure!

I smiled as I tucked my phone and ticket back into my bag. Simon was so formal, signing off after every message. He was a nice guy. I liked all of them, actually, except for Julie.

No sooner had I put everything away than the inspector appeared at the far end of the carriage and I pulled my ticket back out again. It was only at that moment I realised I should have been in carriage E. Fuck. I had caused all that drama and all that spilled coffee and it wasn't even my seat. I looked at the guy, standing by the door, his shirt featuring an unattractive brown stain, and felt a wave of guilt. I hoped he wouldn't realise he had been in the right seat all along when the inspector checked his ticket.

Oh well, if he did, I would give him his seat back. I would even offer to pay for his shirt to be cleaned. Hey – I could offer to buy him a new shirt. Buy 20 shirts!

I sat back and closed my eyes. Life was a wonderful, fragile thing and it could change at any minute – for better or worse: just look at the guy with the coffee all over him. Look at Reginald - that wonderful kind man who was so wounded by events when he was younger that he locked himself away forever.

I was going to start looking at the positives from now on. While things were good, I would learn to count my blessings. From now on, I was determined to enjoy every precious moment that my lovely life had to offer me.

ONE YEAR LATER

Mysterious Invitation WhatsApp Group

Simon Blake

Dear all, I sincerely hope you are keeping well. Did you know that next weekend marks a year since we met up in Gower for Reginald's funeral? Can you believe that? A year! Goodness, doesn't time fly? Kind regards, Simon B

Mike Sween

Hi mate, a year? Hope you're good.

Simon Blake

Yes, I'm very well, thank you, Mike. I wondered whether anyone fancied meeting up to celebrate the occasion and to raise a toast to Reginald? Kind regards, Simon B

Sally Bramley

Hi Simon, Oh yes, I'm up for that. Are you thinking of us all going back to Gower Farm Hotel? The one we all met at before? It would be lovely to see everyone xxxx

Mike Sween

I will if I can, mate, but got so much work on at the moment. Let me have the details and I'll try. Nice to hear from you

Simon Blake

Dear all, That sounds like it might work, then. I will await messages from the others, and see whether anyone else fancies coming along, and will arrange something. I'll have a think about where would be a good place for us all to meet. It would be lovely to see you all again. Kind regards, Simon

MARY'S HOUSE: PRESENT DAY

Have you ever watched those daft shows from Japan? They are on a remote channel way down the list of TV stations. In the one we're watching, couples have to carry each other across a field at great speed while being hotly pursued by men dressed as pink cows, carrying large green flowers which spray blue gunk. Don't ask me why we are watching it.

It's one of those shows that comes on and you think 'what's this rubbish?' but then you end up watching the whole thing, cheering on some random couple from Shirakawa-Go in Takayama, against the reigning champions from Tokyo, and genuinely wanting the underdogs to win.

'Come on Hiromasa and Gyo-Shin,' I scream. I am up out of my seat and shouting at the television.

'You can do it,' shouts Ted.

Next, some cow pats are thrown, for no obvious reason. Then they switch round so the woman is carrying the man as they race back across the field. The commentary team scream, screech, and say how difficult this course is.

'That is not difficult: we could do that!' says Ted.

'No we couldn't, because we're both very heavy and I'm also very weak. If you got onto my back, I'd collapse and maybe even die.'

'No, you wouldn't, we'd be fine. We would definitely beat this old couple from Sendai. Come on, let's try.'

I have a glass in my hand as Ted makes his ridiculous suggestion, and I am not keen on anything that requires me to put down my glass. Ted is insistent though...he pulls me up onto my feet and drops into a deep squat, flexing his muscles like a powerlifter.

'On you get,' he says, clenching still further so the veins in his neck pop out. It's as if he's about to lift a car or push a van down the road, as they do on *World's Strongest Man.*

'I'm not that heavy,' I say, but the groan he gives when I jump onto his back suggests otherwise.

'I can get to the front door,' he says, heaving and panting with the effort of it all.

'Did it!' says Ted, dropping me onto the floor in a rather undignified fashion, and running around the flat with his T-shirt over his head like Ronaldo after he scores a goal.

'I deserve some sort of award. Perhaps I should become a professional weightlifter?' Then he stretches out his arms and shoulder joints as if he has just done a massive workout.

'Okay, okay…' I say. 'You make it sound like you just carried a tank on your back.'

'No, of course not, angel. Sorry. I am just being silly. Now it's your turn. You are the horse and I'm the rider. Brace yourself, I'm climbing on board.'

Ted jumps onto my back without a care for my spine, my internal organs or my knees. My legs give way immediately, and I am sent crashing to the ground.

'I think Hiromasa and Gyo-Shin would beat us easily,' I say, as Ted helps me to my feet.

'Shall we try again?'

'For heaven's sake, Ted, no. Let's not try again. Let's sit down and drink our wine, and not attempt to copy the people in the mad Japanese game show.'

'Does this mean we can't go on there, then?' Ted sounds genuinely disappointed that he won't be able to take on the good people of Sendai.

'No, not with me as your partner. Now - off you go. You need to top up my wine.' I fall back on the sofa and lift my glass to my lips, while he trundles off into the kitchen to bring me the last of the wine.

'Gosh, there's not that much left,' says Ted, returning with the drips left in the bottle and dropping them into my glass. 'Shall I open another one?'

'When, in the history of all the world, have I ever seen fit to dissuade you from opening another bottle?'

'Good point,' he says, disappearing back into the kitchen and emerging a few minutes later with a tantalisingly full bottle. He fills my glass and asks after my battered knees and breaking back.

'They're okay,' I say. 'But my back is hurting right at the bottom. It's a dull ache. What do you think it is?'

'I don't know. What does Dr Google say?'

I reach for my phone, preparing to list my symptoms in an effort to see what injury I may have sustained, when I see there's a pile of WhatsApp messages waiting for me.

'Someone's popular,' says Ted, looking over my shoulder. 'Perhaps it's Weightlifting Today magazine, wanting to do an interview with you?'

'No, it's more exciting than that. The messages are in the Mysterious Invitation WhatsApp group.'

'The what?'

'The guys I met in Wales for the funeral last year. Do you remember? Reginald Charters - the guy who died and left us money.'

'Of course I remember,' says Ted. 'I didn't know you were still in touch with them.'

'No, I'm not. We set up this WhatsApp group but I've not heard from any of them since the day of the funeral.'

I read the messages, as Ted looks over my shoulder.

'Simon's suggesting we meet up.'

'Why?'

'We always said we would. We actually always planned to meet up and try to find the Gower family. Do you remember? They were so kind and welcoming to Reginald's dad when he came over to Wales as an Italian prisoner of war. The private detectives couldn't find them anywhere. We talked about all getting together to find them.'

'Let me know if you're going. I can easily get time off.'

'Oh, you're going to come, are you? I assumed I would just go alone. The others won't have partners with them.'

'No, I'll come.' says Ted with great certainty. 'I'd like to come along and help you.'

'Sure. I'll reply now, and find out what all the details are…'

'What details?' says my flatmate, Juan, wandering into the room after his Pilates class. His face is so bright red it looks as if he has been slapped several times with a large plank of wood.

'I'm back in touch with the Mysterious Invitation people and we're planning to meet up. Ted's coming,' I explain.

'Oh wow, that sounds fun. Is there room for a little one?'

'You want to come, too?'

'Is that okay?'

'Yeah, I guess so, but I don't imagine it will be very interesting.'

'That's okay. I'll keep Ted company.'

'Sure, I'll reply to them now, and tell them I'm in. I'll let you know.'

Mysterious Invitation WhatsApp Group

Mary Brown

Hello, it's me! How are you all? I missed all those messages because my boyfriend was trying to mount me. It didn't go well. Now my knees are sore and my back hurts!

Mary Brown

No, Christ. No. That sounds all wrong. When I say 'mounting me' - I mean from behind. We were copying what they were doing in this late-night Japanese torture show.

Mary Brown

No. No, Blimey

That sounds even worse. Piggy back! He was giving me a goddamn piggyback and I tried to give him one, but I collapsed. Anyway, whatever. I wish you could delete WhatsApp messages. How are you all? Would love to catch up. Can't believe it's been a year!

Simon Blake

Dear Mary, You do make me laugh.

Kind regards, Simon B

Julie Bramley

Me too! Let's all meet up soon.

Matt Prior

Oh hello everyone. And hello Mary. That was funny. If you are meeting in Wales, I'd love to come.

Simon Blake

I wonder whether we should meet in Llandrindod Wells? It's a delightful spa town, and it's the last-known address of Tom and Irene Gower. I'm not suggesting that we track them down or anything, but we could make a few enquiries and see where we get to? And the place is beautiful. Kind regards, Simon B

Matt Prior

Yes, I'll be there. That sounds great.

Mike Sween

I'll come if I can.

Sally Bramley

That sounds lovely. Yes, I'm in. No need for us to go trekking after the Gower family though. Let's just have a lovely weekend and catch up, and raise a glass to Reginald.

Simon Blake

Hear, hear!

Mary Brown

NO. We should totally track them down! We should do a manhunt and try to find them. Let's break into every house in Llandrindod Wells and force them to tell us where the Gower family is. I'm going to come dressed like Miss Marple!

Simon Blake

Goodness. Let's meet up and see how the mood takes us. Very much looking forward to seeing you all.

Kind regards, Simon B

Mary Brown

Me too. Really looking forward to seeing you and hunting the Gower family down like they're wild animals.

PRESENT DAY: LLANDRINDOD-BOUND

The day of departure has come and the three of us charge down the platform to board the train on this rather peculiar mission to join a group of people who I barely know, in a place I've never been to, to track down a family I've never met.

The wild ridiculousness of the situation is reflected in the sight of us: we make for the most remarkable trio, dashing along with our luggage. Juan Pablo is sporting a purple Lycra catsuit under his fake fur coat and a large hat. I set out to look comfortable rather than attractive, in my warm and cosy all-in-one. It's candy-floss pink in colour, and every time I go anywhere I think it's the perfect outfit for travelling because it's all snuggly and lovely, but, also, every time I wear it I regret it instantly and wish I'd opted for something a little more sober. That applies today as well, as I run along, trying to keep up with the guys while looking like their pet Teletubby.

In the front is Ted, taking the lead in his traditional, manly fashion, holding maps as if we are about to go trekking through the Andes. He is double-checking the direction of the train and the precise time it will take to get to Llandrindod Wells as if he were Indiana Jones leading us to escape from the Well of Souls.

'It's a good job I'm here,' he says, and I try ever so hard not to point out that I went off to a remote part of Wales just a year ago on this first mission to meet the mysterious invitation people, entirely alone. I did so with absolutely no problems.

'This is us,' says Ted proudly, swinging open the carriage door and standing back.

'I don't know where we'd be without you,' I say.

Once we have found our seats (Ted insisted on pre-booking), we take our places for the journey and Juan marks his territory by removing his burgundy hat and laying it gently on the coat rack above our heads.

'Tell me a little bit about these people, and what this is all about. Any hotties going?' he asks.

Juan has recently separated from his very hunky personal trainer boyfriend, and he has been like a dog on heat ever since. Honestly, I am tempted to go to the vet to see whether I can get him neutered. Everywhere we go, he asks me whether there is anyone hot there.

'No hotties,' I tell him. 'Well, none you'd be interested in. There was a very beautiful woman called Julie who came, but she was a witch.'

'Oh good,' says Juan. 'I hope she comes. I like the idea of meeting a witch.'

'You wouldn't like her - she was icy cold and self-obsessed. She ended up not getting any of Reginald's money because we were told we had to vote for one person in the group that we liked least and she got the vote.'

'Wow - the dead guy liked to play games, didn't he?'

'Big time. I mean, the whole funeral was full of these odd things he did based on the plays he'd written. It was all so surreal. Julie was really fed up but the rest of us were quietly delighted. She had a sister called Sally who I liked. I hope she comes this weekend. She was very kind and good company.'

'Tell me about the others,' says Juan, leaning over toward me. 'I never realised this funeral was such a riot. They sound like characters from a Victorian novel. We have the glamorous, feuding sisters. What other glamorous lovelies were there?'

'The others were all men,' I say. Ted makes a strange snorting sound of disapproval.

'What was that noise for?'

'I didn't realise you had been gallivanting all over the place with a bunch of men.'

'I'm not sure that going to a funeral qualifies as gallivanting.'

'Carry on, darling,' says Juan.

'So there was Matt Prior - a young Welsh guy. I am not sure whether he is coming or not. He was a good-looking boy - only around 20-years-old but a real sweetheart. Then there was Mike Sween who was quite good-looking and always smartly dressed, works for SKY, I think.'

The truth. Of course, the truth was that I found Mike Sween bloody gorgeous, but if I say that to Ted, given the mood he is in, he will start whimpering and moaning.

'Then the final person to mention is Simon. He was like the leader of the group, because he is older and seemed that much more grown up and sensible than the rest of us. I liked him a lot.'

'The leader? You never mentioned him before. How big is

he?' interrupts Ted. I glance at Juan and he shakes his head, as if advising me not to engage, not to argue with him.

'And that's all?' Juan says. 'I thought there were more of you than that?'

'Nope. Just the six of us...all sitting in a room at this old farmhouse that had been turned into a hotel, wondering why we were there at all. Of course, there should have been someone from the Gower family as well.

'I had a strong feeling that it was Tom and Irene Gower who Reginald felt he owed the most to, because of the kindness they had shown to his father when he came over in the war. But the private detectives never tracked them down. Apparently they tried everything but there was no sight of them anywhere.'

'It's so weird. I thought it was possible to track anyone down.'

'I don't think they had enough time. They only had a week or so to find all of us. If the Gowers had moved abroad, it would have taken much longer.'

'Presumably the private detectives carried on looking for them?'

'No. You would think they would have, but I called them yesterday and was told that Paul - the guy who owns the agency - has been very ill so nothing has happened. There is a lot of money sitting there. I'd love to find them.'

By the time we arrive in Llandrindod Wells it's almost 6pm. It's a cold, sharp winter's night, and the scene that greets us outside the station is picture-postcard perfect: sparkling lights illuminating a village green. Even in the semi-darkness, you can see how beautiful the place is: with lovely dry-stone walls, and bars and restaurants scattered around, all lit by some elegant, old-fashioned street lamps that look as if they have been lifted out of the Edwardian era. It is no wonder the Gower family moved here. It is lovely.

'This place gives me the creeps,' says Juan, pulling his massive fur coat tightly round him. Juan is so incredibly slim, and the coat so large that he looks like he is being eaten by an enormous bear when he does that.

'The creeps? I think it's lovely.'

'It's just so twee. Like the opening scene from a detective series. You know - the lovely, pretty town where nothing goes wrong, then suddenly - bam! Everyone is found murdered.'

'Well, I really hope not,' I say, glancing over at Ted who is too engrossed in the map to join in our debate about whether this place is lovely or Wales' answer to *Midsomer Murders*. I half expect him to pull out a head torch and a compass. Then he lifts his head up and points straight ahead.

'There,' he says, his finger stretched out toward the hotel ahead. 'That's where we're staying.' There is huge pride in his voice, as he nods and smiles to himself.

'Thanks for getting us here safely,' I say, magnanimously.

'Safe for now. Until we are brutally murdered in our beds by the vicar clutching a bell rope,' says Juan.

'Come on, you nutter, let's go and check in then we can get ourselves a drink.'

'A drink from the poisoned well,' he says.

The hotel is very swish, much posher than I thought it would be. Certainly a lot smarter than the farmhouse turned country B&B that I stayed in last time. I suppose I expected much the same thing, but this place is a proper hotel, with people in uniforms and a fancy reception desk. There are signs around the place indicating where the restaurants and bars are, and which way to go for the spa facilities and the gym.

'Ohhh,' I say, pointing at the sign for the swimming pool, and giving Juan a hug.

I have a rather odd relationship with exercise in hotels. It always strikes me as a good idea. Half the problem with going to the gym or to the swimming pool is being bothered to go there in the first place. The thought of the bus, the changing room, exercising, then showering, getting changed and back on the bus again - I mean, who can be bothered with all that faffing around? But hotels seem like a very civilized place in which to exercise because the facilities are right there - down the corridor. It's like having a gym and pool in your own house.

But—and this is quite a big but—hotels also have bars in them, and restaurants, and room service. And a room with a huge bed with a big television in front of it. Now who, in the name of all that is holy, would rather go to the gym than lie on the bed and watch *This Morning,* while a nice man in a smart uniform knocks on the door and hands you the large cheeseburger you ordered?

So, the long and the short of it is that I always take my swimming costume when I go to a hotel because it's a lovely idea, but I've never yet used a hotel pool because room service is a better idea.

We walk across the lobby, toward the reception desk, when Juan spots someone and his interest is immediately piqued.

'Oh hello - here's someone who bats for my team,' he says, letting his enormous coat swing open and pouting off into the distance.

The man he is staring at is tall, neatly dressed and bending over to pick up his bag.

'How on earth can you tell from this distance when the guy's facing away from us?'

'If you know, you know…'

The man moves away from the reception desk and turns round, and then he walks toward us.

'Told you,' says Juan.

'Hello Mary, how lovely to see you.'

'Simon, my goodness, this is good timing. How are you?'

'Very well.'

I can see Juan's eyes light up in disbelief that I know the guy.

'This is Juan, a very good friend of mine,' I say.

'Charmed, I'm sure,' says Juan with a sort of leg bend, like a mini-curtsey. He says his peculiar greeting in such an odd voice that Ted and I both stare at him in alarm.

'This is Ted, my boyfriend,' I say.

Ted offers a much more normal: 'nice to meet you' and the two men shake hands.

'I didn't know you were bringing anyone,' says Simon. 'I regret to say that I came alone.'

'Oh, Ted and Juan just fancied a few days away, so it made sense for them to come,' I say, almost apologetically.

'No - it's great. And you've just enhanced our numbers. It seems that you and I are the only people coming here.'

'Really? Oh. I thought we were going to have a proper one-year reunion.'

'Well, yes, that's exactly what I thought, too. I reserved a load of rooms, and have just had to unreserve them. Still, it is very lovely to see you, Mary, and to meet your friends. Do you fancy dinner tonight? We should make the most of our time here...it is a very beautiful place. We could meet in the restaurant downstairs at eight. It's supposed to be very good.'

'Or at seven?' I venture. I am starving already. If I am forced to wait until 8pm, I will empty the mini-bar.

'Oh right. Yes, that's not a bad idea. You are probably hungry after travelling all day. An early supper it is, then. I will book for four of us, shall I? In Mezzet, just through there.'

We all follow Simon's finger as he points to the restaurant nestled in the corner, to the left of the reception desk.

'Perfect. See you there in an hour.'

'I feel a fool now,' says Ted. 'I thought there was a huge big group going. Now I know it's only the two of you, it feels idiotic that we're all here.'

'No it doesn't, if I'd come back and told you that it was just Simon and me, you would have accused me of all sorts of things. Anyway, some of the others might decide to come out tomorrow, you never know.'

I hope they do. I would like to see Sally again, and obviously it would be rather lovely to get an eyeful of Mighty Mike the Magnificent Stud (that is his official title, but I call him Mike, for short).

Seven o'clock takes a long time to appear. Ted snoozes while I wander round the bedroom, picking things up and putting them back down again while sighing loudly. It is because I am hungry: hunger has the ability to turn me into a recalcitrant teenager as soon as it bites.

I am the same at work: five minutes can take three hours to roll past when we are heading toward lunchtime. I will stand at my till at 12.30pm, unsure whether I am going to make it to my 1pm lunch-break because I am so hungry I can barely breathe. Then I'll serve someone, chat to them, help them take their purchases to the car, help another customer, sweep the whole aisle, bring in goods from the warehouse, rearrange all the pot plants and think - right it must be lunchtime now. But when I look, it's 12.32pm. What? That can't be right. Usain Bolt couldn't have done it that quickly. The clocks are messing with my head. Clocks are evil. I might try to get a government grant to do an investigation into my clock theory.

Anyway, sorry, I got a bit distracted there. The thing is that time drags when I'm hungry. I spend ages unpacking and hanging everything up neatly in the wardrobe with those hangers that don't actually come out, so you have to hang the clothes on them while they're still attached to the rail which involves virtually climbing into the wardrobe. Then I get ready nicely and do my makeup so I look as good as possible. Then finally, finally, the clock deigns to tell me that it is time for food, so Ted and I head downstairs.

'What did you do while I was sleeping?' he asks.

'Mainly worked on my thesis about clocks.'

'What thesis is this?' he asks.

'That they are evil.'

'Sure,' he says, and I find myself smiling. It is joyous to be with a man who can cope with all my eccentricities. I mean - how many guys would say 'sure' when I shared my view that clocks are evil?

We are first to arrive at the restaurant, so we take our seats and order drinks and some nibbles. Around ten minutes later, Juan and Simon arrive - together.

TOGETHER.

'Oh God, what fresh hell is this?' I mutter to Ted, as Simon courteously pulls out a chair for Juan, and my lovely Spanish friend slips into it, fanning his face with his fingers like Marlene Dietrich.

'We met in the lobby just now,' says Simon, perhaps sensing

the inaccurate conclusion I am drifting toward.

'Of course,' I reply, as if I were the sort of person who would ever entertain such a conclusion.

It turns out that Mezzet is the most beautiful restaurant. I am staggered by how tasty all the food is. We have a mosaic of colourful starters in the middle of the table: hummus, vine leaves, tabbouleh, these insanely tasty chargrilled chicken pieces and all sorts of other gorgeous Lebanese bits. Then big salads arrive and baskets of pita bread. It is fantastic, and I have to stop myself from shoving everything into my mouth at record-breaking speed as I try to enjoy all the flavours at once.

I eat so much that I am ready to burst, then Simon says, 'Remember - these are only the starters.'

And I wish I wasn't so insanely greedy. When the main courses arrive, they are a triumph of flavour and size. I have chicken coated in this gorgeous, spicy garlic flavouring that comes with a lovely Greek salad, and the heftiest portion of chips you have ever seen.

They've left some of the dips on the table, so I show just how suave and sophisticated I am by dipping the chips into hummus and tzatziki, while wolfing it all down with glasses of lovely oaky Chardonnay. My favourite.

Most of the talking over dinner is done by Ted and Simon who appear to share a love of map reading and geography.

'No, it's just off the A47, before you get to Norwich...'

'Oh, I know,' says Ted. 'There is a service station there, isn't there?'

Oh my goodness. I try to smile and nod in the right places, but Juan has stopped even trying. He looks like a bored schoolboy as he checks his phone, looks around the restaurant, and slumps further into his seat.

'Are you going to go and look for the Gower family tomorrow?' Juan asks, when he spots me looking at him.

'Probably not,' says Simon, before I have time to answer.

'Oh. Mary said she thought it would be a good idea. Since we're here,' says Juan.

'It feels slightly odd to bother: we know they're not there. If they were there, the private detectives would have found them and given them the money,' Simon replies.

'I don't think the private detectives have been looking for them at all since the funeral. Paul Dillon, the main guy, is ill, apparently. I think it's worth us trying to find them,' I say. 'I mean, I know they aren't there now, but we might be able to find out where they went? We could pop along to the address you have tomorrow. After breakfast?'

Simon is silent, as he seems to be weighing up the options. This is something I never do: if I weighed up the options and thought about the consequences occasionally, I would have had a very different life.

'Maybe we could find out if there's anyone in the area who knew them or was around when they lived here. For the sake of an hour out of our day when we have nothing else planned. Why not?' I add.

'Okay,' says Simon. 'Yes, you're right: we're here, let's go round there in the morning.'

'Can I come?' asks Juan, suddenly awake and back in the room with us.

'Yes, we'll all go,' I say, before Simon can suggest otherwise.

'Let's head there after breakfast,' he says. 'The house is in a little village a short walk from here. The house is called Home Sweet Home.'

1960: PACKING UP

The door to 'Home Sweet Home' was wide open. Tom sat back in the big floral armchair that had been in the family since he was a boy. He lifted his feet onto the stool in front of him, lay his head back and closed his eyes, determined to rest after moving boxes all morning. The breeze from outside wafted in, cooling him down, but he still felt like he was overheating after the exhaustion of all that physical labour. Irene hummed to herself while she made a pot of tea in the kitchen, and from upstairs came the sound of loud music and banging as his son, Tom Junior, packed up all his things.

'There you go, my love: a cup of tea and a couple of biscuits,' said Irene, putting the tray down on the coffee table in front of him. 'What is the door doing open? Shall I shut it?'

'No, leave it open. I like the breeze, and Tom's mates will be here in a minute to help bring the furniture down from upstairs. Have a sit down.'

Irene collapsed into the chair next to him. She looked tired.

She was only 45-years-old and had always been exceptionally beautiful, with perfect skin and delicate features, but today she looked drained. Her complexion had assumed the unattractive pallor of the pale china ornaments staring out at him from the box by his feet. Moving house was a hideous business.

'I'm looking forward to moving, and starting a new job. But let's never move again. You look exhausted, love.'

'I am tired. You know: it is not too late to change your mind. We could stay here. We don't have to move.'

Irene smiled at her husband as she spoke, but he didn't smile back. They had developed very different views about Llandrindod Wells, the place they had called home for over a decade.

She had no desire to move from this lovely area, teeming with glorious countryside, but with an urban heart. There were restaurants aplenty and bars that felt modern and fun. It was a place that felt like home: not like Gower where it was all about farming: morning, noon and night. Irene had never enjoyed their life in farming. She had tolerated it because Tom loved it so much, but it had never been something she enjoyed.

She had persuaded Tom to move from Gower and across the country so she could be near her parents when her son was young. They had settled here, in Llandrindod, a place where there was life and laughter. Irene adored it; she saw people every day, loved the local boutiques and had more friends than she had known in her life before.

Tom had just tolerated it, in the same way as she had tolerated their time on the farm. Now Tom had been offered a job back in the world of farming and she needed to move to the south coast of England with him. It would have been unfair of her to refuse him the chance to take an exciting new job that took him back into farming, even though every fibre of her yearned to stay where she was, in their lovely house, in this beautiful place.

Tom smiled warmly at his wife as he sipped his tea. He was looking forward to moving, and it wasn't fair of Irene to keep telling him how much she wanted to stay. They had been in Llandrindod Wells for so long. It had been the perfect place in which to bring up young Tom after they left the farm, but it was not home; not like Gower had been. He had never quite fitted in the way he hoped he would.

Giving up farming and starting a new way had been a mistake. He had realised that almost straight away. He was a farmer, and a farmer's son, and farming was all he had ever known. Now, at the ripe old age of 47, he had a chance to go back to it. Well, not quite back to hands-on farming...he wouldn't be up at 4am to milk cows, and return with mud under his fingernails after a long day in the fields, but he would be back in that world. He had been offered a job as an agricultural expert at Portsmouth University, where the new degree in land management involved an option called farming studies and farm management. And he —Tom Gower—was going to be teaching them.

A noise outside indicated the arrival of Llyr and Richard; Tom Junior's closest friends.

'The heavy mob have arrived,' said Llyr, popping his head round the door. 'Can we come in, Professor Gower?'

'Very funny,' said Tom. 'I'm not quite a professor.'

'Come in, you clowns,' said Irene, jumping up and hugging them warmly. The boys blushed as she did so. She was by far the best looking of all the mothers: a lovely face, stunning figure, and always dressed so beautifully.

'You have timed it well, the kettle just boiled. Have a seat and I'll call Tom down.'

'No, don't you worry,' said Richard. 'We'll head up and help him to bring all the furniture down, and then we'll stop for tea, if that's okay?'

'Good idea,' said Tom Senior. 'You youngsters get up there and do the heavy lifting. Shout if you need any help from me.'

'No, we will be okay, Grandad. You are too old for this sort of work,' said Llyr.

'He's a cheeky sod,' muttered Tom.

'You'll miss those guys when we move away,' said Irene. 'They've been good friends to all of us.'

Tom nodded. Once again, it felt as if she was criticising their plans to move away, but he would not feel guilty. He had felt awful when he first accepted the job. He was even concerned that she might not come with him. He was also worried that his son wouldn't want to come. But Tom Junior, or TJ as he was known to everyone, had taken the news well. In fact, TJ thought it was a great idea. He had been quietly despairing of the job situation in Wales, after returning from university in Gloucester, and saw it as a sign that he too should be in England. He immediately began applying for jobs in the south, sending off letters for every available management position in the council. His persistence paid off, and before too long he had landed himself a junior management role. So the whole family would move down to the south of England for a totally new life.

'Penny for them,' said Irene as she moved to tape up one of the many boxes lying on the ground in front of them.

'Oh nothing. Just thinking how lucky we are. It is great that TJ is coming with us, and so good that he has found himself a job he likes. It seems strange that this time next week he'll be heading out to work every morning as a manager.'

'I'm very proud of him,' said Irene.

'Me too,' said Tom. 'Very proud. And great that he starts straight away. I'm going to be hanging around for a month before I start...I just want to get going.'

'What do you mean? You'll be spending time with me, and helping me to sort the house out.'

'Yes, yes. Of course. It will be lovely.'

Irene looked unsure.

'It's all going to be okay, you know,' said Tom.

She nodded gently without commenting.

'I love you,' he said.

'I love you, too.' Irene stood up and surveyed the boxes all around. She was determined to keep active so she didn't have time to think too much about everything. Being active would keep her sane.

'So, the question now is - why, oh why, did you let me accumulate so much stuff? Have you seen how much is here? I have already thrown away everything that hasn't been used for years, and taken bags of old clothes to the charity shop. And there's still a ton left.'

Irene pulled the nearest box toward her and glanced inside it.

'Do you think we should take all this stuff? Or just chuck a load more? Oh, look....'

Irene pulled out two photo albums, some newspaper cuttings and various notes and papers from TJ's school when he was young.

'Look at this picture of a dinosaur,' said Irene, holding up the brightly painted picture so Tom could see it.

TJ and his friends descended the stairs as she held the magnificent artwork aloft.

'Actually Mam, that was a picture of Dad. Didn't he have blue overalls on the farm?'

'Yes he did.'

'But why have I got a horn on my face?' asked Tom.

'I think that's supposed to be your nose. You do have a huge hooter, Da.'

The boys joined them as Irene opened one of the photo albums and flicked through it.

'Look at you,' she said to TJ. The picture was of a young boy standing in a field with a handsome young man.

'Marco,' said Irene quietly, looking at her husband. 'That was May 7th, 1945. The day the war was over. We asked Marco to move in with us and live on the farm that day. He was such a lovely guy. So gentle and kind, and such a hard worker. He doted on you, TJ.'

'I remember him,' said Tom Junior. 'Only vaguely, but I do remember. Didn't he make us ice cream once, or something like that?'

'Yes, he did. We gave him some time off and we came back to find that instead of relaxing, he had prepared all this beautiful Italian ice cream for us. I wish we had kept in touch. It was crazy not to stay in contact.'

'Have you not heard anything from him recently?'

'No, not at all. I know they were having a lot of trouble with their son. He was quite a sickly child, and never went out. They withdrew during that time. It was very difficult for them. I sent a card and a letter but never heard back. I guess with all the ice cream parlours opening, and the child being hard work, they just didn't have the time to respond. The boy must be around five or six now, I guess. His name was Joe, wasn't it? The same as Marco's grandfather, and all the ice cream shops were named after him. I hope she's having an easier time of it.'

'You should track them down, love. If the ice cream shops are still going, someone there must know what happened to Marco.'

'Yes, you know, I think I will. Once we get to Southsea and get ourselves settled, I will see whether I can find an address for them and drop them a line. Oh, look. See what we have here.'

Irene pulled out piles of drawings done by Tom Senior. 'I remember you doing all these. I'm so pleased that we still have them.'

'They're brilliant,' said Llyr, descending the stairs ahead of the others. 'Did you really do them, Tom? I didn't know you were an artist?'

The pictures were cartoonish in style, depicting the animals on the farm, and many of them featuring TJ.

'I used to love drawing; I did it whenever I could. I might try and get back to it when we're settled in Southsea.'

'I hate to say anything nice to you, Mr Gower, but these are very good. You should definitely do some more.'

'Yes, I will. Now, you guys, shall we get everything packed up and into the hallway ready for the removal van in the morning? Then we can relax and have some tea and cake.'

'Yes, boss,' chorused the boys as they dragged, lifted, pulled and pushed the boxes containing the lives of the Gower family until they were all piled up by the front door.

1960: A NEW BEGINNING

'Are you nervous?' asked Irene, as she watched her husband get ready for work. She was used to seeing him in overalls in the mornings: clean when he left the house and laced with oil, mud and dirt when he returned. He had been doing manual jobs in Llandrindod Wells. Now here he was, preparing to go to work at a university, all dressed up in a shirt and tie. Irene swept her hand across the shoulder of his jacket. There was no fluff to remove, but she wanted him to feel looked after, and as if he were as clean and presentable as possible.

'I'm terrified,' he said. 'This is a university, for goodness sake. No one in my family has ever been to university, let alone got a job in one. What if I'm useless?'

'You won't be. You're going to be brilliant,' she said. And she knew he would be. The two of them had had some difficulties in their marriage because they were very different people, but his abilities and expertise in farming were beyond debate. He would be great, and love the new job. But she could tell that he was not as convinced, and she could see, by the set of his jaw, that he was clenching his teeth with nerves.

'I will see you tonight, okay?' he said.

'Yes, love. Good luck today. Remember that TJ is bringing Yvonne round later. He wants us to meet her.'

'TJ and his women. How many of them have we met now? And does he really need to bring her round tonight?'

'It's the first girl he's met since we've been down here. He seems to be taking it seriously.'

'Seriously? He's only known her a few weeks.'

'I know, but he likes her. I think this one is different. He seems properly smitten.'

'Okay, okay. I'll see you later.'

Irene stood at the window and watched her husband's back disappear from view.

'You look worried,' said TJ, running down the stairs and past the boxes to stand next to her at the window. TJ had been working at his new job for a few weeks now, and was faring admirably: they had commended him at work; he had met new friends and had even bagged himself a girlfriend. Such was the power of youth that he had slipped into life on the south coast without a backward glance.

It had been different for Irene. She felt lonely and so far away from everyone she loved. She felt like she had no purpose, no point. She rang her friends every day and listened enviously as they spoke of meeting for coffee and how they missed her.

'I am quite worried about him, to be honest. He's been through a lot of changes.'

'Mum, if I can cope with all the changes, so can Dad,' said TJ.

'You're tougher than your father,' she said. 'He's a gentle, sensitive soul. I hope he'll be okay.'

'He will,' said TJ, kissing his mother's head. 'I promise you. It is a five-minute walk to work, and when he gets there, he will be talking about farming all day; the thing he loves most in the world: way more than he loves us. You wait; he will be buzzing by the time he gets home. Now, are you coming to the station with me?'

Irene had fallen into the habit of walking to the station with TJ in the morning to get some exercise and fresh air before returning to open more boxes, and hunt for a job. She was keen to contribute to the household. They were not desperate for money. TJ was paying rent and Tom's income was better than anything he had earned previously, but things were so expensive here, much more so than anywhere they had lived. She also thought it would be good for her, mentally, to be out working, and to feel like she was worth something. She did not want to descend into emotional darkness like she had before. If it hadn't been for the lively spirit of Marco on the farm, she knew she would have found life in Gower, particularly during the war, impossible to deal with.

As she and TJ walked along the seafront, she made herself stop thinking and worrying, and pushed herself to enjoy the feeling of the warm spring breeze ruffling her hair. The water glistened to one side of her, as the morning sunshine played across the sea, glinting and sparkling. On the other side, she looked at the big houses and hotels where people were beginning to wake up and face the day. Irene had always enjoyed early mornings. Even the crazily early alarms they had endured when they were on the farm had not bothered her. She hadn't enjoyed farming, but she had been fine with the early mornings. She was more alive first thing than at any other time.

Along the promenade, they passed dog walkers who nodded and bid them good morning. Out to sea there were swimmers enjoying a refreshing start to the day. Irene watched them with envy. There was something earthy and natural about an early morning swim. She would love to come down one day and join them, but knew she would never have the confidence, or be brave enough to swim by herself.

'Here we are, then,' said TJ, as they approached the train station. 'Remember that Yvonne is coming over tonight. I think you'll really like her.'

'Don't worry, I have not forgotten. I will buy a nice chicken and roast it later. Have a lovely day,' she said to her son, feeling a flutter of sadness as he strode off to catch the train.

1960: MAKING A MARK

Irene had so much to do that she wouldn't get bored, but she had begun to feel lonely in Southsea without people to talk to. She missed having neighbours to call on and seeing friendly faces everywhere. She missed the sense of community that living in a small town for a long time brought. She felt selfish and unreasonable. She had so much: she should be glad that she was healthy and had a kind husband and wonderful son instead of constantly feeling miserable. But she felt lonely, there was no denying it.

Irene sat down on a bench on the seafront and looked out at the dots in the waves: it was the early morning swimmers she had been watching earlier. *Was there some sort of club?* she wondered. There was a small wooden hut on the seafront with towels discarded outside it. Presumably they belonged to the swimmers in the sea. Perhaps that was where they congregated first thing, before hitting the waves. She stood up to go over and find out whether there was anyone in there who could assist her.

'Oh. Was it something I said?'

Irene turned around to see a handsome man had joined her on the other end of the bench. He was mid-50s, at a guess, with lovely, thick, salt-and-pepper hair that gave him the aura of a fading film star. He was smartly dressed as if he were heading off to work, with a briefcase at his feet.

'I didn't mean to startle you. I just saw a beautiful woman, sitting alone on the bench, looking out to sea, and I thought I would join her. But the minute I sat down, the lady stood up.'

'Ha. Nothing personal, I assure you,' said Irene. 'I was watching the swimmers and thought I might head over there and find out a bit more about them and how often they meet.'

'I'll come with you. I'm Mark, by the way.'

She felt wary as she shook hands with the stranger, and felt her cheeks heat as he smiled at her. He was dripping with confidence and bravado. But he had such a nice smile, a kind smile. And it was so nice to talk to someone new.

'Do you live near here?' she asked.

Mark turned and pointed at one of the gorgeous big houses on the seafront. 'Right there,' he said. 'I haven't had to travel far this morning.'

She smiled. 'What a beautiful home. And how lovely to be able to see the sea from the windows. Have you lived there long?'

He shook his head gently. She sensed in him a reluctance to talk about himself, a reluctance that in turn sparked a desire in her to know all about him.

'Where were you before?' she asked.

'Come on,' he said, leading her over to the hut. 'Let's see

who's here. There must be someone here who can tell us all about early morning sea swimming.'

She followed him down the stone steps to the beach and over to where the hut sat, in splendid isolation, accompanied only by the discarded towels of the morning swimmers.

As they neared the small, wooden shed, they saw that it was locked with a rusty padlock that bore the ravages of time.

'Well no one's been in here for a while. Perhaps there is no club. It might just be where they drop their towels,' said Irene.

'Only one way to find out. We will wait until some of them get out of the water and ask them. I will get us a couple of coffees if you want to wait. We could watch the waves for a while, and then talk to the swimmers.'

She had so much to do: unpacking and searching for a job, getting the house ready for Yvonne's visit, preparing and cooking dinner. But the pull of the ocean and this gentle man's company drew her to nod and say that she would like to stay.

Irene headed to the bench to wait, while Mark marched off down the seafront, returning with take-away cups from the café near the pier.

She wasn't a huge fan of coffee; she much preferred tea, but he had offered coffee, and it seemed far more sophisticated than boring old tea, so she sat with it warming her hands, blowing across the dark liquid occasionally and chatting to her new friend.

She told Mark about her husband and son, how they had only just moved down from Wales, and she didn't really know anyone. She explained that she was looking for a job – just basic secretarial work – while she found her feet and got to know more people in the area.

Then she asked about him.

'I've lived in Southsea all my life. I own Grants Estate Agents in Old Portsmouth,' he said. 'There's not much else to know.'

'Do you have a family? Children?' she asked.

He looked down.

'I met Amanda, fell in love, and got married. We bought that beautiful big house on the seafront. Life was wonderful. She died. That's my family story.'

Irene gasped and leaned over to touch his arm. 'I'm so sorry.'

Mark just nodded. 'Look I probably should get to work. Fancy swimming in the morning?'

'I'm not a strong enough swimmer to go out there by myself,' said Irene. 'I love swimming but…'

'Then why don't I come with you? I will meet you here at 7am and we'll have our first sea swim. What do you think?'

'We could do,' said Irene. 'Were you going to come anyway?'

'If you're coming, I'll come.'

'7am?'

'Yes.'

'We'll meet here?'

'Yes,' he said. 'By this hut.'

'Okay. Yes, that would be great. See you then.'

Irene watched Mark as he walked away, raising his arm above his head to bid her goodbye without turning round or breaking his stride.

She put down the paper cup full of coffee. The smell of it was so strong and the prospect of its bitterness so overwhelming, there was no way she could drink it. She should have asked for tea. Why did she ask for coffee in order to seem cool? What an idiot.

Irene walked back home and worked her way through the list of chores that her afternoon presented. But as she stood in a queue in the butchers, picked the nicest vegetables in the greengrocers and looked longingly at the lovely spring outfits that had appeared in the little clothes shop, she couldn't stop thinking about Mark.

There were so many unanswered questions.

He lost his wife. Poor guy. How did she die? When did she die?

Irene pushed the chicken into the oven and set the timer, then she moved the unopened boxes to the room under the stairs so the sitting room looked as warm and welcoming as possible. She had promised herself that she would not do that. Most of the boxes were open now and if she left the unopened ones out in the middle of the room, in plain sight, she would be forced to sort out the contents. By tucking them away, she would be tempted to ignore them for months. But TJ's new girlfriend was coming, so away they went, shoved in and piled high alongside the hoover, the broom and their rickety old ironing board.

While the smell of roasting chicken filtered out of the kitchen and through the house, Irene flicked through the local paper looking for job ads. But her mind wasn't on the task. She thought mainly of Mark. How was he coping without his wife? Did they have children? He hadn't mentioned children. He had been through so much.

There was a reprieve from the tumble of thoughts when TJ came back from work, throwing himself into the house at 3pm after a half-day in the office.

'Day off tomorrow. Yeeeeees!' he said, pulling her in close to him to give her a big hug.

'You look nice,' he said, gently touching her hair.

'Oh, thank you.'

She had tried something a bit different with her hair. No reason. She just thought it might be time for a change. She had also hitched her skirt up a little, to make it look more modern. Young women were wearing their skirts so short these days.

'What have you been up to today?'

'Oh you know – this and that. I met some people on the seafront and I'm going swimming with them tomorrow morning.'

'You look love-struck,' said TJ. 'Like you're a teenage girl who kissed a boy for the first time.'

'What on earth is that supposed to mean?'

'Oh, nothing. Just you, talking about swimming; you look happy. It's a good thing, Mum. Don't snap at me.'

'Oh right. Well, get yourself changed and ready for when Yvonne comes round.'

'Sure,' he said, hugging her again, and wondering why she had suddenly turned so frosty. He was pleased that she wanted to go swimming in the mornings. Christ, women were so complicated.

At 5pm, Tom came home from work earlier than expected, shouting news of his return through the house, as if he were returning victorious from battle. 'Hello, hello, something smells delicious,' he said as he strode into the kitchen, full of joy and happiness.

'You seem pleased. Did it all go well?'

'Great,' he said, with a beaming smile. 'It was really good to be talking about farming again. You know some of those people running the course have never worked as farmers. They know nothing about farming. Their advice to the students and their notes for the students were all wrong. Well, no, not wrong. It was just very theoretical, you know. Farming doesn't actually work that way. I am going to advise them on practical farming methods. I mean, I know there's a difference between the theory and the practical, but there's no point in teaching theoretical farming that bears no resemblance to the realities of running a farm, is there?'

'No,' said, Irene. She pulled the sizzling chicken out of the oven and placed it gently on the side, hoping her husband might come over and start to carve it, then she removed the roast potatoes and lifted the giant pan of vegetables off the stove. The thing was so heavy, it hurt her arm. She gave a small groan, but Tom didn't notice. Then she collected the meat juices to stir into the gravy.

Tom sat down at the kitchen table. 'I think I'm going to make a success of this. It is great to be excited about something for a change. It reminds me of when we set up the ice-cream shop at the farm, for Marco to run. Do you remember? It was an exciting time because it was new and it was all about us and our skills. Now I have the chance to use my skills to teach people properly about farming. Not just from books and notes on the blackboard, but from me – someone who grew up on a farm and knows what it took.'

'I had a nice day, too,' said Irene, not waiting to be asked, as she moved everything off the table in order to lay it for dinner. Why couldn't Tom help with this, instead of leaving it all up to her? 'I sat down by the seafront and ended up chatting to some people who go on morning swims. I am going to go and join them tomorrow. They are meeting at 7am for a swim in the sea.'

It was just a small lie. Barely a lie at all. She'd said 'some people' when it was 'one man', that was all.

'What? You're going to go swimming in the sea first thing in the morning?'

'Tom, it's something I've always fancied doing, and there's a group of them, so I'll be quite safe.'

'Well, make sure you're quiet when you get up. I have a busy day tomorrow. Oh, and I won't be back until late. There is a 'get to know the staff' evening for the freshers that I need to go to. It is going to be strange, but wonderful, getting into college life. They seem like such a nice bunch. I'm looking forward to meeting them all properly tomorrow.'

'Oh, right. What time do you think you'll be back?'

'No idea,' said Tom. 'Difficult to tell. Why, is it a problem?'

'No, not a problem, it's just that I don't really know anyone.'

'You'll get to know people in no time. The swimmers – they might be good fun?'

'Yes, yes. I will be fine. Could you call TJ and Yvonne and tell them dinner's ready?'

'Yvonne's here already?'

'Yes –in the sitting room. I assumed that you'd spoken to them when you came in.'

'No. I didn't realise there was anyone in there. Are they in there with all the mess and unopened boxes?'

'No, I tidied them away, Tom.'

'I wish you'd said that she was here. I'd have gone in to talk to them.'

'You can talk to her over dinner. She's lovely.'

'Who is?'

'Yvonne – TJ's girlfriend. The woman we were just talking about. She's a real sweetheart.'

'Oh good, good. I will go and wash my hands and call them in then. Isn't it great that everything's going so well?'

'It is wonderful, Tom. I'm really pleased.'

The evening passed in a warm glow of friendship and

harmony, as Yvonne told them all about her life, growing up in Brighton, further down the coast. She had moved to Southsea just a year ago, with her older sister, and she worked as a nurse at Portsmouth General.

Yvonne had that kind and gentle disposition that one so readily associates with those in the nursing profession. She was down to earth, sensible and seemed loyal and keen to show how much she adored Irene's only son.

'You're right. She's lovely,' said Tom when the two youngsters had retired to the sitting room, leaving Irene and Tom alone among the detritus of the evening meal. 'I like her. They're a good match.'

'I agree. I hope they make a go of this. It would be nice for him to find someone to settle down with. I know he's only young but it means they can take their time and build the courtship and get to know each other properly.'

Tom gave his wife a hug. 'I'm going to read through some notes, and get an early night before college. I will suggest that TJ walks Yvonne home now. You need to get an early night too, if you're swimming tomorrow.'

'I've got a lot of tidying up to do first,' she said, but Tom had left the room. She heard him talking to TJ as she plunged her hands into the lukewarm soapy water. There was never enough hot water. There were always too many dirty dishes. She was glad she was going swimming in the sea.

Morning came abruptly: the sharp cold of the ocean clashing with the gentle lightness of the emerging sun. Mark swam fearlessly: around her, under her and across her as she laughed, splashed and felt a freedom and delight at being out, and with someone who seemed thrilled in her company. There was something both understated and flamboyant about taking to the seas in the morning, while others still slept. It was the most natural thing in the world to do, yet somehow decadent and wonderful to splash around in the English Channel. She squealed with joy and dived down under the water, only for Mark to pull her back up.

'You are wonderful,' he shouted across the waves as she lifted her head to face the cracks of early morning sunshine breaking through the quiet skies. His words did not seem frightening or inappropriate or anything. Just wonderful. Then the cold gripped her, forcing her to swim faster, and then sprint out across the beach to her towel.

'You okay?' asked Mark, touching her nose gently with the tip of his finger, a move so warm and sincere that it brought tears to her eyes.

On the bench on the seafront, looking out at them, also with tears in his eyes, was her son, Tom Junior.

PRESENT DAY: THE SEARCH BEGINS

'Hello, hello?' I shout through the front door of Home Sweet Home, expecting to see a farmer and his wife standing there, looking exactly like the picture we have of the Gower family from about thirty years ago.

Instead, I am confronted by two girls in their early twenties gleefully sipping some blue drink, possibly 'Wkd', and listening to music that is so loud they have to scream at one another to be heard.

'I don't think that's Tom Gower,' I say to Simon.

'Possibly not. No blue dungarees.'

'Come in, come in, I'm ready for you,' shouts the blonde girl. She has so many earrings decorating her lobes that they have disappeared up her ear and into her mane of bleached blonde hair. If the colour does not give away the fact that her hair is dyed, the jet-black line at her hairline certainly does. I am not being critical: every woman who has had highlights knows all about that evil line that appears at the roots. I am just painting a picture for you, so you know what we are dealing with here.

'You're ready for me? That is wonderful. I'm Mary. How did you know I was coming?'

The two girls look at each other and pull a face which suggests they think the woman who has just walked into their house is nuts.

'Of course we knew you were coming.'

'Okay, that's great, well, this is Simon - he is one of the other guys who was at the funeral, and this is my best friend Juan. My boyfriend, Ted, is waiting outside.'

'Oh. You brought your boyfriend and your friends. Right. Okay. I don't really know what funeral you're talking about, and where's all your stuff?'

'In the hotel,' I reply.

'You'll need it, won't you?'

'Will I?'

'To do my hair. Isn't that why you're here?'

'You want me to do your hair?' I reply. It is all a bit surreal, but if she wants me to do her hair, I will give it a go.

As we're miscommunicating, a lady clutching a large toolbox comes piling through the door, apologising for being late in such a strong Welsh accent that I can't work out whether it's real, or whether she's putting it on for comedy effect. She looks around the room before focusing on dark-stripe woman.

'You must be Bronwyn? I am Melissa...from Melissa's Manes on the High Street. I've come to do your roots.'

'Oh,' exclaims the woman with the dark stripe who we now know to be called Bronwyn. She has a look of confusion on her heavily painted face as she turns to me. 'So, if this is Melissa - who are you? I thought you were the hairdresser.'

'Do you mind if I sit down? Then I can explain.'

Bronwyn looks doubtful...which is fair enough. Why should she allow a total stranger to sit down in her house?

'I'll be really quick,' I offer. 'My name's Mary and I was invited to a stranger's funeral around a year ago…'

'You probably don't need to go into all that,' whispers Simon.

'Okay then. Well, to keep it short - we are looking for the Gower family. They used to live here and we wondered whether you had any idea where they'd moved to after leaving here.'

'We've no idea,' says the other girl. 'Some private detectives came here looking for them around a year ago. I explained to them that we are renting the house from Sam Taylor, who lives over by there, over the road. We don't know anyone who lived here before.'

'Did the detectives talk to Sam Taylor?' I ask.

'I think so, but Sam has only had the house for a couple of years and he'd never heard of the Gower family either, so they left. Are you detectives? Are the Gower family criminals or something?'

'Gosh - no, not criminals. We're trying to find them because they are owed money.'

'Right,' says Bronwyn. 'This all sounds well dodgy to me.'

Despite Simon's earlier insistence that it was not necessary, I decide that it is, and start to regale Melissa with the story of the Gower family. I tell her about the mysterious invitation, the funeral and the money. I explain how incredibly kind the Gower family were to Reginald's parents.

Melissa works on Bronwyn's highlights, while the two of them listen to me, entranced.

'The dead guy sounds like a blinking lunatic, but I love the story of his dad coming over here and everything.'

'I know, right?'

'It's so odd that no one has been able to find the Gower family. Where do you think they are?'

'I've really no idea. We thought we would come here today just to see whether we could find them. I don't know whether you know anyone who's lived in the area for a long time who could help us at all?'

'Of course. This is so exciting. I feel like Inspector Poirot. Let me ring my Nan, she knows people who have lived in the area for years.'

'Thank you so much.'

I call Ted in from outside where he has been languishing against a lamppost, and he joins Simon and I on the sofa, while Juan perches on a small stool with his legs all wrapped around each other as if they have been knitted. We sit there, in a stranger's house, waiting patiently, while the scent of bleach fills the air.

Bronwyn talks in Welsh on the phone while the three of us listen in silence, trying to detect any words that might allow us to understand how the conversation is going.

'When did you say they lived here?' asks Bronwyn.

'We know they moved here soon after the war, so late 40s, early-50s. Unfortunately we don't know how long they stayed here.'

Bronwyn returns to the call and chats away while Simon, Ted and I sit, poised on the edges of our seats. Juan is no longer seated. He has jumped up and is assisting in the hair regrowth touch up, by passing the foils to the hairdresser. Finally, the call ends.

'Okay,' she says. 'It's looking good. Nan has a fancy man called John Morgan who is in a nursing home, and he used to live round here just after the war so might remember them. Visiting time at the home is at 2pm. My Nan told me to tell you that John's memory is not the best, but it is worth a try. Okay?'

'Yes, yes. That would be great,' I say. 'Thank you. Have you got the address?'

'Here you go,' says Bronwyn, scribbling it down on a piece of paper. 'I'll see you there at 2pm. I will get the bus. You won't recognise me, mind. My hair will be lovely.'

'Your hair is lovely already. Thank you,' I say, clutching the piece of paper and preparing to leave.

'Let me just finish these foils,' says Juan. 'I'll be five minutes.'

Ted, Simon and I stand there while Juan plays Vidal Sassoon.

'You've been very helpful,' Melissa tells him. 'Can I ask you something?'

'Of course you can, my love.'

'I'd like to whisper it, please.'

Juan moves in and listens attentively, nodding as Melissa talks, before hugging her affectionately.

'Of course you can, honey,' he says, handing her a foil, and moving over to collect some more.

'She asked whether she could come to the nursing home with us this afternoon, then she can drive Bronwyn in her hairdressing van, whatever that is. I told her that's fine.'

'Of course,' I say, concerned that we will be going fairly

mob-handed to this nursing home, and that might not be the wisest move considering the age of the man we're going to see.

'Now are you okay to do the rest of these foils without me? We'll see you at the nursing home at 2pm.'

PRESENT DAY: MEETING JOHN MORGAN

At 2pm, we are standing outside Gwerin Gyfeillgar Nursing Home on the outskirts of Llandrindod Wells. Have you ever heard of a more Welsh-sounding place? We managed to get lost finding it, of course, so had to keep asking people if they knew where it was. Ted and I put Juan in charge of all direction-related enquiries, just for the sheer joy of hearing our lovely Spanish dancer friend try to get his mouth around the Welsh pronunciations with a lilting Mediterranean accent. None of the people he asked understood a word he said. The whole thing was a joy to watch. While Juan grappled with the native tongue, Simon drove us (very slowly, while wearing his driving gloves) in a Vauxhall Astra built for people half our sizes.

I think both Simon and his car were pleased when we made it. I noticed him wincing at the groan emanating from the suspension when Ted and I got in. I am not sure his little car has ever experienced anything quite like it before.

The girls are waiting for us in Melissa's adorable pink van with 'Melissa's Manes' written in italic on the side, along with various pictures of hairdressing paraphernalia scribed in gold ink. There's a hair dryer, a lady in rollers, brushes and combs - all in glittery gold.

'Isn't it magnificent?' says Bronwyn, gently stroking the outside of Melissa's van. 'I've never seen anything so lovely before. Have you?'

Bronwyn looks much better with her hair done. It's a lovely honey-blonde colour and all swishy and healthy-looking. It is a shame she has done her makeup in such an odd way, with thick black eyeliner extending over her eyes and flicking up towards her eyebrows and a dark lipstick that washes her out.

'Right, let's go. I should warn you that John Morgan likes to be called John Morgan, never John, for some reason. He's very old, so you have to talk in a loud voice, and use simple language or he won't know what's going on and he'll start talking about the war, or something.'

'Sure,' I say. 'I love old people. I met this guy called Frank on a cruise once - he was nearly ninety, and he was great. I spent the whole cruise with him.'

We walk through the corridors, taking in the smells of cabbage and antiseptic that grace the air in all old people's homes. We come to flat seven and knock gently on the door. A carer greets us, carrying a tray of crockery.

'Oh goodness, John Morgan, you have lots of lovely ladies to see you,' she says to him.

Ted coughs lightly.

'Sorry, lots of ladies and one man.' Juan shrugs, and pulls his floppy felt hat down further over his ears.

Mr. Morgan is very old. I know that is stating the obvious.

But he really is quite the oldest person I have ever seen. His eyes are like those of a child, peering out from bunched-up, wrinkled skin. He looks ever so like an iguana. I keep this observation to myself, of course, but the similarity is there. He sits in front of us, without moving or commenting.

'Thank you for letting us come to see you,' I say, leaning over and putting my hand out. John's hands stay firmly in his lap so I just smile. 'My name is Mary.'

'I know that,' he says in a lovely baritone voice, the depth of which belies its owner's fading health. 'You want to know all about the Gower family?'

'Yes, do you know them? Gosh, I wasn't sure whether you'd have come across them.'

'Yes – farmers, weren't they? Came over from Gower after the war. I remember the lady very well. She was an attractive one. Always in her smart clothes. All the boys fancied her but I never quite trusted her. There was something about her that wasn't quite right. They had a young son.'

'Yes, that's right. The son and the father were called Tom. Apparently they called the son Tom Junior.'

'They called him TJ. But I didn't. I called him Tom Junior.'

'You don't know what became of them, do you?'

'Yes, I remember very clearly. They upped and moved down to the south coast, because he had a job at Portsmouth University. We were all very impressed. A university! Teaching farming or something, he was. And that Tom Junior, he had a job working somewhere too. I can't remember where, but it was definitely Portsmouth they went to. Not that long ago, actually.'

'Really? They've only just left here, have they?'

'Yes - very recent. Must have been in the early 60s, I would guess.'

'The early 60s?' we chorus.

I try to ask John Morgan about Irene and why he didn't trust her; more out of nosiness than anything else. But all he will say is that he liked Tom a lot, and he liked to talk about farming with him, whenever he got the chance.

'Tom loved to chat about the farm he had in Gower. I know he wished they had never left. He should not have. He should not have listened to Irene. He should have stood his ground. But, my-oh-my, you should have seen her. I guess she was difficult to turn down, with her miniskirts and boots and her fancy hair and what-not.'

He speaks about Irene until his eyes begin to close and his shoulders droop in weariness. He yawns gently and I can see he is starting to nod off.

'You'll need to leave now,' says the nurse. 'He's exhausted.'

'Of course,' I say. We all bid him a fond farewell, blow kisses and wave, but he has gone, drifted off into sleep.

'I've brought these chocolates for him,' I say, handing the nurse a giant box of Maltesers. 'My friend Frank used to love Maltesers. I thought John might. Frank said he loved them because he could suck them if he didn't have his teeth in, and they tasted just as good. If he doesn't like them, please keep them yourself. You've been very kind to help us like this.'

'Oh, thank you,' she says. 'I hope you find your friends.'

We trundle out of the nursing home, welcoming the cool air as we step onto the pavement. The place is heated to boiling point.

'Come on,' says Simon, leading us all away from the building and to the bench in a small meditation garden they have set up, presumably for springtime when the flowers are out and the sun is shining, and relatives bring their elderly relatives out to get some fresh air. This time of year, it is empty.

We sit down and look at one another.

'Okay, well at least we know where the family went,' I say.

'Yes, we know where they went in 1960. We don't know where they are now.'

'No, I know that, but we've got significantly more to work on now than we had when we first came. We could call Portsmouth University to see whether they have contact details for someone who worked at the college in the early 60s. I know it all sounds a bit unlikely, but you never know.

'This morning we didn't know we were going to walk into a nursing home and talk to someone who knows the Gower family. We have done better than the private detectives already. We should be pleased.'

'You're absolutely right,' says Ted, protectively. 'You should all be very pleased with what you've found out, and now we know they're not here, we can stop looking for them and start enjoying ourselves. I'm up for a boozy, late lunch if anyone else is?'

'Oh, I definitely am,' says Juan. 'More booze than lunch if you don't mind.'

'Me too,' says Melissa, in a move which surprises all of us.

'Me three,' says Bronwyn.

'Sure, yes, lunch sounds great, but I was thinking that we could make some enquiries about the Gower family first. I mean, I was even thinking that if the family is still based down there, we could head for the south coast tomorrow.'

'You really think we should do that?' says Simon, somewhat agitated by the proposal.

'Well, depending on what we find out. If you're up for it, I think we should go.'

'This has got the feeling of a wild goose chase about it,' says Ted. 'We can't keep chasing from one place to the next.'

'I'm not saying that. All I'm suggesting is that we make a few calls.'

'Come on then. Shall we head back to the hotel?'

'Sure,' I say.

'Yep, okay. We'll follow you,' says Melissa.

I climb into Simon's car and wait while he puts on his gloves and adjusts his mirror. There is something quite soothing about his attention to detail. It reminds me of sitting in my grandparents' car when I was younger, waiting as they made every check: petrol, oil, water, spare tyre. They treated every short journey as if they were about to embark on a trek across Africa.

Back at the hotel, we gather in reception to discuss the options. The group is in three minds at this point...there's me who thinks we should hot-foot it to Southsea and keep hot-footing it in pursuit of the Gower family, then there's Juan, Ted and Simon who think we should stay exactly where we are and have a nice relaxing time. Finally, there is Bronwyn and Melissa, both of whom are just glad to be at the party.

We order coffees and teas in reception, and set about making a plan. I call Portsmouth University and ask to be put through to the Department of Agriculture and Farming. There is a lengthy pause.

'We don't have a department like that. The closest thing would be land management. Shall I put you through to them?'

'Sure,' I reply.

I go through to land management where a woman who sounds the same as the last person, tells me that the university no longer runs agricultural courses, and that they are all run by Portsmouth Agricultural College.

'But I'm sure he worked at the university.'

'Well, I'd need to know what department, and there isn't an agricultural and farming department. That's all done at the college.'

I explain briefly that we are trying to locate someone who worked there at the beginning of the 1960s.

'Ah, yes, there was an agriculture department then, but now it's all run by the college. They will have all the records relating to that time,' she says.

I thank her, and turn to the posse. 'Okay, we need to call another number. It's a separate agricultural college.'

I go through the same routine again, asking whether there is anyone who can confirm that a Tom Gower worked there. The woman clicks on a few keys; I hear voices, then more key clicking. 'Yes, he did.'

Found him.

'Would you have any idea where he went when he left? Is he still in touch with the college? Do you know whether he still lives locally?'

'I don't know any of those things, to be honest,' she says. 'Why are you so keen to reach him? Did he teach you?'

'Yes, that's right.'

'Well you're welcome to come down and look through the paperwork here. It's all on microfiche, I'm afraid, but there are records going back to the 50s.'

'Great,' I say, giving the others a thumbs up. 'I look forward to seeing you soon.'

I end the call and look at the group. 'I really, really think we should go to Southsea. They know all about him and say there is a lot of information there.'

Okay, okay, so that is a bit of a lie, but I know I have to say something to motivate them, and persuade them to make the journey. Simon responds by sighing deeply.

'If we do decide to go, we will never all get in my car,' he says. 'I'm not sure I'd trust that thing to go all the way to the south coast with just me in it, let alone you three as well…' I swear he glances at my stomach when he says that.

'We could come with you,' says Melissa. 'I'm not working for the next few days, and I've got a van, in which we do beauty treatments and hair care on the road, so it's got seats, and there's lots of room in it. And I've never been to England.'

'We saw your van at the old people's home. That sounds perfect,' I say, while Simon and Ted exchange glances.

'Are you sure you don't mind driving? It's a long way.'

'Is it further than Cardiff?'

'It's a hell of a lot further than Cardiff. It is on the south coast of England. I'm not sure this is such a good idea,' says Simon.

'Well I can start driving, and if I get fed up someone else can drive. The van is insured regular as we all share it.'

'By 'regular' you mean that anyone is insured to drive? We should definitely check that.'

'Aye, it'll be fine, but we'll go and check.'

The two girls leave and we all look at one another. 'Is anyone else surprised by the fact that a random hairdresser is offering to drive us to Portsmouth in her pink van?' says Simon. 'I don't mean to be ungrateful, but it seems most peculiar.'

'Yes, I don't think we should take her up on it,' says Ted. 'We don't know what we are going to find when we get to

Portsmouth. It might be a wasted trip. It seems very odd to have Melissa and Bronwyn with us.'

'But they want to come,' I say. I like the idea of them joining us. 'Bronwyn lives in the Gower's house now, and they introduced us to John Morgan, so I can see why they're interested.'

'Yes, I suppose,' says Simon. 'But I still think it will be a waste of time.'

'Yes, I vote very strongly that we don't go,' says Ted.

'I vote that we do.'

PRESENT DAY: OFF TO SOUTHSEA

It is quite a perilous journey to Southsea from mid-Wales. Well, it certainly is when the woman driving you has never previously driven more than about 20 miles and has neither understanding of, nor respect for, the speedometer. The van shakes and rattles as she practically stands on the accelerator pedal, flying through rural streets en route to the motorway. 'I've never driven on a motorway before,' Melissa says with glee, as she jumps the car onto a busy roundabout, inches ahead of a Tesco van.

Then she drives onto the motorway and it turns out she quite likes it. We know this from the wild squeal she emits as she moves into the second lane, overtaking the traffic in the inside lane and waving madly at them with her beautifully manicured hands.

Even Bronwyn is looking scared at this point. Up until now, she has been enjoying the thrill of the pedal-to-floor experience, but a look of concern has crept across her face.

'Darling, you don't have to wave every time you overtake someone,' says Juan. 'Your arm will become incredibly tired if you do that every time.'

'I know, but it's so flipping great going past these big lorries. I can't help it.'

'So, you really haven't driven on the motorway before? This is your first time?'

'Yes, I just drive around the town, going to different people's houses to do their hair and beauty. I've never needed to go on the motorway, and I didn't pass my test that long ago.'

'When did you pass it?'

'Last Wednesday,' she says, still waving like the queen as she overtakes a car with a large caravan on the back.

'Right, well, you need to tell us when you get tired, and someone else will drive for you. It would be unwise for you to drive for too long if you haven't been driving for that long.'

'Oh, I've been driving for a long time; I just didn't pass my test till recently.'

'You were driving around before passing your test?'

'Yes,' she says calmly, as she negotiates a lane change with little regard for the other traffic on the motorway.

'You know, Melissa, maybe I should drive now, we don't want you to get too tired,' Ted says.

'Okeydokey.' Melissa pulls into the inside lane, moving to within inches of the bonnet of the car she has just overtaken, forcing them to beep and grind to a halt. She pulls onto the hard shoulder and comes to an emergency stop, throwing us all forward in our seats.

She swings open the driver's door while Ted shouts, 'No, you can't do that...' But it is too late - Melissa's door is wide open and she is out and running around to jump in the back of the van with the rest of us. Cars on the motorway swerve around the open door.

When the back doors of the van open, I jump out and get into the passenger seat, and Ted slides over to take the driving role. We pull back onto the motorway, and though it was incredibly kind of Melissa to drive us, and very generous of her to let us use her van, there isn't a person in that bubble-gum pink motor vehicle who does not give an almighty sigh of relief as Ted moves seamlessly into the traffic. He indicates and checks his mirror as he goes, then moves into the middle lane without waving at any of the vehicles on the road. We soon pass the caravan-towing car that Melissa almost wrote off five minutes earlier, and I see them glance over warily, but Ted continues, building up speed until we are moving at the same speed as all the traffic on the road and are far less of a hazard.

In the end, Ted does all the driving. The plan was for him to swap with Simon at the service station. But Simon spends most of the journey complaining how fast Ted is going every time he nudges close to 70, so we are all very pleased when Ted offers to do the rest of the driving. I think Simon is too. For all his moaning about the speed, he doesn't seem very keen to take the reins. I witnessed Simon's driving yesterday. If he had been behind the steering wheel, we would have taken most of the week to reach the south coast. As it happens, we climb, weary and with aching limbs from the back of the pink van at around 6pm. We have been driving all day, but at least we had a decent break for lunch, and are in Southsea in time for dinner. And yes – you are right – I do measure all journeys by the distance they are between meals!

We park the van along the seafront, outside the Sunnyside Hotel, the cheapest one we could find. I am not sure why we were desperate to find a cheap hotel, since we inherited hundreds of thousands of pounds a year ago, but Simon is one of those guys who could inherit 40 million and still wear the shoes he had worn since he was 14. I didn't want to rock the boat by suggesting that we all step up a notch and get a nice place.

The good news is that Simon and I have decided that we will cover the cost of the girls' hotel and food, because they have been kind enough to come with us. They have been helpful so far. And they're an entertaining duo. And they have a van. And Melissa does such good highlights.

Ted removes the bags from the back of the van and starts to carry them all to the hotel. 'There's no need to carry everyone's bags,' I say, taking mine out of his hands.

'No, we can manage,' say the girls, stepping forward to take theirs, while Simon walks on, into the reception. Ted walks behind him carrying his bag. I look at the girls and we stifle a laugh. Simon is the most extraordinary person, completely self-unaware, kind and lovely, but daft as a brush.

Ted phrases it differently: 'All the girls are managing to carry their bags, and I'm carrying a bloke's. What's wrong with him?'

The hotel is like something out of the 1950s, so we opt out of staying there for dinner, and find a nice little café on the seafront instead. It is called *Shambles* and proudly boasts that it has been there, in the same spot, since 1962.

'Tom and Irene might have come in here,' I comment.

'They could be here tonight,' says Simon, and a sudden knot forms in my stomach. It is like that feeling you get when you are out somewhere and you're told a boy you fancy might be coming. You know - that ball you get inside you that's a mixture of fear and excitement. Well, that is how I feel right now. I really want us to find the Gower family.

'It would be so amazing. Just - so incredible,' I say, while scanning the restaurant for a young man in farming dungarees and wellington boots.

'You know that the chances of Tom or Irene being alive are very remote, don't you?' says Simon. 'We're tracing where they lived in order to find their descendants.'

'Yes, but I don't really want to think about that. I want to think about actually seeing them.'

Ted leans over and squeezes my shoulder.

We are sitting at a far table, against the floor-to-ceiling windows that give us an excellent view of the beach. We watch as waves slap up toward the windows as we sit there enjoying lovely wine and nice food. We are all out tonight except for Juan, who wants to do an online yoga and meditation class instead.

As the others chat and laugh, I sit back and retreat into a dream world...back in the 1960s with Irene sunbathing on the beach and Tom Junior swimming in the sea. It must have been a lovely place to grow up.

'We have to find them. I can sense that they are here somewhere,' I say. 'Wouldn't it be brilliant? I feel so excited I could scream.'

'Let's not start screaming yet. Let's look at the information we've got so far. What do we know, and what do we need to find out?' asks Simon.

'We need to head down to Portsmouth Agricultural College first thing in the morning. That'll give us a better idea of things, and hopefully we'll find someone who knew him or Irene.'

'Sure,' says Simon. 'Let's start there. We could also check births, marriages and deaths in case there's anything listed.'

'They can't be dead,' I say, rather louder than I mean to, but I do feel strongly about finding them.

'I know how keen you are to find them, angel,' says Ted, stroking my arm. 'But they will be over a hundred years old. You're really looking for the grandchildren.'

I lean over to give him a kiss on the cheek as both Simon's phone and my phone bleep in unison on the table in front of us, indicating that there is a message in the 'Mysterious Invitation' group.

There is a message from Sally Bramley.

'I've decided to come and join you. Which hotel in Llandrindod are you staying at?'

I look at Simon. He is still struggling to remember his code to get his phone open so I explain the nature of the message that has been left.

'Shall I go back to her and explain?' I say.

'Yes please,' he says, removing his reading glasses and laying his phone back down on the table, relieved that he doesn't have to tangle with new technology.

Mysterious Invitation WhatsApp Group

Mary Brown

Hi everyone, just a quick update for anyone thinking of coming to join us. We are in Southsea. I know, I know! We only stayed in Llandrindod for one night before discovering that the Gower family moved from their home there in the 1960s. They moved to Southsea which is on the south coast, near

Portsmouth. So that is where we are. Come and join us, Sally. We are at the Sunnyside Hotel.

From the Southsea Six! :)

Sally Bramley

Oh wow. That's much easier. Yes, I will definitely come and join you. I'll be there around 10am tomorrow. Shall I just come straight to the hotel?

Mary Brown

Yes, we will be in the breakfast room. Come and join us for coffee. Can't wait to see you. X

Sally Bramley

PS Who are the six? I am confused! Is everyone there but me? In that case, are there not five of you? X

Mary Brown

Oh, sorry - no. There's me and Simon, then my boyfriend Ted is here and my lovely friend Juan. Also, there is a woman called Bronwyn who was living in the Gower's old house in Llandrindod, who knew someone who said the Gower family had moved to Southsea, and her hairdresser called Melissa who drove us all down here in her van.

Sally Bramley

Wow. That sounds like a riot.

1970: BIG DECISIONS

'Hello, Grants Estate Agents. Irene Gower speaking, can I help you?'

There was a pause while Irene nodded, listening as the house-seller detailed his concerns.

'Sure, I understand, Mr. Davis…' she said, as she heard how he didn't want to drop the asking price, but he was worried about the fact that so few people had been round to view his property.

Irritation had crept into his voice, as if the lack of interest in his house was entirely her doing. As if she were not sending people round on purpose.

'We're doing all we can,' she said. The trouble was that Mr. Davis's house was a poorly decorated, old-fashioned bungalow, and though it was in a decent location, and was roomy inside, the decor was pre-war and very unappealing. It reminded her of going to Tom's house, when they were first courting. The farmhouse had been a whirl of yellow floral wallpaper that had made her wince when she walked inside.

Mr. Davis's place was worse. In the bedroom there was blue wallpaper on the walls that extended right across the ceiling, and the curtains matched. They were exactly the same sky-blue colour and with an identical floral pattern. It looked more like a doll's house than a home for a modern family.

In its day, it had probably been all the rage - that twee early-50s look of endless floral and chintzy wallpaper had been everywhere. But this was the 70s, and the more discerning clientele were opting for much trendier interiors.

'Do you remember we mentioned that it might be nice to decorate?' Irene asked, cautiously. 'Sort of spruce the place up a bit and make it look more modern?'

'What a waste of money,' said Mr. Davis. 'The place is neat and tidy and it's always clean. If someone who moves in here wants to decorate, that is their prerogative, but I am certainly not going to do it when I am about to move out. Where is the sense in that? Can you put me through to your boss? I'm not prepared to talk to his secretary anymore.'

Irene signalled to Mark that she was putting a call through to him. She wasn't Mark's secretary, and the horrible Mr. Davis was well aware of that. She wasn't going to fight against his misogynistic words though; she had done enough of that in the years that she'd worked here. Now she had given in her notice and had just a month left, she would spend those weeks rising above the aggro and sexism that had defined her time working at Mark's estate agency, smile and move on.

She looked over at Mark, still deep in conversation with Mr. Davis, and tapped her watch to indicate that she was leaving. He nodded that it was fine, and then gave her a thumbs up, just to be clear. He was a lovely man. She knew he was heartbroken that she had decided to leave the firm. She had been honest with him, and told him that she had decided to try to make her marriage work, and that they might move away. He had looked devastated, but he had never held it against her. He had not asked for any details. He'd just said that he understood.

Irene grabbed her mac and her handbag and left the office.

Outside it was colder than she had expected, so she slipped on her mac and looked away as a car sped past full of rowdy young men beeping their horn and shouting as they raced past.

She was wearing her new white patent leather boots, the ones that Mark had bought her, with lovely big buttons on the side. They went so well with her black mac with white piping. She loved looking fashionable, but could do without the jeers and lame comments from passing men.

Irene walked along the seafront, past *Shambles* cafe, where they'd spent so much time over the years, and passed the bench that she and Mark now called 'our bench', pausing to think of everything that had happened since she met Mark here. Life was so complicated. But Mark was a good person. She would never regret meeting him or spending time getting to know him.

She glanced at her watch. The appointment was in five minutes, so she kept walking, into the centre of Southsea, along Palace Road and through the familiar yellow door, up the rickety stairs and into the waiting room. Tom was already there. His face lit up when he saw her.

'You look lovely,' he mouthed, so as not to be heard by the others, waiting, like him, for an appointment with the marriage guidance counsellor.

She smiled as she sat down, slipping her sunglasses off her

nose and up into her long brown hair, and reaching for a magazine.

'Tom and Irene Gower, please.'

There was a sigh from a young man in the room who clearly thought it was his turn. Irene lay down the magazine, stood up and followed her husband.

'How are you feeling?' asked Dr Kent, the marriage guidance counsellor who had been advising them for the past few months, as they struggled to get their marriage back on track.

'I feel okay,' said Irene.

'Have you moved back into the family home yet?'

'No, but I have given in my notice at work. Just a few more weeks to go.'

'That's a very positive step. How is that making you feel?'

'I feel a bit nervous about everything at the moment. I have been working at the estate agency for quite a few years, and Mark has been a good friend to me.'

Tom grunted.

'It's true, Tom. We have been over this many times. Nothing has ever happened between us. He is a friend, and he is my boss. I moved out of the house because we were arguing all the time, not because of Mark. I needed to get my head together. It was never because of Mark.'

Irene was aware of how angry Tom was about her friendship with Mark. TJ had seen them swimming in the sea one morning and taken it badly, assumed she was having an affair and told Tom. There appeared to be nothing she could do to convince him that there was no affair. Mark was a friend, and that was all.

'Is there anything else bothering you?' asked the doctor. 'You said that everything is making you feel nervous at the moment.'

'Just the usual worries. My son TJ is living in Brighton with his wife, Yvonne, and I miss them. He doesn't call much. He blames me for everything that happened, of course. They have a little boy called Andrew who is 18 months old, and his wife is heavily pregnant with their next one. I wish I could be more involved...'

'How does it make you feel when you're not very involved?'

'I feel shut out. I feel like I have lost my son and lost my husband and wrecked my family, but I didn't do anything wrong.'

'You had an affair.' said Tom. He said this every time. Every time.

Irene felt her sadness turn to anger. 'No I didn't. I met a friend, and the friend offered me a job. That's all.'

'But he wanted to have an affair with you. You can't pretend he didn't.'

'Tom, we've been over this and over it. I did not have an affair with anyone. He might have wanted to, but I did not. Never. I wasn't even tempted. I was flattered by his attention at the beginning, but we fell into a friendship very quickly.'

'And have you made a decision about Brighton yet?'

Irene looked down at her hands at this question, so the counsellor looked instead at Tom.

'I've been offered early retirement from Portsmouth College, and some part-time work at a college in Brighton, if I want it,' he said. 'And the Brighton Argus want me to do some cartoons for them. We will have enough money. Irene will not have to work. The kids are settled there and our grandchildren are there. We should go.'

'How about you, Irene?'

Irene continued to stare down at her hands. 'It feels risky.'

'Risky in what way?'

'Well, we'll move to a place where we don't know many people, and will be stuck together, and it might be the end of it all.'

'It might not,' said Tom. 'It could be the making of us…'

Irene looked over at him. She had made up her mind about moving along the coast, but she didn't want to discuss it now. She planned to talk to Tom directly, not through their counsellor.

But Tom seemed so small and helpless, slumped in the chair, practically begging her to do something to help save their marriage, and she didn't want to wait any longer.

'I think we should move to Brighton.'

Tom's grey eyes widened and a smile spread across the entire width of his face. She might never be in love with this man again, she might not feel a rush of excitement when he walked into the room, but he was her husband, and this was her family. And this was her chance to put everything right.

'Let's move to Brighton,' she confirmed.

The counsellor asked her why, of course. All the counsellor seemed to do was ask why she was doing things and how it all made her feel.

'Because I think it would do us all a lot of good. It would enable me to spend more time with TJ and Yvonne, and give us a very real chance of repairing our relationship.'

'And how do you feel when you say that?' asked the counsellor.

'I feel good,' she said, because saying anything else would have opened up the gates of interrogation even further. In truth, she felt nervous. She had moved out of the family home a few years ago when TJ moved to Brighton because it had become unbearable. Tom would accuse her of cheating on a daily basis because she worked with Mark every day, and Tom knew they went swimming together in the mornings. In truth, nothing had happened between her and Mark.

Not once.

The only thing she had lied to Tom about was telling him that she had never fancied Mark, and never wanted anything to happen. That was wholly untrue. She had desperately wanted something to happen. Desperately. But she was always constrained by the vows she had made all those years ago, and her sense of devotion and propriety.

'I wish you well,' said the counsellor. 'I'm always here if you need me, or I can refer you to someone in Brighton, if that would be easier.'

They walked single file down the old stairs and out to a bright and sunny day.

'I'll miss Southsea,' she said.

'But Brighton's beautiful,' replied Tom. 'Are you coming home, now?'

'I've got something to do first,' she said. 'I'll come over later.'

Irene walked over to the phone box and rang Mark.

'Can you meet me at *Shambles*?' she said. 'I have something to tell you.'

1973: LIFE IN BRIGHTON

Irene walked back from the telephone box with her hands pushed deep into her pockets and her collar up despite the warmth of the midday sun: shielding herself from the world. It was as if she were hiding away; protecting a great, dark secret. She let herself into the roomy apartment that she and Tom were renting, and slumped across the sofa.

'Where've you been?' asked Tom.

'For a walk on the seafront,' she said. It wasn't a lie. She went on regular walks along the seafront, but they always ended with her in the phone box, ringing Mark. She never mentioned that bit. Or how much she missed him.

'Are you ready for this lunch?'

'I'll get ready now. I won't be long.'

Irene knew exactly what she would wear. She slipped on her new flared trousers, some wedge shoes and a fitted polo-neck jumper in a lovely burnt orange colour. It wasn't what most people would be wearing, but she did not care. She wanted to look fashionable. It is what Jane would have wanted. She threw a crocheted handbag over her shoulder and headed back into the sitting room.

Tom stood and looked her up and down.

'Is that appropriate?' he said.

'Why wouldn't it be?'

'I don't know. It's a memorial service for Jane. Won't people be dressed more formally? I am wearing a jacket and tie. I got the impression that others would be, too.'

'You want me to wear a jacket and tie?'

'No, of course not. I am sure you are fine dressed the way you are. You look very fashionable. Come on, let's go.'

Irene sighed heavily, to emphasise her frustration at him, while he led the way down the stairs and out of their pretty Brighton flat. But she knew deep down that he was right. She probably should have dressed more soberly, but she did not want to sit and remember Jane while dressed in black. Jane was so vibrant, joyful and wonderful.

Irene had become very close to Yvonne's mother, Jane, since moving to Brighton. The two of them had become inseparable...meeting for drinks and in cafes for cups of tea.

Then, a year ago, aged 59, Jane died. It was sudden and unexpected - a stroke brought on by a blood disorder that no one knew she had. Something called Factor V Leiden, inherited from both her parents, it turned out, which made it particularly dangerous. In the year since Jane's death, the family had investigated the blood disorder and ruminated many times, over many drinks, on how, if only they had known, they could have done something about it.

They could have sought treatment, had her monitored regularly by her doctor, done anything within their power to stop her from dying such a sudden, brutal death at such a young age. But no one had known. How could they?

Simon, Yvonne's father, who Irene had also got on with well, had become withdrawn and quiet since his wife's death, no longer the active member of their family group, organising get-togethers, walks along the beach, barbecues and picnics. He was a lovely man, very kind and good fun, and Irene liked him enormously, but she hated the way he had become such a shadow of his former self. Today, there was a small gathering at Simon's to remember Jane, one year on.

'Sorry,' she said to Tom, as they sat in traffic just minutes from Simon's house. 'I should have dressed in black. You are right. It is just that I cannot bear that she is gone. I cannot bear the reality of her not being there with Simon anymore. She always wore such bright, modern and lovely clothes. I guess I wanted to reflect that. But you're right. You are absolutely right. I'm sorry I snapped at you.'

Tom smiled at her and squeezed her knee in an affectionate gesture. 'I know you were very close to her, and I understand. Don't worry; you'll be the best dressed person there as you always are, wherever we go.'

There were around 20 people gathered at Simon's house, all of them in black. Sod them. Irene was wearing the most modern outfit she owned because that is what Jane would have wanted. She wondered whether any of these people really knew Jane like she had.

She glanced around the room at the familiar faces, nodding and smiling in recognition, while inside she felt she might shrivel up and die with the pain of all this. A year had gone by since Jane's death, but she felt no closer to coping with the loss of her great friend.

Jane had kept her from crumbling when Irene had first moved to Brighton. Jane had been a joyful reminder that life could be fun and enjoyable.

One by one, Jane's closest friends walked to the front of the room and told stories about her, and the fun times they'd had. Irene told them about the time the two of them had gone out late, and begged the barman not to chuck them out at 10.30pm, urging him to give them one more drink until a loud voice behind them told them to go. They spun round to see a cross-looking police officer standing, glaring at them.

'Jane gave him a kiss on the cheek and we both ran out. He looked furious, but we ended up becoming really good friends with him.'

'You sure did!' came a loud voice. It was George - the officer they had met that night.

Simon smiled, enjoying the memory of his lovely, sociable wife. He had heard the stories of Jane and Irene's nights out before, and always enjoyed them. He loved the memories of his wife as this wonderful life force, this bringer-together of people. This kind, beautiful, gentle woman.

He looked over and caught Irene's eye, smiling warmly at her. He was so glad the two of them had come to mean so much to each other. He was aware how much colour, life and joy Irene had brought to Jane.

Irene returned the smile. She couldn't tell all of the stories to the assembled guests, not that they did anything terrible, but they hadn't always been the best behaved of people. For example, she couldn't talk about the time they drove to Southsea so that she could see Mark one last time. She could never tell them how Jane urged her to spend time alone with him while Jane went for a long walk along the seafront to give them space. She would never tell anyone what had happened.

1973: REMEMBERING JANE

Irene had been so low when she first arrived in Brighton. No one knew how much she had loved Mark. Then she told Jane, and they spoke about it endlessly. Jane never judged or commented, she just listened, and took Irene on nights out that allowed her to forget about everything and enjoy herself.

'Irene, is there anything else you'd like to say about Jane?'

Simon looked almost pleading as he spoke, as if desperate for Irene to continue with the tributes to his late wife.

'Of course,' she said, stepping forward to the front of the group. There was no story that she particularly wanted to tell, but for Simon's sake, she wanted to offer some words about the beautiful woman he had lost.

'I didn't know Jane when I first moved to Brighton. Well, we knew each other through the kids, and obviously saw one another when the wedding was being planned, but we weren't close. We were very much parents of the marrying couple rather than friends.'

Irene paused to gather herself. She didn't want to cry. This was not a time for shedding tears; it was a time for recalling the beauty, joy and wonder of Jane.

'Then I moved to this town from a place where I'd had a job and lots of friends, and felt quite lonely. Jane picked me up and took me out and introduced me to everyone she knew.

'Gosh, in many ways it seems like an eternity since she died, and in other ways it feels like it was just last week. Life has changed so much without her here. I miss hearing her voice, seeing her, spending time with her; I miss just knowing that she exists in the world.

'People say that time is a great healer. Who are the people who say that? They are frauds. Time has not healed anything. The more time goes by, the more I miss her. I hate that her family will be growing without her to see, and every time anything happens to me, I long to share it with her and feel desperately sad that I cannot.

'The Jane-shaped hole in my life is still there - like a deep, raw, ugly wound that will never heal. All I'm able to do now is cope with the wound. I have learned not to prod it or to think about it all the time, and though it is always there and always will be, I can exist with it.

'I know that all of you will feel the same, because we all loved Jane deeply. There will always be a void.'

There was loud applause when Irene finished her little speech but as she walked back to stand next to Tom, she felt disappointed. She hadn't meant to give a talk full of misery and woe. She had meant to talk about the fun and joy of the woman.

'That was lovely,' said Tom.

'It was nowhere near lovely enough, it was all wrong,' she said. Then she watched as Tom's face fell. And realised she'd said the wrong thing again. The man must feel as if he could do nothing right.

'I just mean that I should have been a bit more upbeat,' said Irene. 'But, thanks.'

Irene looked up to see Yvonne waddling across the sitting room toward them. Her heavily-pregnant tummy stood proud in front of her. This was to be her son's second child - a little girl.

'How's it going?' Irene asked.

'As well as can be expected considering how rotten the whole damn thing is,' said Yvonne. 'Your words were lovely, thank you, Irene.'

'Gosh, it's the least I could do. I loved your mum very much.'

A silence settled between the women. Irene had always liked Yvonne, but she was not the easiest person to chat to. She seemed outgoing and lively when she first started dating TJ, but in company she was quite shy and never really spoke unless spoken to.

'How's the pregnancy going?'

'Seven weeks to go. I'm just hoping and praying that she hasn't got the horrible blood thing that killed Mum.'

Blood tests, since Jane's death, had revealed that Yvonne had the disorder, but only mildly. Luckily their son, Andrew, did not have it.

'Whatever happens, this little girl will be loved and cherished, and if she has the blood disorder, which seems really unlikely, then we'll deal with it, and get her the best treatment possible.'

Irene was cleaning the house, organising bags of old clothes to take to the charity shop, and throwing out anything that didn't have an immediate use, one bright morning in early May. She had become a grandmother two weeks earlier to a lovely little girl called Sophia Jane. The baby had been born a few weeks early, but was putting on weight, and getting healthier every day.

Irene filled up another bag. It was such a small flat; she had to make sure there was no clutter lying around or it started to feel uncomfortably full. Then the phone rang.

'Hi, it's Simon,' said a small, shaky voice. 'We've had some bad news.'

'Oh no, what's happened?' said Irene, dropping the rubbish bag she held in her left hand and cupping the phone.

'It's the baby. Sophia Jane has the same blood disorder. She has it badly. It is terrible news. I don't know what we're going to do.'

Irene listened as Simon explained the condition in detail. Sophia's disorder meant she was 20 times more likely to have a heart attack or stroke than if she had been born without the gene.

1974: NEW YORK CALLING

The months passed so quickly after the initial diagnosis. Spring rolled into summer, before winter's frosty hands touched their lives, then spring swept in again - majestically painting all the colours back into their garden, into the sky and onto trees. It was soon Sophia Jane's first birthday, and the anniversary of Jane's death. Thoughts of Jane were warmer and less fraught this time. Irene still sobbed, alone, as she thought of her friend, but it was hard to be morbid when pink balloons and teddy bears filled her son and daughter-in-law's house.

'Come for dinner next week,' said Yvonne. 'It would be lovely to see you and Tom when the kids are in bed and we can talk properly.'

'Of course. What a lovely idea. Will Simon be there?'

'Yes, I'll make sure he's there, too.'

Tom smiled warmly when she told him about the dinner. He was in such a good mood all the time these days. He had been working more and more for the Brighton Argus, producing cartoons for them every day. They had even given him the title of 'Art Director (cartoons)' and Tom was to find good new cartoonists as well as producing his own pieces of art. Nothing fazed him. He was happy, content and loving life.

The day of the dinner, Irene sensed something was wrong. She tried to dismiss her negative feelings because she was well aware that she had a tendency to expect the worst. But when they arrived at her son's house, the feelings multiplied...there was a tension in the air and a feeling of doom all around.

TJ and Yvonne sat quietly, close together and holding hands, something that Irene was quietly pleased about. She had feared that their announcement would be that they were splitting up. She couldn't think of anything else quite dramatic enough to warrant this demand for an evening get-together.

'We've got some news,' said TJ suddenly, prompting all talking to stop, and all heads to swivel in his direction.

'We have been told that treatment for Sophia and Yvonne's illness is available.'

'Oh, that's amazing,' said Tom, jumping to his feet. 'I'm so pleased. What will it involve? When can she have it?'

'There's a small problem, and this is the bit you're not going to like. There is a treatment available but it's in America, at the Bellevue Hospital in New York,' said TJ.

'We've done lots of research and we've talked about it endlessly, and we think we should go.'

'But, how long would you be there for? What about work?' said Irene. She struggled to share Tom's instant delight in the idea. Of course, Sophia's health meant everything, but the family had established themselves so well in Brighton, they had so many friends and TJ was happy and successful. Was it worth them upping and moving to the other side of the world?

'Will it be expensive?' she asked.

'No,' said Yvonne, in her first foray into the conversation. 'I was talking to Dad about it and he thinks we might be able to go there without any charge, under the new healthcare policy in the country.'

Irene felt a twinge of pain. Why had they spoken to Simon but not to Tom and her? She looked at TJ who dropped his gaze in a manner that hinted at embarrassment.

'There's a new system in the USA, called the Medicare program. It started in 1965. It's a kind of social insurance program to provide health insurance coverage to people who are either age 65 and over, or who meet other special criteria.'

'One slight problem with that might be that you're not 65 and over, and you're not American citizens,' said Irene, still hurt that TJ hadn't come to them to discuss the situation, as well as talking to Simon.

'No, well that's what I was worried about, too,' said Simon. 'But the special criteria is for people who are suffering from illnesses that the American hospitals are keen to learn more about. If that's the case, they will take her and all treatment will be free.'

'And you think that Sophia's blood disorder might be something they are keen to find out more about?' said Tom.

'I wrote to them and asked exactly that. I enclosed her medical information and a letter from the doctor, and I got this back,' said Simon, handing over an envelope. Irene felt another wave of sadness. How long had Simon known?

Inside the envelope was confirmation that the hospital in New York was interested in working with Sophia on a new drug they were developing. The only one of its kind in the world.

'But how would you even do that? TJ would have to give up his job, you would take the kids away from everything they know. And us? We'd be devastated if you were so far away.'

'I know,' said TJ. 'I know, Mum. But if there's a chance of helping Sophia while she's young enough to respond to treatment, we have to go.'

PRESENT DAY: LET THE SEARCH BEGIN

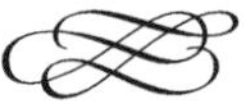

Good God alive, what were we drinking last night? I have woken up this morning in the tiny bed (it says it is a double bed, but I am not convinced they know who they are dealing with here. Ted and I come to over 40 stone between us).

'Are you awake?' I ask Ted, even though I know he is asleep because I can hear him snoring gently. He's got one of those snuffly snores, not the mad warthog snore that previous boyfriends have had, that you can hear halfway round the M25. No, thank God. Ted has a much gentler noise emanating from his open mouth and flared nostrils as he sleeps. I am not saying it's attractive, but at least it is fairly quiet.

'Ted, Ted,' I repeat. I now seem determined to wake him up for no good reason. It's only 7am, and we haven't arranged to meet the others for breakfast until nine, but I feel the need to chat to him about everything that has been going on.

Eventually the snuffling comes to a sudden stop and he murmurs and opens his eyes, looking over at me all alarmed.

'What happened?' he asks.

'Nothing happened,' I say.

'The car crashed into reception…'

'What are you talking about?'

I thought the car crashed, was that in my dream?'

'It was in your dream,' I say, leaning over and giving him a kiss on the cheek before instantly regretting it when I get a nose full of his garlicky morning breath.

'I had this dream but there was this car full of people that had come swerving off the motorway and crashed into reception.'

'It doesn't take a genius to work out how that dream happened, given the way Melissa was driving that pink van yesterday.'

'I know,' says Ted. 'Can you believe she's never driven more than about five miles in any one trip before, then suddenly she announces she's happy to drive us hundreds of miles across motorways to the south coast? Bloody bonkers.'

There are many things that I love very much about Ted, and one of the things I really adore is the way we can chat, and compare notes on what happens.

'Do you think we'll ever find the Gower family?' I ask.

'I think so. With your determination, Melissa's pink van and Simon's driving gloves we can't possibly fail.'

I give him a big hug. 'It is a shame they don't have a more uncommon surname, isn't it?'

'Yes, it might help a bit if they were called the Jabberwocky-Bockersnappers or something,' he replies, and this amuses me a lot. I howl and snort with laughter in an undignified way and throw myself into his arms and within minutes my clothes are off and we are doing what two people in love tend to do.

'I'm glad I said 'Jabberwocky-Bockersnappers', Ted reflects, as we lie in bed afterward. 'I might start using that name in daily discourse.'

'It might lose its ability to amuse me if you do that, though.'

He nods, gently, while his eyes start to close, but I am not having any of it - I want to take us right back to where we were before all the bockersnapping started...chasing the Gower family.

'I'm glad Sally's coming today. She's quite sensible, and I guess the more of us there are here, the more phoning around and visiting people we can do. Then hopefully we will get some positive leads. If we could just find the details for any relations or friends at all, we could pass them on to the private detectives, and make sure the family gets the money that's owing to them.'

'Have you spoken to the private detective firm at all?' asks Ted.

'Yes - I already told you. The guy running the firm is really ill. It means we are on our own here. We have to find them.'

Ted smiles broadly as I am speaking.

'What are you smiling at?'

'You,' he says.

'What have I done that's so funny?'

'Well, you love it, don't you? I know you genuinely want to find them in order to give them the money, but you love things like this. You should have been a bloody private detective. As soon as there's any mystery to solve, you're on it.'

'You're so right. I watch police programmes all the time, and I definitely could solve half the crimes before them.'

Ted and I are first into the breakfast room, and make the most of the rather delicious buffet before the others arrive. It is continental, which is really the lowest form of hotel buffet, but at least they do fried breakfasts, although you have to order them. We decide that we will nibble away on the continental buffet until the others arrive, then make as if we've had nothing to eat, and order our breakfasts from the menu.

This is another thing that I dearly love about Ted. He is as obsessed by hotel breakfast buffets as I am. Or, should I say, he's got the same obsession with food as I have. We try hard not to indulge our every food desire, but we do gain the greatest of pleasures from eating together.

I've just sat down with my second plate of bread rolls, bits of ham, rather rubbery cheese, a small yoghurt, melon and a couple of gherkins and olives, when we see Melissa and Bronwyn. They are shortly followed by Juan who does a sort of skip and twirl to come and greet us.

'We missed you last night,' I say.

'I should have come, darling, but I really wanted to do the yoga class and it was two hours long. I ended up drinking a couple of gins in the bar here afterward, before crashing out. Then I heard the girls come back, so I joined them for one last drink. Which became several, of course, and then I got into a bit of hair dyeing. Do we have a plan for today?'

'We start with the Agricultural College and see what that brings,' I say, as Simon joins us. Melissa shuffles down toward me so he can fit on the table. I notice that she has pink streaks in the front of her hair where once it was auburn.

'We decided to have a little experiment last night,' she says, as she catches me looking. She flicks the pink-tinted strands through her fingers as she speaks. 'Juan did it.'

'It looks nice,' I say. 'Perhaps I should get something like that done, Ted?'

'Please don't,' he says. Then he looks at Melissa. 'It looks fantastic on you; I just don't think it would look that great on Mary.'

'Good save,' I say under my breath and he gives me a mini high-five before I start work on the bread rolls in front of me.

'So, tell me a little bit about who's coming today,' says Melissa. 'Juan was explaining to me last night while I painted his nails, but he wasn't really sure.'

'Her name's Sally,' I say, looking over at Juan's fingernails. They are a deep blackcurrant shade. Quite nice, actually.

'She was at the funeral with her sister, Julie. There was this really awful thing we had to do, right at the end. It was to vote off one of the people who was there, meaning they would get no money. Well, Sally's sister was the one we voted off, because she was really arrogant. I feel guilty about the whole thing, but she wasn't a very nice person, and we were forced to vote or none of us would get any money.

'I felt really sorry for Sally. She tried hard to defend her sister, but Julie was unpleasant. I'm intrigued to see what happened with Julie after the will reading, and how the two of them are now.'

'Me too,' says Simon.

We order our breakfasts, opting for large fry-ups, because we are not entirely sure when we will next be stopping to eat. I say that, but I am very aware that there will be plenty of chances to eat throughout the day. But the menu is more than I can resist... the thought of lovely crispy bacon and scrambled eggs with tomatoes, mushrooms and sausages...sheer heaven. I place my order for the largest breakfast they do, ask for a cappuccino and promise myself that I will start dieting tomorrow.

'Good Lord alive!' says Simon, utterly transfixed as the waitress lays my plate down on the table.

'It's not that big,' I say.

'Are you not seeing what I'm seeing?' he says.

'Well, yes – it's a big breakfast, but we're not sure when we'll have lunch.'

'No, not breakfast. Look out through that window and tell me what you see.'

'Holy mother of God!'

'What is it?' chorus Juan, Melissa and Bronwyn.

'You know we told you about Julie?'

'Yes.'

'Well that rather glamorous woman out there, wiggling toward the front entrance on sky-high stilettos, is her.'

'The one you voted off?'

'Yes.'

'So, she got no money?'

'Yes.'

'So, this is quite embarrassing then?'

'Yes.'

I had forgotten just how beautiful Julie is. Or maybe I just blocked it out of my mind. I remember that she was very attractive, but the vision that walks through the old-fashioned breakfast room, past the tables of elderly diners, all of whom look up wide-eyed at the beauty that has appeared in their midst, is quite magical. She is like a Hollywood movie star, and the whole place seems transformed by her presence. By the time she reaches us, floating gracefully along in a simple black shift dress, black heels and clutching some designer handbag, the whole room is entranced.

'Hello everyone,' says Sally.

'Surprise! I bet you didn't expect to see me, did you?' says Julie, a smile reaching across her perfect face as she speaks. She is wearing bright red lipstick, and her cat-like eyes are painted in the darkest black. 'Is this really the best hotel you could find? It's like that dreadful place we stayed in for the funeral. What was that place? Half farm, half rundown, dilapidated old building.'

We all look at her. No one speaks.

'I'm Ted,' says my boyfriend, easing himself up out of his chair and leaning across to shake her hand. She shakes his hand back with a half-smile, looking at him suspiciously. 'Do you work for the hotel?' she asks.

'No, I'm Mary's boyfriend.'

She looks from him to me and I see that smile playing on her lips again. She does not comment, but turns to her sister and asks her for a black coffee. Quite why Julie herself cannot approach the waitress with the order is a mystery, but she doesn't, just sits down as elegantly as a princess and waits for her sister to do the work for her. Then we all sit in a very uncomfortable silence and wonder how we should proceed.

'I don't know whether you remember me, but I'm Simon,' says our tour leader. He folds away the copy of the *Daily Telegraph* that he has been perusing, and looks up at the two women.

Julie ignores him, but Sally smiles graciously. 'Gosh Simon, of course I remember you. How are you doing? Everything okay?'

'Everything is great. I'm afraid we've done quite a trek in search of this Gower family, but we know they lived in Southsea, so hopefully we will be able to track them down today.'

'That would be wonderful,' says Sally. 'I'd love to meet them, after all we heard about them. It sounds like they were incredibly kind to Reginald's father.'

'Oh, I'm so excited about meeting them,' I say. 'I just can't think about anything else. Can you imagine what it will be like when we see them, standing there, in front of us?'

While we speak of our excitement, Julie sits silently, sipping her coffee, still wearing her sunglasses. She looks around the room imperiously...looking without really seeing. She scans the people, the furniture and the decor without appearing to take much of it in. Then she turns her attention to me. 'Mary, do you have an address for the Gower family?'

I have just loaded a fork with a huge pile of bacon and eggs and slipped it into my mouth as she asks her question. I masticate wildly, but then lovely Melissa steps in.

'We don't have an address,' says Melissa. 'But this guy in a nursing home in Wales told us that the Gower family moved down here so that's why we are here.'

I have become used to Melissa's garbled voice: her strong Welsh accent and the way she gallops away through sentences. In fact, I have come to think of it as rather endearing. But the look on Julie's face suggests she finds it irritating.

'I don't understand a word of that. Sorry, who are you?'

'I'm Melissa, I was doing Bronny's hair and she is living in the house that the Gower family used to live in like ages ago. And I was there doing the highlights because she needed her roots done and they came and then I knew this guy and he was in a nursing home.'

'Mary, it is a very simple question, do you have an address for the Gower family, or not?' says Julie, cutting off Melissa with her sharp tongue.

Oh God, why did Sally have to bring her horrible sister? And why does the horrible sister make me feel so inadequate, jittery and like I am back in school?

'Are you struggling to understand?' says Ted, rising to his feet. 'It's as if you're simple or something. Melissa just explained that we don't know where they are living yet, and we are here because a guy at a nursing home in Wales, who once knew them, said they came here to live. The whole purpose of us being here is to find an address. If you have any clever ideas as to how we might do that, we'd all love to hear them.'

I do not think I have ever been prouder of Ted.

'I wasn't aware that your name was Mary,' says Julie, but I can see that she looks stung by his rebuke. For a second I feel sorry for her. It must be horrible to be so disliked. All the beauty in the world will not win you friends and influence if you are mean and nasty all the time.

'No, my name is Ted. But when you're rude and aggressive to Mary it'll be me who answers you.'

I love Ted for intervening in heroic fashion, but I have never needed anyone to answer for me and I slightly resent his claim that he will be replying on my behalf from now on. I am also well aware that if we sit here fighting and back talking one another, we will never find the Gower family.

'Okay, let's try and put all this behind us, and focus, shall we?' I say, like a frustrated teacher of misbehaving teenagers.

'Yes, goodness, yes,' says Simon. 'We have so much to do, let's all try and get on, please.'

'The starting point is obviously the Agricultural College. I was thinking last night that maybe we could look in local newspaper cuttings for any stories. I wonder whether local newspapers are online. That would definitely be worth checking.'

As I speak, I see Melissa and Bronwyn pick up their phones. It is a matter of minutes before they tell me that many of the archives of the *Portsmouth News* are online, so I put them in charge of finding any mentions of Tom or Irene Gower.

Julie stays silent through the whole exchange, and then she asks one simple question that answers all my questions about why she has come to Southsea to join the search.

'Is Mike coming?' she asks.

Until she mentions him, I had forgotten about Julie's fascination with Mike Sween. Clearly, she still holds a torch for him.

'I don't think so, Julie. He's not really responded to the various messages.'

'I'll drop him a text, and see whether I can motivate him to come.'

'Great,' I say.

PRESENT DAY: BACK TO COLLEGE

We all bundle into Melissa's hairdressing van (I say 'all of us,' but Julie insists on taking a cab), and head the short distance to Highbury in search of the college.

Despite our best efforts to put Simon in the driving seat, Melissa insists on taking the wheel and driving like a woman possessed through the streets of Portsmouth. There's something paradoxical about being in a vehicle with a recklessly fast driver, because whilst you're driving at the speed of light and not really stopping at red lights and junctions, and thus reach your destination more quickly, the whole thing feels much longer because you're experiencing every second that passes with such morbid dread, that every second lasts a lifetime.

By the time we reach the college, I am 94-years-old.

'Hello,' I say to the austere-looking woman on reception. 'I don't know whether you can help me, I called earlier. I'm trying to track down a man who was a lecturer at Portsmouth Agricultural College in the 60s and 70s.'

There is a long silence and I think she is going to tell me she cannot help.

'We have an extensive library department here, but all records are stored on microfiche. I'm afraid they haven't been transferred onto the computers, so it's a bit of a laborious task, but you're welcome to come in and look through.'

'That would be brilliant,' I say. 'Can we come now?'

'Yes, let me book you in. What's your name?'

'Mary Brown,' I say, before explaining to her that, ideally, eight of us would like to come.

'The most we can take is two. I'm afraid the microfiche is only available on one computer, so only two people can sit at it.'

'Okay then, can you put my name down and the other name is Simon Blake.'

'All done,' she says, handing me two lanyards.

I think there might be a little bit of quibbling when I tell the others that only two people can be in the microfiche department at any one time, and that I have given mine and Simon's names. There isn't though. It seems that looking through old microfiches in the stuffy old library of a remote agricultural college isn't what most people think of as great fun, so they are quite happy to let Simon and me do the task.

'Darling, I will be looking around all the boutiques in the local town,' says Juan. 'Old Portsmouth has nice shops, according to the lady on reception in the hotel. I need new sequined dancing tights.'

'No, you don't,' I say.

'I do,' he responds.

'You wouldn't want to get yourself some nice jeans or jogging bottoms instead?'

'Nope.'

'I'll be in the pub having pie and chips and a sneaky pint if anyone wants to join me,' says Ted.

There are no takers. To be honest, Ted looks relieved. Simon and I leave Julie and Sally deciding where they will go, and walk toward the college.

'Wait for us two before having lunch, won't you?' I say to Ted. 'Then Simon and I can give you all the feedback as we eat.'

'Sure,' says Ted, in a way that indicates that he has no intention of waiting for anyone, even though we have just enjoyed a huge cooked breakfast.

Walking into the college is an astonishing experience. Have you been into a college or university recently? I haven't. I walk into the library expecting it to be a bit like school, but inside it is more like a business... All very formal and sensibly set out, with our pass cards needed to get past all the security systems, and all these employees who look as if they're working in Deutsche Bank or something.

We go through to the small area at the back of the library where the computer terminals sit. The microfiche machine is very old-fashioned looking compared to the rest of the library, and clearly doesn't get much use by the students. It has a tatty note Sellotaped on the top saying 'microfiche only'.

A kindly librarian assists us in operating the machine, and pulls up the tapes from 1960.

That is when I realise what a massive undertaking this is. There are tonnes of tapes. 'We might be here for weeks,' I say to Simon.

'I know. I hope to goodness he didn't start work at this

college in 1970 or something. It's going to take us forever to get through each week, never mind having to go through decades.'

'We definitely should have brought snacks.'

'I'm sure we'll survive.'

The microfiche tapes contain the college newsletters, or 'bulletins' as they call them. I scan through, looking for the name 'Tom Gower'.

It takes two hours of searching before we finally spot his name.

'The college is pleased to welcome Mr. Tom Gower,' I shriek.

'Oh, finally,' says Simon, in a more muted voice.

'It says that Tom will be a lecturer in the agriculture department, teaching first-year students the basics of dairy farming. Tom is a former farmer himself, so I am sure he will have lots of information and experience to pass on to our students. We wish him all the best.'

Simon looms over me to get a better look at the screen, and for some reason I think he's going to give me a high-five, so I put out my hand, but he just looks at me and I feel a complete fool, so I drop my hand back down and turn to the microfiche.

Tom Gower started here in 1960. Great. But what does that mean? How is that relevant to where he is now?

'You know what we're going to have to do, don't you?' I say to Simon.

'I was thinking exactly the same thing,' said Simon. 'Knowing when he started is interesting, but not especially useful. We're going to have to find out when he left, and hope it says where he went after leaving.'

'But it won't say that. These are school bulletins. They are only going to say they are sorry to see him go.'

'It might say: 'We wish him well at Bath College' or something.'

'That's true,' I concede.

And so we turn our attention back to the microfiche. We read and read and flick through the tapes and read some more. Hours are passing, darkness is descending outside. I am becoming irritated and annoyed that the others are all out shopping, drinking and enjoying themselves and I am stuck in here. Then I remind myself that this was my choice. I wanted to be here, in the thick of it.

So I carry on reading.

The two of us are dizzy and frustrated before we finally find it, in a bulletin sent in 1969, announcing that Mr. Tom Gower will be retiring from his position as head of agriculture.

'Ooooooo,' we chorus. 'Head of Agriculture. He had a few promotions along the way.'

Then, joy of joys, a picture of Mr. Gower, with his wife Irene.

'Oh my God - look how beautiful she is. Gosh, I didn't imagine her looking like that.'

'Read here,' says Simon, pointing to the text on the screen. It says she's been working at Grant's Estate Agents.'

We take pictures of everything we have found, clicking away at the screen in order to capture the information.

'All dates, and all names,' I say. 'We might have to contact some of the other people who were working there at the time. Make sure you have their names.'

Simon clicks away on his camera, as if he is the paparazzi.

'I've got everything,' he says, as we switch off the computer, pile all the microfiche tapes together, and head out of the library.

It is 4pm when we walk out into the natural light and almost flinch from the intensity of it. Like that feeling you get when you walk out of the cinema in the middle of the day, and are astonished to find it light outside.

'We've got a bit of research to do, haven't we?' I say to Simon, as we stand there, breathing in the fresh air and mulling over our options.

'Let's go to the estate agents,' he says, decisively.

He seems more engaged with the process now, which cheers me no end. I thought it was me against the world in the battle to find the Gowers.

I google Grants Estate Agents and discover it's still operating and based just a little further along the seafront, so I message the group to tell them to meet us there.

'Estate agents? You and Simon have decided to buy a house together here, have you?' asks Ted.

'Ha, ha. It's where Irene Gower worked.'

'Oooooo,' says Ted. 'I'll see you there.'

The estate agents' office looks shabby, to be honest. It has a rundown appearance, as if it hasn't quite moved into the twenty-first century. Other estate agents nearby have glossy exteriors, with screens in the windows, flicking between different houses that are for sale. In Grant's Estate Agents' window, there is a collection of small cards, barely bigger than postcards with pictures of houses on them. The paint around the windows is peeling and is an unattractive moss-green colour.

Why would they allow that to happen when it is next to sparkling white, clean and elegant rival firms? There is no way anyone would ever choose to go in this one rather than the others.

I push the door open and see the surprise on the face of the young woman sitting there, as if confirming my thoughts about the place. What if Irene still works here? This could be her daughter. They might have had another child after Tom Junior.

'Sorry to disturb you, but I am looking for Irene Gower,' I say. 'She used to work here.'

'Sorry, I don't know anyone by that name,' says the woman.

'Would you have any records, by any chance, of staff who worked here in, like, the 1960s and 70s?'

'The 60s and 70s? I don't think we've been here that long.'

'Is there any way you could find out?'

'The agency is owned by a guy called Gary Grant. I could call him?'

'Yes please.'

The receptionist rings her boss, and we all stand there in silence as she asks him whether he has ever heard of Irene Gower.

'He wants to talk to you,' she says, handing over her mobile phone.

'My name's Gary, I'm the owner of the business. Can I ask why you want to know?' he says.

'I'm trying to track down Irene Gower,' I say. 'She worked at this company in the late 60s.'

'Who are you? Are you related to her?'

'No. It's a complicated story, but she was very kind to a man once. The man's son passed away a year ago and left a lot of money. He wanted to let her have a big amount of it, but no one can find her or her husband. I was also left money, and I just want to find her, so the money can be passed on. We're a bit short on information, but we know she worked at the estate agents, and wondered whether you might be able to help?'

'Right.'

'Do you think you might be able to?'

'My grandpa used to own the estate agents. He definitely knew Irene.'

'Oh good. I'd like to visit her.'

'Heavens, she'd be over a hundred years old by now. I don't imagine she's still alive.'

'Yes, sorry. I mean - do you know where any of her descendants might be? Do you know her son TJ?'

'Look, I never knew her. I just know that she worked here and that she broke my grandpa's heart and ruined his life.'

'What?'

'My grandpa was infatuated with her. When he died, twenty years ago, we found letters they were sending to one another, long after she'd moved away.'

'Are you sure? She was married, though. To Tom Gower.'

'I'm sure.'

'And do you know where they moved?'

'To Brighton,' he says. 'In the letters my grandpa is asking her whether she moved there to get away from him. She replies that she moved there because her son and grandchild are living there.'

'Do you know if she's still living in Brighton?'

'No idea. In one of the letters, she encloses a picture that her husband drew of her, and mentions that he has been doing cartoons for the *Brighton Argus*. That's all I know, I'm afraid. I can't say I'm very impressed with a woman who gets her husband to draw her, then sends it to another man, but - there you go. Nothing I've heard about that woman impresses me much.'

'Thank you so much for your time. You've been really helpful,' I tell Gary.

I don't like the way he talks about Irene. I feel strangely attached to the Gower family, and quite defensive of them, but she does sound like a right old minx.

'They are in Brighton,' I say, as we leave the estate agents. I have decided not to share the romantic entanglements of our target with them all just yet. I don't want them to be put off her, and decide they want to end the search. 'Tom was working for the *Brighton Argus*. Might be worth going to Brighton?'

'Well, phone them first, Mary. I'd rather not subject myself to another long journey unless it's absolutely necessary,' says Simon.

'Of course,' I reply. Why is no one else as ridiculously excited by all this as I am? I want to get straight on the road and off to Brighton. Instead, I dial the number for the *Brighton Argus*.

'Hello, my name's Mary Brown. I wonder whether I could talk to someone who deals with the cartoonists on the paper, please.'

'Can you let me know what it's to do with?'

'Well, it's a bit complicated, but I am trying to track down a cartoonist who worked on the paper many years ago. Or, rather, I am trying to track down his family. I just wondered whether there was anyone on the paper still in touch with him or his family who could help me.'

'Right,' says the receptionist, with very little confidence in her voice. 'I'll put you through to the art desk, and someone there might be able to help.'

'Hello, Sandra speaking,' come the dulcet tones of someone with a very strong Essex accent. I go through the rigmarole of explaining what I am after, and wait for a couple of seconds while she clearly thinks about how to get rid of me.

'Have you checked our site online to see whether he's still here?' she says.

'No, he's definitely not still there. I didn't know whether anyone working there now had stayed in touch with him after he left.'

'Hang on one second,' she says. 'Could you tell me what the name was again?'

'Tom Gower.'

She disappears from the line and I prepare myself for the news that no one at the newspaper remembers him, but instead she has an idea. She tells me that my best bet would be to talk to Russell Clow. He is retired now, but started work on the paper when he was 18, back in the late 60s, and he worked for the paper all his life until retiring six or seven years ago.

'Can I take your number, and I'll ring him and see whether he's willing to talk to you?'

It is only 20 minutes later when the phone rings. The woman from the Brighton Argus tells me that Russell Clow remembers Tom Gower very clearly, and he is happy to meet me in the morning if I want to come to the paper's offices.

I give a squeal of delight at this point, and say that I would love to come and meet him. 'I'll come to the offices at 11am.'

'Eleven am in Brighton?' says Simon. 'I think we've done quite enough trekking across the country, haven't we? I suggest we have a look round Southsea, then head back to Wales tomorrow. We have tried our best. We can't keep going like this.'

'No! We have to go to Brighton,' I say. 'We have to.'

'No, come on, Mary, enough is enough,' says Ted.

But I know I can win him round again.

Mysterious Invitation WhatsApp Group

Mary Brown

Hi everyone... Guess what? We are off again! We are heading to Brighton, because we have discovered that is where they moved after Southsea. Anyone coming to join us?

Mike Sween

Yeah, I'll come down for a couple of days. Where will you be staying?

Julie Bramley

Hey you, looking forward to seeing you tomorrow. If you want to come tonight instead, I am free for dinner. xx

Mike Sween

I can't make it until the morning, but look forward to seeing you all around 10.30am.

Simon Blake

I have just booked us all into the Holiday Inn on Brighton Seafront

Mary Brown

Hey Mike - looking forward to seeing you tomorrow. PS Holiday Inn on the seafront looks better in the brochure than it sounds!

Mike Sween

Ha, ha. Thanks Mary. That's a relief!

Julie Bramley

And if you do decide to come down tonight, my offer of dinner still stands… much love xxx

PRESENT DAY: BRIGHTON BOUND

Early the next morning, we all climb into the pink hairdressing van. The luggage is piled into the tiny boot that isn't really a boot at all so it spills over into the back so it's all lying next to us.

'This is cosy, isn't it?' says Sally, rather understating things, as we sit down, all squashed up next to one another. Julie comes with us in the van, which is remarkable. I fully expect her to call a chauffeur-driven car, or have unicorns summoned to fly her there, but in the end, she decides to honour us with her presence. She snags the only single seat, so she is not shoved up against anyone else, and sits in splendid isolation, looking remote and judgmental as the van winds its way through Southsea and off toward Brighton.

Julie is completely overdressed, as we knew she would be. Mike will be waiting for us when we get to the hotel so she has made every effort to impress. She wears a fitted purple dress, sky-high cream pumps and her cream coat draped over her shoulders without putting her arms into it. This is something that no one in real life ever does. It is only TV presenters and models on those fashion slots on *This Morning* who wear coats like capes. The rest of us normal human beings would spend our entire days picking them up off the floor if we did that. Julie doesn't, of course, but then she could hardly be described as 'normal' with her ridiculously pretty face, gorgeous hair, and ankles the width of a pencil.

'Will it take long?' she asks, like a petulant five-year-old, before returning to study her phone.

'It takes about an hour and a quarter, depending on the traffic,' says Simon knowledgeably. 'But the route takes us along the seafront all the way so it should be a very pleasant trip.'

'Gosh, yes, because staring at the sea for over an hour is exactly what I want to do first thing in the morning.'

I pull my notebook out of my bag and start to jot down some thoughts, listing the questions I need to ask of Russell when we get to the *Brighton Argus*.

When did Tom work for the Brighton Argus?

Why did he leave? What did he go on to do next?

His address?

Any close friends who might still be in touch with the family.

TJ. What about him? Did he marry? What is his wife's name? Can we track her down?

'We'll head to the hotel first, shall we?' says Simon.

'Yes. Let's go there, drop everything off, and have a chat, to make sure we know exactly what we want to find out, and then head for the *Brighton Argus* at 11am. I hope they are still living in this area.'

'The children could well be. The family moved around so much, they might well want to settle somewhere and put some roots down. People are less inclined to move around when they are older. I guess one gets to the stage when one just stays where one is. I certainly feel like I'm approaching that stage of life myself.'

The van winds its way through the narrow, pretty streets just off the seafront, until it comes to a standstill next to a big hotel. I am not a fan of these huge corporate hotels. I much prefer a little, country hotel. But it is cheap, looks nice on the website, and is well located for the newspaper headquarters situated in the next street. Also, we don't know the area, and this place looks as good as any other.

We walk into the hotel reception and I am aware straight away that Mike is around somewhere because of the change in Julie. She fusses with her hair and smooths down her dress. She looks like a woman on a mission. Whatever else happens in Brighton, at least we will have the joy of watching Julie pursue Mike in the hope of rekindling the romance they shared in Wales.

Sure enough, he is there in the reception area, ready to meet us when we walk in. He is tall, tanned and handsome in jeans, a white shirt and a cream linen jacket with a flash of foppish blue handkerchief emerging from his top pocket. He is very handsome. His hair is longer than it was before. It lends him an English gentleman air, kind of like Hugh Grant in *Four Weddings and a Funeral*, but bigger and more head turning. 'Oh darling,' declares Julie, wiggling her way up to him and kissing him on the cheek. 'You look absolutely gorgeous. How have you been?' She is standing very close to him and stroking his arm as she speaks. Next to him is a woman from the hotel. She is dressed in a knee-length navy skirt that looks two sizes too big for her, a white jumper that is pulled down over her hands in that annoying way, thick tights and flat, black shoes. She looks like every receptionist ever.

We all pile up to him, hug him, and say how pleased we are that he is here.

'We'll have to update you on everything that's happened. It's been quite a journey,' I tell him, and he smiles warmly and gives me a big hug.

'It's so nice to see you, Mary. I am dying to hear all about what you have been up to. Now there's someone I need to introduce you to.' He steps to one side, and introduces the hotel receptionist woman.

'This is Polly,' he says. I shake hands with her and tell her what a nice hotel it is. She looks quite surprised by this. Then I introduce Ted, and Juan.

'How long have you worked here?' I ask.

'No, Polly is my girlfriend.'

Now I cannot begin to explain to you the look that crosses the delicate features of our supermodel friend when Mike makes this unlikely announcement. Julie looks distraught and horrified in equal measure. I am not sure whether she is more worried about the fact that he has a girlfriend, or that the girlfriend is so plain. I don't mean to be mean, but Polly really is one hundred percent girl next door, with her mousy blonde hair and sensible clothes. She appears to have a very slim figure, but she is drowned in the skirt and loose-fitting jumper. She is not wearing a scrap of makeup, unlike Julie. The latter is painted thickly with the stuff, and looks like she has stepped off the cover of *Vogue*.

'Your girlfriend?' she says.

'Yes, my girlfriend.'

Julie laughs, turns and walks away.

We stand there in stunned silence.

I am about to say something like 'thank you for coming' or 'let me tell you what we've been up to' to fill the emptiness caused by Julie's sudden departure when the click-clack of heels in the foyer informs us that she is on the way back.

She charges along without any of the hip swaying, chin-raising haughtiness that she usually displays.

'Really, Mike? Really?' she shouts at him.

'Yes, she's really my girlfriend,' Mike says. 'Her name is Polly and she works at SKY, don't you sweetheart?'

Polly nods, looking a little confused and unaware of why she's provoked this reaction in Julie.

'You're at SKY, are you?' says Julie. 'Goodness me. Not on screen I imagine?'

I see Mike's eyes narrow. 'What do you mean by that?'

'Let's be honest, Mike. She does not look like a TV star. Does she?'

'Thank goodness, she doesn't. She looks lovely, natural, and attractive. She is an incredibly kind, sweet person. And we're very much in love.'

I watch as Julie's eyes darken, and wish someone would come along with popcorn. This is likely to be quite a scene.

'Did you know that Mike and I had a brief fling?' Julie says.

Polly continues to look baffled by everything.

'I didn't know that,' she says, with a beautiful voice.

I am dying to tell her what a lovely voice she has, but decide not to intervene at this juncture.

'Yes. We had a very steamy passionate fling. It was momentous.'

'Oh, for goodness sake, Julie. We spent one night together

over a year ago.' He puts his arm around Polly and pulls her close to him.

'I could have any man I want. But I thought that you and I had something special.'

'Julie, we had one night together. A year ago. This is all very embarrassing and making Polly feel uncomfortable.'

'So what does 'Polly' do at SKY then?' Julie asks. For some reason she makes quotation marks in the air as she says Polly's name. 'Does she make the tea or something?'

'I do voice-overs, programme announcements and links between programmes. I also do quite a lot of voiceovers for films.' Polly seems to be gaining some confidence. And that voice of hers is quite lovely.

'I can see why you would do voice over work. You have a beautiful voice,' I say.

Julie laughs. 'I thought you were going to say that you can see why she does voice-overs - because she's too ugly to be on screen. That would be nearer the truth.'

'How dare you?' Mike says so loud that I jump a little and take a step back. 'If you were a man, I would hit you.'

'Now, come on,' says Ted, stepping between them. 'This is getting ridiculous. Everyone needs to calm down. Julie, why don't you go to your room, and let's all catch up for lunch later, shall we?'

This seems like a reasonable suggestion, but Julie is having none of it.

'You are crazy,' she shouts. 'Absolutely crazy. You could have had me, and you've gone for her instead.'

'I did have you,' says Mike. 'And it wasn't up to much. I have met someone here that I love desperately. I want to spend the rest of my life with her. I hope you meet someone that you feel similarly about, one day. Until that day, keep away from me, and particularly keep away from Polly. Let us all get through the next few days in as dignified a way as possible.'

'You're a fool,' barks Julie, but I can hear a slight crack in her voice, giving away how upset she is. Then she stomps off in the direction of the lift. She has left her bag behind, with her key lying on top of it. I realise she's going to have to stomp back and pick them up. Despite disliking her intensely, I feel a wave of warmth toward her. I do not want her to have to go through that humiliation. So, I pick up her key and her bag and run after her, handing them to her. She gives me a look of tenderness that I have never seen in her face before. Her eyes are full of tears, and I long to hug her, but I am scared of how she will react, so I back off and rejoin the group. Ted hugs me and kisses me lightly on my forehead. 'Well done, sweetheart,' he says, 'That was a very kind thing to do.'

'Well,' says Simon, when the lift has taken Julie out of earshot. 'That was all a bit dramatic, but welcome all the same, Polly. The rest of us are very happy to see you.'

'Thank you,' she says.

I glance at my watch while everyone collects their bags and arranges to meet in the dining room for lunch at 1pm.

'We have an appointment at the *Brighton Argus* in 20 minutes,' I say to Simon. 'Are you ready?'

'I'll be five minutes,' he says. 'I just have to visit the little boys' room.'

I kiss Ted on the cheek before we leave, then text him while we are walking to the newspaper. 'Make sure you send full reports on everything going on there. I need to know what happens, how mad Julie goes, and whether Polly ever cracks and punches her'

'You can count on me,' he texts back.

The *Brighton Argus* buzzes with life and activity. I thought local newspapers were sleepy. Not this place. Journalists rush around and clocks on the wall indicate the time in New York, Los Angeles, and London. I am struggling to see why they need to know the time anywhere but Brighton, but still, it gives the place an air of importance and an aura of discipline, hard work and creativity.

It also gives me a strange confidence in our ability to find out all about Tom Gower.

We are standing at the entrance to the impressive newsroom when I see an elderly man lift himself out of his seat on the far side of the news desk and walk over to us, smiling.

'I'm Russell,' he says.

'Oh, nice to meet you. My name's Mary and this is Simon.' We all shake hands, and he invites us to a small studio that has been setup with a couple of microphones and a green screen.

'Are we going to make a show?' I say, lightly.

'No. This used to be a meeting room; obviously, they do all sorts of high-tech nonsense in here now. Just ignore all the stuff.'

'So, you do TV and radio recordings here?'

'Not me. I retired years ago, but the website has lots of videos on it, so I guess this is where they record them. Now, what can I do for you?'

'Okay. This is very complicated, so bear with me.' I tell him the story of the funeral, and the money and the fact that the Gower family were missing, and how much Reginald had wanted the money to go to Tom's descendants as a gesture of thanks.

'That's good to hear,' says Russell. 'Tom was a very decent man. Too decent in a way.'

'How?'

'Well, he would have made a much better cartoonist if he'd been more aggressive; spikier. His drawings were good, and his ideas were good, but he never pushed things far enough to make people gasp.'

'Gosh, that's really interesting. So, he wasn't nasty enough?'

'Well, it's not that you have to be nasty, but you need an edge.'

'Oh, okay. Did you work with Tom much?'

'Yes, I was a runner for the photographers, taking their films back to the offices after they had shot them. These were the days way before digital cameras, so every photographer would have a runner who would get the films back to the office ready to be processed. I had moved to the art desk by the time Tom started. I guess he would have been in his mid-50s. And I was about 21. I was his assistant.

'He wasn't based in the office, but he submitted cartoons. I used to cycle to his house to get them and bring them in here. He was a lovely chap. He had a very beautiful wife as I remember. Yes, Irene. I say, she was very beautiful. I think they had some relationship problems, though, didn't they?'

'Oh, did they? That is interesting. I thought that maybe they had. We talked to a guy in Southsea who worked at the estate agents where she used to work. He said his grandpa and her had this thing going.'

'The estate agent. Yes, my goodness. I remember something about that. I can't remember the chap's name now, but Tom used to mention him. He said he was glad they were away from Southsea, but he always wondered whether Irene was still in touch with the guy. I don't know whether they were actually having an affair or not, but it was something that always played on Tom's mind.'

'Do you know what happened to him after he left?'

'After America, you mean?'

'I mean after he left the *Brighton Argus*.'

'Oh, I see. The last I heard was that the whole family was in the USA.'

Simon and I stand there in sombre silence, grimly realising that there is no way we will find the family now.

'Are his grandchildren still in the USA?'

'I don't know. I never knew much about the grandchildren. They were very little when he was working for us. The younger grandchild had an illness that they were all very worried about, and there was a treatment being developed at a hospital in New York. They went out there to be a test case. We kept in touch for a while. Then lost touch, as is always the case.

'He said that the treatment had worked well. As far as I can remember. I mean, I don't suppose this is any use to you at all, is it?'

'It's very useful,' I say. 'I had hoped that the family might still be living around here, but knowing they are not, and are not even in the country, has saved us a lot of time.'

'I'm so sorry I can't be any more help. They all settled in New York. I mean the grandchildren would be all grown up by now, wouldn't they? They probably have children of their own.'

'Yes, they would. Well, thank you for your time.'

'No problem at all,' he says. 'Just a thought, but I'll look up the name of the illness the little girl had, and the name of the hospital they went to in New York. If you can't find them, and the money is just sitting there, you could donate it to them. He felt passionately about everything the hospital was doing.'

'Thanks, yes, that would be great,' I say. 'Then we can put all of that to the private detectives and know that the money is somewhere Tom and Irene would have approved.'

Simon and I walk back to the hotel in silence. I feel like I have been beaten up. There is no way we will find them now. At lunch, everyone asks me to update them on the situation.

'Okay,' I say, standing up and shrugging my shoulders. 'Tom and Irene Gower did live in Brighton, and it sounds like he made a real success of it as a cartoonist, but the family upped and left and went off to live in America.'

There is a huge groan.

'I know. I am really disappointed, too. But Russell, the guy on the newspaper in Brighton who knew Tom, said that his grandchild had a blood disorder and they went to the USA because there was a hospital in New York who offered to try to help. Then they settled there.'

Later that night, I tell Ted everything, about the estate agent telling me about the affair, and Russell all but confirming it. Then I sit on the edge of the bed to take my eye makeup off.

'I can't believe we won't find them,' I say, embarrassingly close to tears. Ted wraps his arms around me and pulls me into him. 'I feel so sad. I feel really sad for Tom. If Irene had an affair and he knew about it, it must have been awful.'

'We don't know that he knew about it. He might have thought they were happy together.'

'I guess, but people tend to, don't they? I bet he did know. It must have been awful for him. And their grandchildren getting sick and having to go over to New York. That must have been hard.'

'Yes. New York in the 60s and 70s was not as it is today. It would have all been quite a change from working on the farm in Gower.'

And that's when I burst into tears...crying big, fat, ugly tears into my boyfriend's shirt.

'Come on, sweetheart, we have done everything we can. You've been amazing, but we can't go over to New York.'

'Can't we?'

'No.'

1978: FEARS FOR SIMON

Irene handed the last of the dishes to Tom, and reached into the soapy water to pull out the plug. Tom seemed lost in a world of his own as he dried the bowl and put it into the cupboard.

They had reached a comfortable place in their lives, existing together in some sort of harmony after all the disruptions. She still spoke to Mark occasionally, but he had long moved on...he had children and a young grandson called Gary. The calls they shared were fewer these days and her memories of him, though still warming and plentiful, were definitely dimmed by time.

'I must call TJ later,' she said to her husband, as she wiped around the sink and threw the cloth across the taps to dry. 'Did you know they have been in New York for five years now? It was five years ago today that they left. Sophia is eight-years-old. It is crazy how time flies.'

'It's crazy but they've done so well. All set up, and with Sophia having responded to the drugs. I'm proud of them.'

Irene smiled, agreeing with her husband, while walking into the sitting room to make the trans-Atlantic call. She was delighted that everything was working out for them, but devastated that they had decided to stay in New York, rather than come home. She felt as if she wasn't part of their lives, and was missing seeing the grandchildren grow up. Then, there was Simon. She didn't know how much to tell them, but Simon was very unwell. He had a leaky heart valve that required a complicated operation. He had urged Irene not to mention it to Yvonne and TJ, but it was difficult. She felt bad for not telling them.

TJ picked up the phone in New York and realised straight away that it was his mother calling…that familiar long-distance hum that preceded her words. The faltering speech and the endless wait for her to respond to a question. The phone calls home were always very difficult. Not so much now that they were settled in, but to start with, it had been a real problem to keep the conversations with his mother light and chatty.

He had not wanted to burden her with any of his problems, but the truth was that New York had not proven to be the easiest place to settle into when he and the family had first arrived on that dark winter's evening five years ago, clutching their young children and wondering whether they had done the right thing.

They had feared for themselves in a city that they had been warned was dirty and dangerous...traipsing bags and cases onto buses, and avoiding the underground as they found their way to their Manhattan apartment.

They had been worried about so much. Were they wise to give Sophia drugs that were not approved and still in the experimental stage? Should TJ have left his job? Would they ever fit in?

He had never wanted to share any of his fears with his mother, so he would always keep the conversation light and tell her about the magnificence of the huge building in which he now worked, and how well he was doing.

As they chatted on this occasion, it was Irene who was trying hard to keep things light, and avoid mentioning Simon. If Yvonne's dad could recover without needing surgery, she could tell them without worrying them. To mention it now felt cruel when they were so far away.

When TJ asked about Simon, she said that he was very tired, but otherwise seemed well. Then she came off the phone and thought long and hard about whether she had done the right thing. Shouldn't she just tell the truth?

Six months after the phone call, it was Tom, not Irene, who phoned to break the news: Simon had gone in to surgery for a double heart by-pass and to fix a leaky valve.

A week later, Tom was forced to ring again to tell TJ that he would be wise to come back, as Simon was drifting in and out of consciousness and might not recover.

The days after the phone call were spent in a blur of hoping and praying that Yvonne and TJ would arrive back before Simon died.

They did.

Just.

Whether by force of sheer will or by luck, Simon clung to life until his daughter and her family returned from New York. He was able to smile at them as they came in to see him, and squeeze his daughter's hand one last time before slipping away from them forever.

1990: NEW YORK

They all sat around the table, smiling, laughing and hoping that Tom understood what was happening. Irene put the birthday cake down on the table in front of him. It was a superman cake, as he had requested, and had a collection of candles on the top. Not the 75 that would have been required to match his age, but lots of them, all flickering brightly.

'Blow them out, Dad,' said TJ, putting his arm around his dad's shoulder with such affection that Irene felt a rise of warmth inside her. She loved them both so much.

Tom looked blankly at the cake, and then put his arm out, into the flames of the candles. TJ reached over to pull his arm out of danger's way, while Yvonne pulled the cake back. Tom stared at his shirt where the cuff was burned, leaving a scorched mark.

'Shall we get you to bed, now?' said Irene, moving round to her husband's side, and checking the burned cuff to make sure there wasn't a burned wrist beneath it.

'Bedtime in Gower,' said Tom standing up. He was being far more cooperative than he usually was. Perhaps he was tired. Perhaps the smell of burning had scared him. Who knew? It was impossible to know how he was feeling for vast swathes of time. On other occasions, he would scream at everyone and tell them exactly how he felt and what he thought of them.

'Sophia, can you put down the magazine and go and help your mother?' said Irene, as she led Tom upstairs. She was tired and fed up, and could see Yvonne rushing around to tidy the place up, while an 18-year-old, who should know better, slumped in the corner to check the new fashions in her weekly magazine.

'Up to bed in Gower,' said Tom.

'We are in New York now though, aren't we? Not in Gower anymore. Up we go.'

By the time she had got her husband to sleep, and come back downstairs, she was grateful for the tidied room and large drink waiting for her on the kitchen table.

She sat down next to her son, Yvonne and her grandson Andrew. Sophia sat in the sitting room, talking on the phone, Irene's phone, while chewing gum. Irene hated to complain about her all the time, but by the time Irene was 18, she was out working. At least Andrew showed interest in the family, and was helpful and kind. He had recently graduated from university and was applying for jobs. No one seemed to have any expectations of Sophia, and it drove Irene nuts. What sort of 18-year-old comes round to her grandparents' place to visit her very sick grandfather, then picks up the phone and starts calling her friends, without even asking whether she can use the phone?

Jane most definitely would not have approved of her granddaughter's slovenly ways.

'What are we going to do?' said TJ, taking his mother's hands.

'Make her help around the house more. Insist she gets a job. There are lots of things you could do.'

'No, not Sophia,' said Yvonne, who had begun to despair of the way in which Irene treated Sophia, expecting her to do so much more around the house because she was a girl. It was 1990, not the 1950s.

'I meant Dad,' said TJ, being much gentler with his mother than Yvonne felt inclined to be.

'There's nothing we can do. I'll look after him.'

'But, Mum, that's so difficult. It's okay when we are all here to help, but when you are on your own you can't possibly be expected to watch him all the time. He nearly set fire to himself just then, and that's with us all sitting around. He is going to hurt himself. We have to think about putting him in a home.'

'Absolutely not,' said Irene. 'No way on earth am I dumping him when he's at his most vulnerable. I will look after him. Perhaps Sophia could come over here and help me, from time to time?'

Yvonne stood up and walked away, over to the kettle in the corner of the room. She had no intention of making coffee: she just needed to remove herself from the conversation.

'Will you at least think about putting him into care, Mum? It could be better for all of us. Dad most of all,' said TJ.

'I have thought about it, and have decided not to.'

Irene's reluctance to confine her husband to a home was motivated by a deep-seated love for the man she married when barely out of her teens, and also a splinter of guilt. She'd put him through so much pain. Now, when he needed her, when they were in a foreign country, so far from the life he had been born into, she would look after him, as he had looked after and tolerated her so many times.

They had come to New York to look after their family, and now the family needed to look after them. That is how the world worked, and Irene felt angry and frustrated with Yvonne for not wanting any pressures on her own family, and for wanting Tom's problems confined to a discreet home on the other side of town. Well, that would not be happening.

'Your father would have sacrificed everything he has, and everything he is, for you,' she said, doing nothing to hide the bitterness she felt. 'He's desperately ill and in need of help. Now we will give everything for him.'

TJ put his arms around his mother. 'Of course, we will, Mum. We'll make sure everyone comes over to help.'

'Thank you. It is the least we can all do. If you could come over and just spend time with him, talking to him, it would make the world of difference,' she said, addressing her comments to the whole room, but meaning them mostly for Yvonne and Sophia who always seemed so indulged and selfish.

TJ promised that everyone would help, and Irene excused herself and headed upstairs to sit by Tom. She hated what dementia had done to him. It had stolen everything from him - his abilities and all his senses. Worst of all, the disease had taken his memories. He could remember things from long ago, and spoke frequently about the farm, asking whether Marco was coping okay, and whether the cows had been milked, but he remembered nothing of the things they were doing in the present day.

Irene was beside him most of the time, but she would leave

the room for just a minute and he had no recollection of her ever having been there.

'I haven't seen you for years,' he would screech at her.

Her husband had always had such a friendly, easy-going personality, but the loss of so much had left him pricklier and less amiable than at any time before.

He could no longer drive, keep up with a normal conversation, recall the names of the people closest to him or do his precious drawing. He was still the person Irene loved, but he was not well. He was struggling, had lost his independence, his ability to cope, and all the treasured memories of their recent time together.

Four weeks later, when Tom was only 75 years and a month old, he had a heart attack in the night. Irene heard a gasp for breath and a struggle next to her. She turned and put on the light to see him lying there, pale, not moving, but breathing gently. His eyes flickered as she jumped out of bed, and ran round to stand next to him.

'Shall I call an ambulance? Are you okay?'

He breathed shallowly and soon he was gasping for breath.

'Don't leave me,' she said. 'Not after all we've been through, Tom. Please don't leave me now.'

His eyes closed as he gasped, more shallowly this time. Irene issued a silent prayer to God, saying sorry for everything she had done wrong, saying sorry for not completely loving this wonderful man as she should have. I promise, Lord, if you spare him, I will devote my life to him, I will do anything, anything. Please, please don't take him from me.

Tom opened his eyes and looked into the face of his wife. 'I adored you from the moment I first saw you,' he said. 'I'll love you forever. Please take me back to Gower. Please. Back to Gower.'

'I love you too, Tom. I love you more than anything in the world. You are the finest man I ever met.'

PRESENT DAY: FUNERAL PLANS

'Cheers,' I say, raising my glass and waiting for the others to raise theirs in reply.

'To the Mysterious Invitation Group,' says Simon.

'To us.'

I look around the table...this rabble of individuals with so very little in common, flung together because our relatives were once tangentially connected to a man who died.

'Thank you all so much for coming,' I say, taking on a leadership role. For some reason, it feels as if it is I who have pushed the whole thing forward more than anyone else has, so I should express gratitude to them for coming on the ride.

'The only person not here is Matt,' I say, suddenly realising that everyone else is now here, around the table.

'It's a shame he couldn't come,' says Sally. Julie doesn't speak, but she says a great deal with her eyes, as she glares unremittingly at Mike and Polly, occasionally shaking her head as if to reconfirm to everyone that she is still in a state of shock and incomprehension about the situation.

Melissa and Bronwyn haven't joined us this evening. They have gone out into Llandrindod, to some lively bar, presumably to tell all their friends about this bizarre group of people they met. They seemed genuinely thrilled to have come with us on our little adventure to England, having never been out of the area. Bronwyn even confessed that she had never stayed in a hotel before, so the whole thing must have been an incredible adventure. I am glad about that. I am also glad we have found some sort of solution to our problem. Even though it's not really a solution at all, and certainly not what we hoped for.

We are stuck with the fact that the family moved to America and settled there.

'Shall I call Matt?' I say. 'I could put him on loudspeaker so everyone can say hello to him.'

'Oh yes, do,' says Sally. 'Then he'll feel like he's here with us, and he'll know we haven't forgotten about him.'

We call his mobile, but get the answer phone, so we raise our glasses and offer a loud cheer to tell him we are thinking of him and wish he were with us.

I tell him I will call him back when I am at home and fully update him on what happened.

'I should ring the private detectives, shouldn't I?' I say. 'Just to tell them what we've managed to discover. I'll pass on the details of the Bellevue Hospital.'

'Yes, absolutely,' says Simon. 'I'm happy to call them if you want. They need to know about the research project. That's where the Gowers' money should be directed.'

'I'll do it now,' I say. 'Before I forget.'

Again, I have the phone on loudspeaker, as I ring and ask the receptionist to put me through to Paul Dillon.

'I'm so sorry. I can't do that. Is there anyone else here who can help?'

'No, I really need to speak to him.'

I make faces at the others around the table, and Simon shrugs back at me, as if to say 'what is wrong with them? Why can't they just put you through to Paul, for goodness' sake?'

'Can you tell me who's speaking?'

'My name's Mary Brown. It is quite a complicated story but he will really want to hear what I have to say. It is about Reginald Charters who died a year ago. I was invited to the funeral.'

'Oh, gosh, yes. I remember that.'

'So, can you put me through to him?'

'No, I'm afraid not. He passed a few days ago.'

'He passed?' I take the phone off the loudspeaker.

'Yes, he died. He had cancer. I don't know whether you knew that?'

'Oh, my goodness, I'm so sorry. I knew he was ill, but I didn't realise he was that bad. That is terrible news. I'm very sorry.'

'Did you want details of the funeral? I know he was very fond of you, the way you stepped up to give a talk on the day of the funeral. That was an incredible gesture.'

'Thank you. Yes, let me have the funeral details...'

The woman on the phone tells me it will take place on Friday at 11am. 'It's at the same church as Reginald's funeral.'

'Thank you so much. I'll see you on Friday.'

Ted and Juan have their arms folded defensively. They have heard me make another plan, and they are clearly worried it is going to entail a drive across mountains and wild terrain in search of something that isn't there.

'Paul died,' I say bluntly, turning to the group. 'I'm really tempted to go to the funeral. It's at the same church as Reginald's.'

'What?' says Julie. 'What would possess you to go back to that godforsaken place?'

'I don't know, really. I just feel like it would be a nice thing to do. And there'll be people there from the area who we can talk to about what we discovered.'

'No,' says Ted. 'Honestly, love, let's just go home now.'

'I know it sounds mad, but it's not that far away.'

'It is quite far away,' says Mike. 'It's the other side of Wales.'

'Yeah, but it's not as far as we have been. We could go over there for the funeral, and then go on the train back from there. What do you think?'

Ted drops his head into his hands. I give him a little hug and tell him I am glad he's so keen, which makes the others laugh. 'I know you probably think I'm mad but I'd so hoped to find the Gower family, and going back to where we all first met a year ago feels like a nice thing to do. Like some sort of resolution, even if it's not the one we were after.'

'If you want to go, we'll go,' says Ted.

'I want to go.'

'Actually, I'd quite like to go,' says Simon.

'Oh goodness, if you are going, I'll come,' says Sally.

'Well, I was going to get a lift back with you, Sally. So, I'll come too,' says Julie, in a move that surprises everyone.

We look at Mike. 'Yeah, why not?' he says. 'Let's go to Gower for the funeral.'

. . .

Mysterious Invitation WhatsApp Group

Mary Brown:

Hi Matt, I just left a message for you. Since then, we have decided to head to Gower. It's Paul Dillon's funeral on Friday (the private detective). It would be lovely if you could come. It is back at the church where Reginald's funeral was held. Call me when you can.

Mike Sween:

Come on, mate. Come and join us

Simon Blake:

It would be lovely to see you, if you can make it, Matt. Kind regards, Simon

Sally Bramley:

Hope to see you! X

PRESENT DAY: GOWER FARM HOTEL

It is very odd to be back at the Gower Farm Hotel, and it is strange to be going to the funeral of someone I know, but to which I haven't, strictly speaking, been invited.

Such a change from a year ago when we were invited to the funeral of someone we didn't know, but to which we had been invited.

How about that for a story with a ridiculous beginning and a ridiculous end? We are soon going to be back in the same church, at the same place, with many of the same people.

'I feel a bit odd, now we're here at the hotel,' says Ted. 'Don't you?'

'No,' I say. 'I'm really glad we came.'

'But you didn't really know this guy. You only met him once.'

'Which is once more than I met the last guy whose funeral I came to here.'

'Well, I feel odd, even if you don't.'

The hotel looks a bit different from last time we were here. Lots of renovations are going on. There are workmen buzzing around the place, and the sound of hammers bashing and saws cutting, as we get ready for the day ahead.

Ted looks very smart in his makeshift black outfit. I had to go to a shop in Llandrindod Wells and buy a black dress because I obviously didn't think to bring a funeral outfit with me.

In the end, I had to opt for a sort of tent creation. That was the only item that went anywhere near to getting over my tummy and my bum. It is made of linen and is deeply unflattering, so I am trying to make it look better with the addition of lots of makeup. But now I look like I'm going for a night out on the town, rather than going to a funeral, so I am wiping some of the makeup off and trying to work out where the thin line is between demure respectability and high-end hooker. Funnily enough, the line is not as clear as you might imagine it would be.

There is a knock on the door, and I answer to see Sally standing there, dressed in her black and looking really lovely. 'Oh, you look nice,' she says.

'No, you look nice,' I reply. 'I look odd. This was the only thing I could find to wear. And now I think I might have too much makeup on.'

'Stop it. You look perfect. Absolutely perfect. Oh, and your husband looks handsome.'

'Why thank you, ma'am,' says Ted, leading us down the rickety stairs that I first walked down a year ago, in a state of utter confusion, and some trepidation, out to the side of the building toward the church.

We walk in and join the other Mysterious Invitation people, so we are all sitting together in one pew. I spot Matt at the end, and wave and blow kisses until Ted tells me to stop.

'Inappropriate,' he whispers, as I drop my hand.

The service is quite long, and some of the readings are in Welsh, which doesn't allow us to feel part of the whole thing. But it is lovely and warm, and there are loads of people there, including the tallest vicar I have ever seen. He must be about seven feet tall. Clearly there is a lot of affection for the local private detective who has been working on the High Street for his entire life. I spend time trying to work out who the people in the church are, but it is very hard when everyone is sitting there in black, crying.

So, I decide to relax and enjoy it as much as I can. After the service, there is a burial, but it is for close family and friends, so instead we are invited back to Paul's house, where there is a small buffet and the chance to share memories about him. We all stand together, the interlopers who have travelled across Wales to be here. Then we walk as one behind the crowds of people leaving the church and on to Paul's house.

'Hello, don't think we've met,' says a voice, as a man in a green suit catches up with us. 'I'm John, Paul's brother.'

'Oh, it's lovely to meet you. I'm so sorry for your loss.'

'Thank you, dear, but I refuse to be downbeat about it. He lived a good life and had been ill for a long time. In the end, his passing was a mercy; he was in so much pain. Now's the time to celebrate a life well lived. That's why I refuse to wear black.'

I introduce myself and the others to him, and begin to tell the story of how we all met Paul.

'Oh, my goodness. I heard about that. Paul told me all about it. What an astonishing thing to happen. Did they ever find the other family? The one that was missing on the funeral day?'

'No, they didn't. They were called the Gower family, and we've been rushing around this past week, to see whether we can find them.'

'Any luck?' he asks, as we walk into Paul's house.

'No, we started in Llandrindod Wells which was the last address we had for them, and found they'd gone to Southsea, then to Brighton, then to America. We went to Southsea and Brighton, but drew the line at making a trans-Atlantic search for them.'

John smiles. 'You've been on quite an adventure. There might be someone here who knows what happened to them. It would be worth having a chat with a few people.'

'I will,' I say. 'But I might have a bite to eat first.'

We all move through to the buffet, and join the queue for food, then find a quiet corner in which to eat.

'Shall we head off after this?' says Ted. 'It's a long train ride home, and it would be nice to be back before it's too late.'

'Sure,' I say. 'But give me ten minutes. I will go, circulate, and find out whether there is anyone here who knows the Gower family, and then we will go. Okay?'

I put down my plate and walk back into the main room, scanning the people who are standing around, before moving up to one small group and introducing myself.

'I wonder…you don't know the Gower family, by any chance, do you? They used to live here, on the farm, many years ago.'

'Sorry, no,' says the woman, and the others in her group shake their heads.

'They owned Gower Farm?'

'I'm sorry, I don't know them.'

I slip away and edge my way into a group of older people who might have known Tom and Irene, or known of them.

'Oh, yes. My parents knew them when they were here. They moved to north Wales, I think.'

'Yes,' I say. 'Then they moved to England.'

'To England?'

'Yes, down to the south coast. Then they moved to New York.'

'No,' comes the reply. 'Goodness me weren't they adventurous?'

'Their granddaughter wasn't well, so they moved there to get treatment for her.'

'Yes, that's right,' comes a strong, deep voice from beside me. It is the vicar, smiling down at me from his considerable height. 'They moved back to Wales after that.'

'Really? Did they? Really?'

'Yes, Tom Gower was buried here. It must have been 25 or 30 years ago now. His wife settled somewhere near Port Eynon, I think. That's a little place on the coast. Irene lived a long life and only died a few years ago.'

'Gosh. Are other members of the family around?'

'TJ is still alive, but in a nursing home, I think. I know that Yvonne, his wife, died years ago. His son Andrew is living in Germany, but Andrew's sons, Eddie and Charlie, are in the country. They have just finished university.'

'Gosh. So, when Paul was hunting for the family last year, they were right under his nose?'

'Well, no, the boys weren't around here then. They were away at uni. Paul would not have known that they had come back to the area. Tom was buried here because he wanted to be near the farm, but their funerals were actually held in Port Eynon. No one realised the family was back in Wales. I didn't until I saw the graves and met Charlie and Eddie there.'

'Gosh. One of the reasons I am keen to find them is to make sure they know about some money that has been left to them. Is anyone in touch with Andrew or his kids? Is there any way you could pass a note to them if I left one with you?'

'Or you could go and talk to them. Charlie and Eddie are staying at the Gower House Hotel while they are back from uni. They're helping with refurbishments there.'

PRESENT DAY: MEETING CHARLIE & EDDIE

I head back to Ted, and the group, and tell them the news.

'I promise we'll go after this, Ted, but I have to go and meet Tom and Irene's great-grandchildren first, after everything we've been through to try and find them.'

We all gather our coats and bags, walk back to the hotel, and I approach the receptionist and ask her where I might find the Gower brothers. Then we all take a seat in reception to await their arrival.

It is not long before two tall, handsome and charming young men appear in reception, eager to talk to us about their family.

I explain to them all about the funeral a year ago. I tell them the story about Marco going to work on their great-grandfather's farm and how kind Tom and Irene were to him. I tell them about Marco's theatrical son, Joe, who was shunned by society so changed his name to Reginald and decided to hand his wealth over to those who had treated him and his father well.

They take the news of the money being left to them with wide-eyed amazement.

'Are you sure? I mean, I never even met this guy Reginald, or his dad.'

'Nor us,' I say.

'We went to the funeral and no one there had met Reginald,' explains Simon. 'It was the most peculiar experience.'

'God, I can imagine,' say Charlie and Eddie, together.

'Do you want to come with us, to the graveyard? We were about to go down there and put flowers on our grandma Yvonne's grave. Our great-grandma and grandpa are right next to her.'

'Gosh, yes, I'd love to,' I say, and we follow Charlie and Eddie as they walk past the gravestones and under a little archway through to a second graveyard, and follow them to the graves of Tom and Irene.

'Here,' says Charlie, and I actually gasp when I see two headstones, standing right next to one another. At the bottom of each one, it says: Unedig gyda'n gilydd yn y nefoedd.

'What does that mean?' I ask Charlie.

'United again in heaven,' he says, and I start to cry a little.

I know it sounds silly, because I didn't know Tom and Irene at all. In fact, I had never even been to Wales before we received the invitation to the funeral a year ago, but I just feel so glad that it worked out for those two in the end, despite some hair-raising moments along the way.

'It looks like Irene realised how much she loved Tom in the final years of their lives. That's really touching,' I say, while the others look at me as if I have entirely lost my mind. I seem to be so much more invested in this family than anyone else. I love that they are now together for eternity. Let's just hope that Mark isn't wherever they are going, or it all might go pear-shaped again.

Charlie and Eddie lay flowers on the graves, and we stand back and watch in silence. Charlie hands me a flower to put across the graves of Tom and Irene, and I step forward and lay it down, feeling so emotional, I am struggling to control my sobbing. I cast an eye along the group...the Mysterious Invitation gang all together at Tom and Irene's graves a year after the funeral. There is something quite magical about it all.

Then we all walk back through the archway, past the church, and back up the road toward the hotel.

'What do you think you'll do with the money?' I ask.

'We won't get it, will we?' says Charlie. 'I thought the money was for Tom and Irene.'

'No, it's very much for you. Reginald made a point of stating that the money should go to the youngest living relatives. That is you two. He would be very keen for you to have it. You'll be able to set yourselves up for life.'

They look at me, then at each other, and then back at me again.

'Really? The money is for us? Literally for us, and not a sort of pot of money for the family to share?'

'Nope. All for you. You have your great-grandparents to thank. They were both so kind to Reginald's father that Reginald felt moved to leave a lot of money to you.'

'It's lovely to hear something like that about one of your relatives,' says Charlie.

'I know,' I say. 'When we were at the funeral a year ago, we all said the same. I'm very proud that someone I'm related to behaved so kindly that a dying man's last wish was to reward him.'

Once we are back at the hotel, I feel like it is not our place to stay any longer, so we decide to head off, and go into town to Joe's Ice Cream Parlour and experience one of his gorgeous ice creams before getting the train home.

We bid farewell to Charlie and Eddie, and all exchange numbers, and then we head off to indulge ourselves. All six of us, and our entourage, off to enjoy the creamy Italian taste that we have heard so much about.

We seat ourselves in the fifties-style ice cream parlour and order the biggest ice creams they have.

I cannot tell you how beautiful it tastes: rich and creamy. It is gorgeous, full of fresh strawberries, nuts and sauce. Ted has the fudge one, and it's not only full of fudge, it's packed with fudge brownie, toffee sauce, pecan nuts and tonnes of caramel and chocolate.

'Best ice cream ever,' says Ted. 'Really first class.'

Then we all raise our ice cream dishes in a toast.

'To Reginald.'

'I know this has been a really unusual trip,' I say to Ted, whilst the others chat amongst themselves. 'And you and Juan must have been bored out of your mind at times, but I'm really glad it ended like this.'

'What? In an ice-cream shop?'

'Well - yes - I'm very glad about that, but I'm mainly pleased that our journey finished with us finding those lovely young men. I feel like our cross-country trip was all worth it.'

'Yeah,' says Ted, licking out his bowl like a four-year-old. 'I had my doubts when we drove to Brighton in that pink hairdressing van, but it all turned out well in the end. Well done, Mary Brown. I salute you.'

EPILOGUE

A couple of months after our trip to Wales, I am woken early on a Saturday morning by a text.

Hello. Do you remember us? It's Charlie and Eddie Gower here. I hope you are well and made it back home to England safely. We just wanted to share some news with you.

We have decided to put our money together and we are going to buy Gower Farm.

It means we will own the farm that our great-grandpa had when he was younger...the one that Marco came over to in the war. We thought Reginald would approve.

We are also going to send money over to our auntie at the hospital in New York.

You and Ted are welcome to come to our farm, anytime. Tell Ted to bring his wellies, though, because we will be putting him to work!

Thanks for making all that effort to find us.

Please come and visit us!

Lots of love,

Charlie & Eddie Gower

Copyright Notice

Mysterious Invitation is a work of fiction.

Names, characters, places and incidents are the products of the author's imagination, or are used fictitiously. Any resemblance to actual events, locales, businesses or persons, living or dead, is entirely coincidental.

Printed in the United Kingdom

FIRST EDITION

❀ Created with Vellum

ALSO BY BERNICE BLOOM

Want to read more?

Mary Brown is the star of the *Adorable Fat Girl* series of comedy books. All available on Amazon.

UK: https://www.amazon.co.uk/Bernice-Bloom/e/B01MPZ5SBA/ref=dp_byline_cont_pop_ebooks_1

US: https://www.amazon.com/Bernice-Bloom/e/B01MPZ5SBA?ref=sr_ntt_srch_lnk_1&qid=1618151377&sr=8-1

Or, search 'Bernice Bloom' on Amazon, or see: www.berniceblooom.com for more information

The next book in the series is: *Confessions of an Adorable Fat Girl,* which follows Mary on the adventure of a lifetime, featuring a trip to visit Charlie and Eddie on Gower Farm.

My Book

If you need any more information, or want a list of all the books, you can contact us on: bernicenovelist@gmail.com

Thank you so much for your support x